Olivia nodded toward the window. "Jillian and I have seen Carson out back practicing at the hoop. If he makes the team, I promised Jillian we'll go to the games when I'm free to take her."

Jeff turned to face her. "If you're working, and you're all right with it, she can come with me. I plan to get to every single game."

Same as an attentive dad. That thought popped up, and equally fast, Olivia resisted it. Jeff wasn't Jillian's dad. Carson wasn't her brother. Olivia was presuming something she wasn't sure she was ready for. "I wouldn't want to impose. That's taking on a lot."

"Not really." Jeff frowned. "Those two are growing up friends. They're creating memories that include each other, right down to picking out Christmas trees."

"Yes," Olivia said, not adding the part about their appearing to be siblings. Some days, a life with Jeff was so possible, so real, it left her shaky with fear.

Dear Reader,

Nearly five years after he lost the family's sheep ranch and left town in a huff, Jeff Stanhope is back in Adelaide Creek—and he's not alone. He's guardian to fourteen-year-old Carson Moore, whose mother recently died. Jeff is about to reopen a once-thriving lodge in town. Radiologist Olivia Donoghue is starting over. Eleven-year-old Jillian's leukemia is in remission, and Olivia has landed a new job in the small town of her dreams.

With the holidays on the horizon, October is a great time to begin building new lives in Adelaide Creek. Halloween brings a bump in the road for Carson, and for Olivia and Jeff, too. They got off to a rocky start, but both insist the subject of romance is off their radars. A family Thanksgiving at the ranch gives way to snowy days and the arrival of a couple of four-legged newcomers, along with a sleigh. If Olivia and Jeff can listen to their hearts, Christmas at the lodge could be magical—even charmed.

I hope you enjoy Olivia and Jeff's story, and please visit my website, virginiamccullough.com, to sign up for my newsletter and see what I'm up to next. You'll find me on Twitter and Facebook, too.

To holiday romances,

Virginia McCullough

HEARTWARMING

The Doc's Holiday Homecoming

—

Virginia McCullough

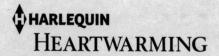

HARLEQUIN
HEARTWARMING

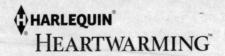

ISBN-13: 978-1-335-58476-2

Recycling programs
for this product may
not exist in your area.

The Doc's Holiday Homecoming

Copyright © 2022 by Virginia McCullough

For questions and comments about the quality of this book,
please contact us at CustomerService@Harlequin.com.

Harlequin Enterprises ULC
22 Adelaide St. West, 41st Floor
Toronto, Ontario M5H 4E3, Canada
www.Harlequin.com

Printed in U.S.A.

Virginia McCullough grew up in Chicago, but she's lived in many other exciting locales, from the coast of Maine to western North Carolina and, for the last several years, northeastern Wisconsin. She's enjoyed a long career writing nonfiction books as a coauthor and ghostwriter, but now she tells stories her fictional characters whisper in her ear. Seven romance novels later, *The Rancher's Wyoming Twins* is the first of her latest miniseries, Back to Adelaide Creek, for Harlequin Heartwarming readers. When she's not writing, Virginia reads other authors' books, wanders on trails and in parks near her home, and dreams about future road trips.

Books by Virginia McCullough

Harlequin Heartwarming

Girl in the Spotlight
Something to Treasure
Love, Unexpected

Back to Bluestone River

A Family for Jason
The Christmas Kiss
A Bridge Home

Back to Adelaide Creek

The Rancher's Wyoming Twins

Visit the Author Profile page
at Harlequin.com for more titles.

To Phyllis Whitney and Elisabeth Ogilvie,
two trailblazers of romance—they led the way
and many of us happily followed.

CHAPTER ONE

DESPITE THE URGE to climb back into his truck and drive away, Jeff Stanhope kept his feet planted on the dusty ground and stared across the acre of front yard at the house he'd grown up in. Memories of his childhood and teenage years crept out of their hiding places as he watched more than a dozen men and women and a couple of children gathered around picnic tables and the grill. The Stanhope ranch had once been a magnet for friends and neighbors to come together for a barbecue on many a weekend afternoon. Picking out the people he recognized wasn't much of a challenge. Almost everyone had played some part in his past.

At the moment, only one person really mattered. Jeff smiled as Heather stepped away from a cluster of women. Then she crossed her arms over her chest and stared. At him.

The sight of his kid sister both lifted his

heart and quieted the anxiety needling his gut all day, and yesterday, and countless days before that. He waved and nearly laughed out loud in relief when Heather began to saunter his way. Her deep frown and narrowed eyes didn't matter. That fierce look of disapproval was temporary. She wouldn't stay mad at him forever.

"That's your sister, huh?" Carson asked.

Jeff pivoted to the fourteen-year-old who stood a few feet behind him and off to the side. "Yep, that's Heather. Follow me, Carson." He pointed to the dog. "Keep an eye on Winnie."

"Uh, are you sure you want me with you? She's kinda eyeing you, and not in a good way," Carson said. "Seems she's having a party and we're crashing it."

Jeff offered a sheepish smile to Carson. "What can I say? You were right. You told me I should call first. Too late now." Jeff picked up his pace and opened his arms as he approached Heather. He had no doubt she would step right into them.

Not quite.

His sister stopped a few feet short of him. "A heads-up would have been nice," she said. "It's called an RSVP." She planted her hands on her hips. "Maybe send a text, the way most people living in this century would." She glanced at Carson, and that's when the smile Jeff remembered transformed her face. When she extended her hand to the boy, he shook it, a little awkwardly and with his fair skin turning pink. "It's good to meet you, Carson. I—we—are glad you're here."

"I guess you're having a barbecue," Carson said.

"What's going on?" Jeff asked.

"We're celebrating," Heather said flatly, shaking her head. Finally, she curled up a corner of her mouth in a lopsided smile, not warm and welcoming like the one she offered Carson, but it was a start. "We're celebrating my wedding, you dolt. We had a lovely cere-mony here last week. It's not as if you didn't know Matt and I were getting married."

"C'mon, Heather," Jeff said. "Last week, we were still clearing out the apartment and donating the furniture, not to mention load-ing the truck and getting ready to hit the road. You didn't give us much lead time." Why would she? He'd ignored most of her texts and emails since leaving town. He hadn't ig-nored the one about the wedding, though.

News of her marriage had come as a shock. She'd never mentioned any guy, let alone this Mathis—Matt—Burton before. How did she expect him to react when he found out her husband-to-be was the guy who'd bought their ranch? A ranch the Stanhopes had established and run through the best and worst of times for almost five generations until a foreclosure changed everything.

Jeff tried to push those facts aside, at least until he and Heather had a good long talk.

"Anyway, you have made it to our party— late." Heather's grimace showed her impatience. She opened her mouth as if to say something, but apparently changed her mind because she shifted her gaze from him and again focused on Carson. "Why don't you come with me, Carson? I'll introduce you to our family and some of our best friends." She cocked her head toward the crowd. "We're celebrating another wildly happy occasion, the arrival of my friends Olivia Donoghue and her daughter, Jillian. They've moved here, too, and just arrived."

"I told Carson about them," Jeff interjected, "so he knows who they are." Heather could be furious with him for a good long while, and that would be a small price to pay for all his mistakes. As long as she kept smiling at Carson and making him feel welcome, Jeff's heart would turn to mush and he'd be grateful to Heather forever. Later, he'd figure out how to mend fences. He hadn't seen her since he'd run away from Adelaide Creek almost five years ago. Jeff had talked to her only a handful of times in those years. That lapse was on him, though. Not one bit of it was her fault.

"This is Winnie," Carson said. The brown-and-white dog with floppy ears and an endearing face raised her head at the sound of her name. "I bet you wonder what's happening around here, don't you, Win?" He turned to Heather. "She's a mix of a lot of things, probably basset hound because of her long ears, but my mom thought she had some terrier in her, too." The teenager paused and jabbed his thumb at Jeff. "He helped us pick her out at the shelter."

"That was a couple of years ago," Jeff explained, but immediately realized it wasn't necessary to add anything. Carson had it covered. When it came to Winnie he had no trouble talking. Could be that Carson and Winnie would do all the ice breaking for Jeff.

Carson Moore, who'd turned fourteen mere days before they left Seattle, was the catalyst for Jeff's decision to come back home to Adelaide Creek. He'd weighed other options, but not for long. Now that his life had changed in a big way the strong pull back to his roots made the choice an easy one, at least as far as major life-altering actions went. Once he'd made up his mind he was quick to get the move underway. Maybe it was the whirlwind of the past weeks, but now Jeff needed a minute to get his bearings.

Along with memories of barbecues and parties, unpleasant reminders surfaced of the last time he'd made the trip up this same long road to the ranch, driving this very truck. On that day, Jeff had left the motor running while he raced to the barn and gathered the hand tools he'd left behind. He ignored the new owner's attempt to be cordial and have a conversation extending beyond a quick hello. Angry and bitter over losing the sheep ranch he'd been raised on—and the only way of life he knew—Jeff had gone beyond ordinary rudeness to open hostility. He'd packed what he'd wanted and sped away, tires screeching.

Since he prided himself on his ability to

control his emotions, he'd had to live with that embarrassing moment and other regrets about how he behaved. Besides, his anger hadn't solved any problems. His rude departure left him feeling that he'd dishonored his parents and the many generations of Stanhopes that came before him. This time, though, he intended to make peace with Matt Burton, the man he'd treated poorly that day. Whether it suited him or not, the Burtons, all of them, were his family now.

"Winnie is quite a beauty," Heather said, leaning over to pet the dog. "Welcome to our ranch, Miss Winnie. Let's introduce you to everyone." She grinned. "Come on, Carson."

The boy and Winnie followed Heather, leaving Jeff to adjust to his surroundings. The only thing that had changed since he'd left was almost everything. For starters, he wasn't the same bitter man who'd gone away. He still labeled himself a loner, but time had smoothed his rougher edges. He couldn't afford to aim anger and resentment at anyone, not now that he had Carson to take care of.

Carson already towered over Heather, not much more than five feet and a couple of inches tall. She pointed this way and that to indicate the landmarks of the ranch, the barn and the stables behind it and the corral and field where the horses hung out. She gestured into the distance where sheep dotted the pasture, patchy now in the fall. Jeff was itching to get himself a horse to ride. He'd get one for Carson, too, when the boy finally caught a touch of horse fever.

Some changes he observed were for the better. The old frame house he'd said goodbye to had once accumulated a long list of needed repairs and updates. From what he could see in front of him, quite a few items on that list had been scratched off, starting with the coat of white paint on the house that left it standing pretty and proud. Heather and Matt had also put pumpkins on the steps to a new wraparound porch, and pots of deep red and golden mums sat on the railing. It was a warm day, and heavy cloud cover had blocked the earlier bright sunlight, but the colors surrounding him were typical signs of mid-October.

Some things were the same, as they should be. For one thing, his sister's curious light brown eyes and smile reminded him of the sunny girl she'd been. As a teenager, she'd been a good student and not a bad catcher on the softball team, but she'd been truly serious about only two things. First, riding her horse and pal, Velvet, and second, doing well in nursing school. Today, celebrating her new life, Jeff could see no trace of the brokenhearted woman who'd departed Adelaide Creek at the same time he had. She'd headed for points east for the first of a series of temporary nursing assignments, while he pointed his truck west.

Even before they'd gone their separate ways years ago, he'd struggled to think of her as more than the little girl he'd taught to ride horses as well as take good care of them. Now here she was, all grown up, married and stepmom to a set of twins. Not that he understood how any of that happened. Not yet, anyway. Call him suspicious, but how could his sister fall for Matt Burton? But here she was, living in the same house on the same ranch she'd grown up on.

As they got deeper into the yard, Jeff saw a guy around his own age serving up hot dogs and burgers. Jeff immediately recognized him as Burton. Matt was chatting with Heather's best friend, Bethany, and her parents, Jen and

Dan Hoover. Those three were fixtures in his childhood. He'd never have imagined being so happy to see them.

Heather turned her head and beamed at him as she pointed to two little kids zipping across the yard. "See what being a maid of honor at Bethany's wedding led to? I married the best man and those little cuties are my new seven-year-old twins." Heather stopped walking and lightly put her hand on Carson's arm to hold him back. "The redheaded girl chasing them is Jillian. She's eleven. This time last year, she was my patient, but now she's a special friend."

Carson pointed back to Jeff. "He, well, he sort of told me the story of how she'd been sick. But she's well now, right?"

"I'm glad Jeff explained her situation. Yes, her cancer—leukemia—is in remission." Heather waved to a woman who was watching them from her seat at the bottom of what appeared to Jeff to be a pyramid made of crates. "That's Jillian's mom, my friend Olivia Donoghue."

"A doctor," Carson said.

Jeff picked up Carson's eager tone. Heather's expression showed some surprise, but she confirmed that Olivia was indeed a radiologist. Later, Jeff would fill in more details about Carson's injuries, especially about his multifractured ankle, mostly healed now. He still had some tough physical therapy ahead, though. The same was true for the deep slash running the length of his arm below his elbow, ending along the outside of his hand. Those two injuries were the trauma to his body, wounds the doctors and physical therapists assured Carson would heal in time. The emotional fallout was still ongoing. And not limited to Carson, Jeff admitted. The memories of the accident that mangled Carson's arm and ankle and had killed Karen, the boy's mom, still had the power to keep Jeff up at night. Maybe they always would.

"How about I introduce you to the kids, Carson?" Heather asked. "They're younger, but they're your family now." She paused and put her hand on his arm. "These relationships can get a little complicated. Believe me, Matt and I understand that."

Carson acknowledged Heather's words with a subtle nod and followed her.

Heather gave Jeff's shoulder a playful shove. "Go introduce yourself. Matt is eager to…

well, to really meet you for the first time. So is Olivia." Her smile faded a little. "They're getting tired of hearing me talk about my big, bad older brother. Now they finally get to see you in the flesh."

"Will do." Jeff noted that she kept up her cool distance from him, but none of that bled over to Carson. Heather led the boy to the pyramid of crates where the kids had gathered. It pained Jeff to see the injured teen trying so hard to walk as if nothing was wrong with his ankle. He'd gone from the wheelchair to a walker and then a cane in record time, even while deep in emotional shock. Only in the last couple of weeks had Carson regained the mental energy to grasp that despite the seriousness of the injuries, physically he'd been fortunate and escaped permanent damage. The long-sleeved hoodie he wore today hid most of the scar on his arm and hand. Healing couldn't come fast enough for Carson, who was determined to start practicing dunks and jump shots at the first opportunity.

Getting Carson on the back of a horse was going to be trickier, but understandable, considering the kid came from busy Seattle streets. He'd grown up playing on concrete sidewalks and in neighborhood parks. Not a barn or a pasture in sight. Because of that, Carson didn't view horses as creatures with a special mystique. He didn't link them to adventure and freedom, not the way Jeff—and Heather—always had and probably always would. On that point, he and Carson weren't on the same page or even reading from the same book.

After Carson made it clear he had no interest in horses, Jeff left the topic alone so far, but one day soon he'd nudge Carson and remind him that Seattle was the past. His immediate future was in this Wyoming town, Adelaide Creek, with its population of fewer than five hundred. The best way to explore the rocky ledges and hills and the grassy basins where the sheep grazed was on the back of a horse. Jeff knew that truth from experience that ran so deep he felt it in his bones.

For a couple of flashing seconds, Jeff longed to be alone in the stable instead of meandering toward the grill where his new brother-in-law was flipping burgers and turning hot dogs. How was it a grown man, thirty-six years old, could feel so awkward and self-conscious and out of place, as if he didn't really belong where he was born? Carson, the fish out of water, seemed more at ease than Jeff himself.

Carson already had his phone out and was recording a video of the kids playing. He was using his stiff right hand and the sleeve of his oversize sweatshirt had slid down his arm, exposing the scar, the visible reminder of his losses. As much as Jeff wanted to know what went through the boy's mind when he confronted this permanent scar, Jeff didn't ask outright. He didn't want Carson to feel pressured to come up with answers to tough questions, but did his aching ankle or the red slash on his arm trigger memories of the crash?

As he watched Carson interact with the kids, it struck him that the boy's all-is-right-with-the-world smile was missing from the scene. He used to amuse his mom by making silly faces, but for now those attempts to be funny had disappeared with most of the familiar routines, people and places in Carson's life. It hadn't taken much to make Karen laugh at her son's antics. More important than that, she never missed a chance to let her son know he was the best thing that ever happened to her.

Jeff had known Carson before his voice changed and he'd begun to fill out and grow into the high school athlete he aspired to be. Jeff also had been amused by the sharp, lively kid. The reminiscing made Jeff forget about meeting Matt and instead, he kept his eyes on Carson and Heather. He could hope to see the lightness in Carson make a comeback, but Jeff wouldn't fool himself, either. The boy's happy childhood had come to an abrupt— and cruel—end.

"It's not often I get to be a guest at such a special party." The voice came from a woman approaching Jeff from the side. "Your sister is pretty special."

"Yes, Olivia Donoghue, she is," Jeff replied, deliberately using her full name. Her reputation preceded her, but he was thrown by how strikingly beautiful she was. If he'd been wearing a hat he'd have touched the brim and lowered his chin in the manner of a true Western gentleman. "I hear this is a welcome party for you and your little girl."

Olivia grinned. "I know. How fun is that? Celebrating a wedding and welcoming Jillian and me to Adelaide Creek."

He'd never quite understood the notion of a melodic voice. Now he did, and it knocked him off-kilter. So did the woman who produced the melody with her words. She was a few inches taller than Heather, and Olivia's shoulder-length hair was more red than brown. The cotton jacket she wore exactly matched her blue-gray eyes.

"I don't suppose we need a formal introduction, Mr. Jeff Stanhope." Her already faint smile disappeared when she added, "Although I only know you as the perpetually long-lost brother of my good friend. You'll have to fill in the rest."

Nothing timid about Olivia. It was his turn to come up with a response, a little challenging now that her musical voice had hit a flat note.

"Well, I'm here now." Jeff gestured toward the clusters of people. "I'm guessing you've met some of these folks during your vacation here this summer." He smiled. "See? I heard about your visit that morphed into pulling up stakes in Minnesota and moving here. I'm not completely out of the loop." He paused. "At least not lately."

"Oh, no need to defend yourself. I shouldn't be snarky," Olivia said. "It's just that your sister lived in my house while she helped me take care of my daughter through her long treatment. We got to be good friends, so I know how disappointed she was that you didn't stay in touch. She was hurt…big-time." Olivia's eyes opened wide and she put her hand over her mouth. She closed her big eyes for a second before opening them again. "Oops…talk about nervy. And *none* of my business."

"No, it sure isn't." He did hesitate to let his irritation come through in his voice. "But I'll grant you this, Olivia, I can't say you lied."

"I had no call—"

Jeff raised his hand, palm out, to stop her from explaining. "When I figure out why I cut myself off from everything and everyone I ever cared about, I'll let you in on it."

Olivia had made an unforgettable first impression, but he knew her by reputation, too. To use the basketball lingo Carson tossed into conversations, Heather's close friend started out with a couple of points already on the board. Jeff admired a woman willing to upend her whole life and move to Adelaide Creek, after only a two-week visit. He knew from Heather's emails, the ones he'd mostly left unanswered, that Olivia and her daughter had endured a difficult, life-threatening time.

"Uh, how about if I get out of your business

and introduce you to my favorite person?" Olivia's distinctive voice was back. "Jillian is eleven and loves horses. She's already at home here in Adelaide Creek."

Jeff glanced at Matt in the distance, still talking to a group of people around the grill. He'd meet his new brother-in-law soon enough. Jeff swept his arm ahead. "Lead the way, Olivia. While we're there, I also need to make my own introductions. As of last week, I'm Nick and Lucy's uncle."

Jillian sat between the twins on the bottom level of the pyramid perch, which was off to the side of the house and driveway. Carson stood a little apart with his injured foot resting on the edge of one of the crate risers. Phone in hand, he was leaning forward and talking to the younger kids while Winnie sniffed the little kids' shoes. Based on his body language, the way he nodded along with the kids as they talked, Carson was probably asking questions about the pyramid. The boy's gaze followed where the kids were pointing, and he appeared to be completely focused on the pair of younger children. A pleasant sense of satisfaction rippled through Jeff. After arriving only minutes ago, Carson looked the part of an older cousin interacting with little kids eager to soak up his attention.

"This must be pretty exciting for Lucy and Nick," Jeff said. "They have a new mom and Carson is their cousin now. By choice, I suppose we could say."

"The best kind of relatives," Olivia said dryly. "The ones we get to choose."

"I'd agree with you on that, but for the fact Carson's mom died." Jeff thought it best to remind her of the most important part of the boy's story, since at least at the moment it dominated everything. "What I mean is the boy doesn't have any family now, except for those of us who choose him." There was Carson's grandma, Karen's mom, but she was in an assisted living facility and too frail to take on a teenager, no matter how much she loved him. Carson promised to stay in touch with her through texts and videos to let her know how he was doing in his new home. That was a promise Jeff intended to help the boy keep. Carson had already texted photos and video of the scenery on their drive from Seattle to Adelaide Creek.

"From what Heather tells me, *you* decided

to make him your family. True?" Olivia gave him an expectant look.

He didn't have time to explain how and why that had happened, because the twins rushed toward him, putting their kid brakes on at the last minute or they'd have barreled into him. Jillian followed, but Carson lagged behind with Winnie and another dog.

"Did you know you're our uncle now?" Nick asked, pointing to Jeff. "Uncle Matt is our uncle, too, but he does the same stuff as dads do."

Jeff tapped his temple. "Let me think. Heather is my sister. And you two are now her kids. Whaddya know? You're right. That makes me your uncle Jeff." He grinned at both kids. "And I'd be proud if you called me that."

"So, that means Carson is our new cousin." Lucy's face lit up. "Wow, we have a much bigger family now. It grew a lot in a week… seven days."

Olivia laughed. "It's a little hard to keep track of, huh?"

Not to the kids, Jeff thought. It was all part of their changing lives.

"Heather said we have lots of friends, too,"

Nick said. "We have Olivia and Jillian. And now Winnie."

Winnie was busy sniffing the other dog, who tolerated the interest without returning it.

"What's your dog's name?" Jeff asked.

"Scrambler," Nick said. "See? He likes Winnie already."

"He started out life as our gram's dog," Lucy explained. "Now he belongs to everybody. He follows us everywhere."

Jeff nodded to the redhead. "And you must be Jillian. I've heard lots of good things about you."

"Heather told me you really love horses," Jillian declared as she got to her feet.

Her wide-eyed expression reminded Jeff of Heather when the subject of horses came up. "I'll bet you do, too, huh. I can see you have that special I-love-horses sparkle in your eyes." Jeff said. He glanced at Carson, but if the boy heard Jillian, he wasn't letting on. Instead, he'd backed up and turned his attention to the two dogs. He'd also taken his foot off the riser, but was resting his weight on his good ankle, using his injured one only for balance. He'd have been more comfortable with his cane to lean on, but he'd made the choice to leave it in the truck. Jeff couldn't convince him to bring it along.

"I love, love, love horses." Jillian raised herself up on her tiptoes and crossed her hands over her heart. It seemed she had more to say, but stopped when her mom more or less interrupted and gestured toward the pyramid.

"Matt built that contraption," she said. "He and his mom, Stacey, dubbed it the Twins Topper. It looked kind of dangerous to me at first," Olivia said, talking fast and way too loud. "Nothing more than a pile of flimsy crates attached to each other, but I inspected it and saw that Matt had driven the stakes deep into the ground and all the connections holding the crates together are strong." She stopped to take a breath. "So, it's much sturdier than it seems."

"Can't say I was worried," Jeff said, puzzled by the way Olivia abruptly interrupted Jillian and changed the direction of the conversation. Maybe Jillian wanted to extol the world of horses, but Olivia sure didn't. "But then, being raised on a ranch kind of increases the chances to get banged up some."

"I was thinking of Carson as well as Jillian," Olivia said, formal and cool. "Heather mentioned that he's recovering from a couple of serious injuries, so I assume you don't want him climbing about on crates. Obviously, I had to check it out before I'd let Jillian on it."

"I suppose so, but Carson's older—and healing fast. He's pretty much testing himself and figuring out how much he can do." He conceded nothing, but he kept a pleasant tone. He knew next to nothing about Matt, but based on Heather's description Jeff was certain his new brother-in-law wouldn't put the twins at risk. "After what your little girl has been through, you probably have your own feelings about that."

Olivia nodded and then hurried away from his side and closer to Jillian and the twins. Man, he was trying to be reasonable, but Olivia was all over the place, warm and friendly one second, cool and standoffish the next. She'd made a couple of things clear, though, including her unsolicited bad opinion of him.

TALK ABOUT A first impression gone wrong. Please, give her the previous five minutes back and Olivia would start over and do much, much better. As she watched Jeff walk away, she resolved that from now on she'd watch her tongue when it came to his relationship with Heather. As was only right, she'd leave that to the two of them. At the same time, she might have known Jillian would plunge right into a conversation with Jeff about horses. In her daughter's mind, Heather's legendary horse-loving brother was a kindred spirit. Maybe it was inevitable that Jillian end up a girl devoted to horses and riding, but not when her body was still recovering from the effects of chemotherapy. Even if the assault to her body wasn't obvious to the untrained eye, Olivia had absorbed almost too much information about what chemo could do to a child.

Then there was Jeff himself. Olivia had seen photos and even his mother's paintings of him done over a period of years. No way had those images prepared Olivia for the real guy. They hadn't done him justice, not even close. He had a presence about him that went beyond his thick dark hair and deep-set eyes that brought to mind luscious dark chocolate. With his wide shoulders and muscular arms, he had a body sculpted by the physical work of ranching or more recently, crewing on trawlers and freighters.

Olivia had expected him to be more as Heather described him, still hardened and bitter about losing his family's legacy, this very ranch. If those old feelings were still a part of Jeff, he wasn't showing them at the moment. At least not today, and not with Carson nearby. Whatever. It wasn't her job to analyze any of this. His feelings about this ranch and his former home were completely irrelevant. She had formed an opinion that would guide all her dealings with the man. No matter how friendly, even charming Jeff Stanhope might be, he was a runner. A man who ran away from anything that smacked of responsibility. Like her dad. And Jillian's father. She didn't need a third runner messing up her life.

On the other hand, she had to accept other realities. No matter why Jeff had all but broken his ties with Heather in the past, today he was an important connection for Olivia and Jillian here in Adelaide Creek. Her new home of the heart, Olivia had whispered when she'd made the unexpectedly—and blissfully easy—decision to leave her hospital job in Minnesota and build a new life here in Wyoming with Jillian. Whether she took to Jeff or not, he was Heather's brother and civility was in order.

Until August, when she and Jillian visited Heather for a vacation, the notion of a true home-of-the-heart had seemed ridiculous—at least for her. Then, she'd driven into Heather's hometown for the first time and everything changed. Maybe it was the canopy of cottonwoods that greeted her coming into town. Or it could have been the diner or the combination grocery store–gift shop that were the heart of Merchant Street, the social and business center of Adelaide Creek.

Olivia had warm feelings about most everywhere she'd ever lived, but this was the only time in her life she'd fallen deeply in love with a place—and it made her believe life could be magical again. Exactly two months from the day Olivia decided to make the move, she and Jillian again drove their packed-to-the-gills car past the Welcome To Adelaide Creek sign on the road into town. Jillian clapped and yelled, "Yay! We're here in our new town." Olivia couldn't have expressed it any better herself.

Their two-week visit hadn't been perfect, not with the scorching summer heat wave to contend with. It might have deterred other people, but not her, or Jillian. Today's October air was a gift filled with its own special scents of the ranch mixed with roasting corn and burgers on the grill. In contrast to the earlier light, heavier clouds darkened the sky and rolled toward the ranch. If those clouds kept coming and emptied, Heather and Matt would be thrilled. Party or no party, they were desperate for rain.

Watching the four kids play with the two dogs, Olivia thought about the way all the pieces of her move had fallen into place. Within days of coming back from her visit to Heather, Olivia decided to take on the challenge of pulling up stakes again, but this time to claim her true home. Even with Jillian in remission, Olivia was painfully aware that no guarantees existed, so why not take her chances?

She sold her house in Red Wing only a couple of days after listing it with an agent. Then, in the course of researching possible openings for an experienced radiologist, she'd come across articles about a shake-up in how radiology, and most medical services, was delivered in the largest health care network in Adams

County, geographically large with a small population. When those changes led to a new position for a diagnostic radiologist based in the hospital in Landrum, Olivia jumped on it and an offer came fast.

The only loose end had been a place to live. That problem had been solved when Heather and Matt decided to go to the courthouse and get married without fanfare and throw this party later. That left Heather's cozy converted bunkhouse available for her and Jillian to settle into only yesterday as their first-stop home.

Observing her surroundings now, watching Jillian with the other children, Olivia felt as if the stars approved of her decision, too, and lined up to give her a path to her new home. Being rooted in science, she usually didn't think about the hand of fate or any such thing, but maybe she believed in it now, at least a little bit.

She was still deep in thought when Matt and Jeff approached. Seeing Matt, Jillian raced over to him. She nervously laced her fingers together and held them against her chest. "Uh, Matt, would it be okay if I went to the corral to see the horses? I won't touch them or anything.

I just want to see them up close." She spoke fast as if that was a sure way to get to a yes.

"Let's slow it down, Jillian." Olivia could see the end of the corral, but no horses.

As if reading her mind, Jillian said, "Lucy said the horses are behind the stables, so you can't see them from here."

"Of course, it's okay," Matt said, grinning. "Most of our horses welcome some human company."

"If you don't mind, Jillian, I'd enjoy tagging along with you," Jeff said. "I haven't had a chance to say hello yet, either. Heather's mentioned a horse named Pebbles she's fond of. I'd like to get a look at her."

So much for her words about taking it slow. They blew away on the wind.

"C'mon, Mom," Jillian said as she ran ahead.

"Okay, okay."

"Hey, Carson, do you want to come with us?" Jeff said, passing the teenager where he was watching the twins playing with the dogs.

"Where are you going?" Nick shouted.

"Just to visit the horses," Matt said.

Predictably, the twins immediately hurried off the pyramid and joined Jillian. Carson stayed behind.

"Nah, you go on. I'm good. Hungry, actually. I'll go grab a burger." Carson spoke while already in motion toward the grill, where Heather had taken Matt's place.

"Carson will never be far from a friendly face around here," Olivia said, falling into line.

Jeff smiled brightly, as if he appreciated her words. "That's what I count on to make this huge change easier for him."

Jillian and the twins were already on the lower bar of the corral fence and some horses were ambling over. Olivia lightly caught Jeff's arm to stop his forward progress. "If it's all the same to you, I'd just as soon no one hype the joys of horseback riding to Jillian—at least not yet."

"With my sister around—and Matt—that might be hard to accomplish," Jeff said, his tone blunt and objective. "They ride all the time. Matt buys and leases horses. It's part of day-to-day life around here."

"I get that," Olivia said through clenched jaws. "I'm not that dense. Jillian *will* learn to ride one day. But she needs a little more recovery time before that happens."

Jeff raised his hands defensively. "Okay,

Olivia. I get your point, but she can be relaxed around horses and enjoy their company without being encouraged to ride them."

That stopped her, sort of. But unlike Heather, Jeff couldn't know what Jillian had been through. "You can't see it, Jeff, and Jillian doesn't *feel* it, but her body is weakened from the chemotherapy." She wrapped her hands around the back of her neck to release some of the tension in her neck. These conversations about what Jillian was ready for had a way of making Olivia stressed, even brittle. She sighed and added, "Those chemicals saved her, but remission from leukemia doesn't come without paying a heavy price."

Jeff's eyes showed concern. "That's probably a conversation you should have with Matt and Heather. I can only imagine what you've been through." He offered a troubled smile. "Whether I'm happy with it or not, I don't even own any horses yet. That step is still in the future."

Maybe that was true, but Olivia couldn't seem to leave well enough alone. "But Jillian has heard Heather talk about how you taught her to ride and she painted a vivid picture of the pair of you practically living on your horses." Olivia sighed.

Jeff didn't offer a response but watched her with anticipation.

Apparently, it was up to her to bring the conversation to a cordial end. "Speaking of painting pictures, one of your mother's oil paintings of you and Heather on your horses is hanging in the bunkhouse. Jillian loves that painting, and when she hears your name, she thinks horses. I guess that's why I'm going on and on to you." That and whatever else it was about the man that made her nervous and kept her talking way too much.

Jeff smiled. "Well, what Heather says is true. We rode when we herded sheep, and we rode for the joy of it. It was like breathing. But how you handle Jillian and her desire to ride is entirely up to you."

Olivia heard Jeff's matter-of-fact tone and snickered. She put her hand to her forehead. "Wow, listen to me. I can talk about Jillian being obsessed with horses, but I'm the one who can't let it go." She filled her lungs with air and exhaled. "I'm sorry. I'm going to stop bringing this up."

Jeff scanned the area around them, as if

wanting to be sure no one could hear him. "I haven't shared my plans for the lodge with anyone yet, not even Heather. But right now I'm certain I won't be ready to teach anyone to ride, adults or kids, anytime soon. You've got my word on that. If I end up teaching at all, it will be next summer at the earliest." Jeff grinned. "That's our secret."

"Okay, then, no one will hear about your plan from me." She made an X over her heart. "I promise."

Jeff glanced over her shoulder. "That sky is getting darker still—and fast." She turned and he pointed beyond the corral and the pasture to see massive charcoal clouds moving in quickly and sweeping away the lighter clouds. Large, heavy raindrops suddenly plunked down on their skin. "This isn't ordinary rain, Olivia."

Olivia spotted Matt on the other side of the corral where several horses grazed in the pasture. He shouted something over his shoulder, but she couldn't hear him.

"Matt probably wants to bring the horses in," Jeff said, breaking into a fast run. By the time Olivia reached him, Jeff had hustled all three kids off the fence and into the barn with

Scrambler. He was on his way out to the corral to help Matt move the horses.

Olivia went from a fast walk to a jog, but then stopped to glance behind her. Heather and the other guests were ferrying food from the yard to the house. With Winnie dancing at his feet, Carson was helping Stacey yank the cloths off the tables before they blew away. It took only a minute or two to transform the yard from festive to forlorn.

Olivia considered heading for the house to lend a hand, but Jillian was already in the barn. Besides, Carson was now coming her way with the dog at his side. He was hobbling a little as he tried to speed up.

"Why don't you go into the house, Carson?"

"No, I need to get to the barn, or the stable. That's where Jeff is." His dark blue eyes communicated urgency, but something else as well.

"Okay, let's hurry," she said, realizing that Carson's need to find shelter with Jeff was stronger than a desire to be warm and dry in the house with the others. Olivia joined the teenager and the two made it to the stable right before a booming crack of thunder. A bolt of lightning quickly followed and lit up everything outside and inside.

Joining the kids at the open end of the building, Olivia drew them farther inside. Along with the younger kids, she stayed back from the wide doors and out of the way as Matt and Jeff led the horses into their stalls. Then the two men ran back outside to where a couple of straggler horses stood close together in the wooden shelter in the pasture. Winnie stayed almost glued to Carson, but Scrambler started barking at the two men and had to be coaxed deeper inside.

More thunder rumbled and rapid lightning illuminated the space around the buildings. Jillian was laughing along with the twins, who were jumping around in excitement over the storm and the whoosh of the wind. Even when a limb from a cottonwood between the house and the barn crashed to the ground, the three younger kids showed no fear. Lightning and thunder were continuous now, with almost no break between the strikes in the sky and the deafening roars.

Olivia glanced at Carson, old enough to know this was a no-joke storm. Subdued, he leaned against the doorjamb, almost frozen in place. But then he pulled out his phone. When Olivia followed the angle of his arm and his gaze, she realized he was recording every step Jeff took as he secured the horses. The rain poured down fast and hard, already rapidly creating ponds and streams in the ground around the buildings. Jeff's hair was plastered down and rain dripped off his face. His clothes were soaked through.

With the kids staying close to her, Olivia wanted to shout out to Carson to reassure him that everything was under control and would be fine. But she knew no such thing. Carson lowered his phone and stopped recording, but he never took his gaze off Jeff. Wanting him to move back from the doors, Olivia called his name. When he turned around, his eyes were filled with fear.

CHAPTER TWO

JEFF INHALED THE smell of the bacon sizzling in the pan, gave the scrambled eggs a final stir, and then flipped the last of the golden brown buttermilk pancakes. Perfection. "Hey, Carson, grab a couple of plates on your way to the counter. And knives and forks, too."

Trying not to be obvious about it, Jeff kept his eye on Carson wincing as he pushed to the edge of the couch before standing. The lingering aches in his leg didn't appear to distract him from whatever he was staring at on his phone.

Jeff transferred the eggs and bacon to a platter and put it on the breakfast bar. "Leave the phone on the coffee table. You know the rules."

Carson's stone-face expression didn't ease, but he dutifully left the phone on the coffee table and retrieved the plates from the cabinet. "Who came up with that rule anyway?" he muttered, not looking at Jeff.

Pretending surprise, Jeff exclaimed, "He speaks! I have proof, even if I don't always agree with the words that come out of his mouth." Smiling, he added, "In case you forgot, making rules is my superpower—one of them anyway."

One side of the teenager's mouth curled up. Sliding his own phone down to the far end of the breakfast bar, Jeff perched on a stool across from Carson. Jeff pushed the platter closer to the boy and told him to help himself. Carson wasted no time piling his plate high with the food. He drowned the pancakes in syrup and added an extra dollop on the eggs for good measure.

As the two ate a breakfast worth bragging about, Jeff silently assessed Carson. He searched for signs of…of what? At this point, he couldn't define exactly what he was expecting to see. Between Carson's growth spurt over the last year and his deeper voice, he was a lanky teenager now, not the child he'd been not so long ago. Before the accident, Carson had been an okay soccer player, but the basketball court was a different story. Both an excellent shooter and above-average shot blocker, he had star potential, at least when he regained the strength he'd lost.

In spite of his injuries, Carson was still a healthy kid with broadening shoulders and muscular legs. Physically, at least. It was harder to get a bead on what was going on inside Carson. From the first days in the hospital after the accident, everyone who dealt with the teenager told him—even promised him—that time would heal his broken heart. But if Jeff added up everything Carson had been through over the last few months, the teen showed amazing resilience. Never notably shy, Carson had easily mingled with the others at the ranch, especially the younger kids. Until the storm brought the party to an abrupt end, it had been an okay first day in Adelaide Creek.

"Is your leg giving you a little trouble this morning?" Jeff asked.

Carson shrugged. "It's just stiff." As he spoke, the teenager glanced at the long scar on his forearm and hand. It would be many months before the redness faded, and despite the surgeon's meticulous suturing, Carson would always have a scar. Meanwhile, thanks to PT, his muscle strength was coming back.

Jeff bit his tongue to keep from commenting about Carson hurting a little. His entire team of doctors and physical therapists had repeatedly warned Carson about being on his feet too long or moving too fast.

"I was running around a lot at the ranch on Saturday, you know, chasing the kids and dogs," Carson admitted, "and trying to get to the barn in the downpour."

"A boy who hails from Seattle knows a little something about rain," Jeff teased.

"Rain, lots of it, but not many wild storms with that much lightning. And the tree branches crashing. It went on for a long time." Carson stabbed a pancake with his fork with a little more force than necessary. "Weren't you scared out in the open space with Matt and the horses?"

"A little," Jeff admitted. Mostly though, he'd been impressed by how naturally he and Matt fell into a rhythm in order to work together to calm the horses and get them safely into the stables. "The thing is, sometimes the only rain you get around here for a good long while comes with a violent storm. But with the snow, it's a little different. We only get that much excitement with a full-blown blizzard a couple of times a year."

"That's cool," Carson said, glancing at the windows with a view of the mostly bare trees that exposed the footpaths through the woods. "I wouldn't mind seeing more snow than we got in the city."

"As for your ankle, you don't need to chase Winnie today," Jeff said. "I'll do that. Besides, the dog and I have a lot to do here at the lodge."

Carson looked down at Winnie, who was curled up at his feet. "Good girl." In a stern parental voice, he said, "We'll have to limit the time you can hang with Scrambler, won't we? He's a bad influence. We don't want you picking up bad habits. No begging for food in this house."

"Winnie with her fine manners was a popular newcomer at the party," Jeff said, smiling.

Carson agreed with a nod before helping himself to a couple more pancakes off the platter.

As if he hadn't seen Carson's wavy sandy blond hair before that minute, Jeff noted that it not only covered his ears, but the back fringe was saying hello to the neck of his T-shirt. How had Jeff missed that? "After I pick you up at school today, we'll get you a haircut." He ran his hand down the back of his own head. Shaggier than he usually wore. "I'll get one, too. I think I saw a drop-in shop when we drove through town. We can give it a try. Okay?"

Carson nodded, but didn't look up. Jeff hadn't expected him to argue or balk, especially about something as ordinary as an overdue haircut. The boy rarely objected to Jeff's directives, but he also seldom offered much in the way of opinions when it came to the personal side of things. On the other hand, Jeff groaned inside at his own lapse. He should have taken care of the boy's haircut before they'd left Seattle, so he'd be ready for his first day at a new school. Sometimes it seemed he'd failed one more test that measured what kind of guardian he was turning out to be.

Observing Carson fuel himself for the day ahead, Jeff wished he could get the teenager to open up more. When it was only the two of them, Jeff had to work hard to draw him out. He used to be such a talkative kid, but even limiting the time he could isolate with his phone and tablet hadn't coaxed him out of this quiet phase. That made his sociable banter with Heather and Matt—and Olivia—reassuring. Unlike a lot of teenagers, he seemed okay being around the younger kids, even recording their antics, which brought out their inner performers. The twins were excited about having a new cousin to go along with their new mom.

Jeff checked the time and pushed away from the breakfast bar, making a quick decision to clean up the plates and platters later.

"Do I have to start school today?" Carson asked, reluctantly sliding off the high stool. "Why can't I wait a day or two before enrolling?"

At times it was so tempting to take the path of least resistance and let Carson get his own way. What difference would a day make? But Jeff's better judgment kicked in fast. "Because I can't think of a good reason not to get that part of your life underway," Jeff said. "And I'll bet you can't think of one, either."

Carson stared down at Winnie, who was on her feet and staring back as if waiting for directions. "Winnie will be lonely without me." Carson smirked. "How about that for a reason?"

"As reasons go, it's pretty weak," Jeff said, smirking back. "I'll keep her company around here. She knows me pretty well." Memories flashed in his head. Karen had specifically asked Jeff to come along to help pick out a dog, but Carson was the first to spot the dog with her floppy ears, about a year old and eager to play. Or maybe it was Winnie who spotted the eleven-year-old and chose him. Sometimes it seemed Winnie was smart enough to pick the child whose heart was ready. Whatever. Winnie had become a prized addition to the family before the door of the shelter closed behind them.

"You hear that?" Carson said, leaning over to rub Winnie's jowls. "You get to help Jeff do whatever it is he does. So, if it gets dull around here, you blame him, not me."

Carson had often talked to Winnie as his way of teasing his mom and sometimes Jeff. A quirky habit, but usually fun. After Karen died, the boy had little to say to the dog or anyone, but he rarely let Winnie out of his sight. Jeff's heart hitched hearing a touch of Carson's ribbing make a comeback. He was happy to play along. "Dull? She's going to make the rounds of her brand-new home. There's nothing boring about the woods and cabins and the roads and paths to travel to get to them."

Amused, Carson shrugged and picked a route through a pile of still unpacked boxes on the way to his room and came out with his backpack. Battered and faded, the dark blue pack with half a dozen zippered pockets had seen much better days. But Jeff knew not to offer to get him a new one. He'd tried that already. Twice. But Karen had given Carson that backpack and he wasn't interested in replacing it.

Jeff left the house first and gave Carson a minute to say goodbye to Winnie for the day. He could tease Carson about Winnie having him at her beck and call, but Jeff would always be grateful for that good-natured dog. Even in fresh, sharp pain in the ER cubicle, Carson never forgot about Winnie and urged Jeff to go home and check on her and make sure to walk her. Later, home from the hospital, even on the darkest days of Carson's grief, he'd never neglected Winnie. Over these last four months, it seemed as if the two grieved the loss of Karen together.

When Carson climbed into the front seat of the truck, minus his cane, Jeff forced himself to keep his suggestions to himself. Instead, he shifted the subject to the school bus route. "I was thinking I'll drive you every day this first week. By that time, you'll be added to the bus schedule. I assume that's okay with you."

Carson nodded, but then blurted, "So, when I'm getting registered at the school, what are you going to call me? I mean, am I your foster kid?"

Jeff jolted, not only at the question, which came out of the blue, but at Carson's higher than normal pitch and his loud voice. Fortunately, he didn't have to search for an answer. "No, you're not my foster child, Carson." Carson knew it was quite the opposite. "You never were. I'm your guardian—your *legal* guardian—from now until you're an adult." Jeff tilted his head toward the seat behind him. "I've got the papers in that file to prove it, so there won't be any questions or misunderstandings. Not at the school or from any of the medical folks you'll be seeing to follow your treatment."

Everything about Carson's situation was a matter of public record, and that included the death of both parents. Carson's father had been gone for several years and Jeff had his death certificate in the file, along with Karen's. He'd included copies of the boy's school records just in case of glitches in the digital transfer between the schools.

When the accident first happened, Jeff hadn't been sure what Carson would want. Had he even known how limited his options were? With both parents gone and his grandmother unable to take care of him, foster care loomed. On the second day in the hospital, the fog of Carson's hours-long surgery had cleared and in that sterile, impersonal room, he was bombarded by the enormity of the loss that turned his world upside down. It had been left to Jeff to confirm what Carson already knew on some level, that his mother had been killed. Instantly, so she didn't suffer. Carson had nodded, and covered his eyes with his uninjured forearm. Vulnerable and fragile, Carson turned to Jeff and whispered, "I'm alone now. I don't have family or anyone."

Without hesitation, Jeff uttered the words that changed everything. "You have me, Carson. I'm not going anywhere." He heard himself say out loud what he'd been mulling over since he'd sat by himself, holding his head in his hands, in the family waiting room. He hadn't been confident he could pull it off, though, especially when social workers and an attorney acting as Carson's legal advocate fired questions at him. He'd had to fill out forms that were many pages long. He'd supplied all the facts of his past, grateful that he'd stayed out of trouble, with the exception of one misdemeanor for underage drinking in his freshman year in college. That hadn't raised an eyebrow.

Gradually, as the challenge he was taking on became increasingly real, doubts crept in. He spent a few nights pacing around the apartment questioning his fitness to take care of Carson, knowing he could never be a true substitute for Carson's mom.

Still, he didn't back out and take off. Resolve had taken over. Carson was not going to become another orphaned teen struggling to find his way in the foster care system. The decision was etched in concrete. And maybe he nursed nagging doubts about his ability to do a good job of caring for Carson, but considering the alternatives, he never regretted his choice.

Now, on the way to his new school, Jeff's answer satisfied Carson because he was quiet for the rest of the drive on the cloudy morning. The drive was only twenty minutes or so and took them along the flat stretch of road where sheep grazed on one side and cattle on the other. Hay bales dotted the fields or were stacked near barns and stables. When the road climbed and then dipped again, scraggly woods took over the ground between the rocky hills and ledges. The faint pink of the earlier sunrise bled through a mostly gray sky.

Carson didn't speak again until they turned the corner onto the main road to the high school in Landrum. "This place sure isn't like Seattle. There're hardly any cars on the road."

Exactly the way Jeff preferred his traffic. Very light. He'd never adjusted to Seattle's legendary crowded streets and highways and traffic inching along. Give Jeff empty roads and more sheep and horses than people and he was happy. "It hasn't changed much around here. Heather and I took the school bus to Landrum every day. Only heavy snow slowed us down."

"Nick and Lucy were telling me that a blizzard is coming," Carson said. "I thought they meant today, but they said the snow would come in November."

"They were giving you fair warning," Jeff said, amused. "Those two are characters, aren't they?"

"They think I'm cool, ya know. First, they got a new mom. Now an uncle who showed up out of nowhere." He waited a few seconds before adding, "And the uncle guy dragged some kid they never heard of along with him, so now I'm their cousin."

Jeff had more than one reaction to Carson's description, but this wasn't the time to delve too deeply into the conversation of how people can end up belonging to each other. Their situation was new to him, too. Instead, he stuck to safer ground. "The bigger their family gets the better the twins like it. How fun is that?"

Carson fell silent again and stared out the window for the last few minutes of the ride that took them to the edge of central Landrum, where the high school stood. This relatively new single-story building designed with spokes coming from a central hub had replaced the square three-story brick building. The old school still stood and separated the new high school from the middle school.

A huge parking lot and athletic field lay behind all three buildings. The old stadium was
still in place across the field.

"No stairs to navigate," Jeff said when
they'd parked and he led them inside. A security guard pointed the way to the main office,
where they were whisked into a counselor's
office. Jeff carried a leather portfolio his dad
had given him years ago, and now Jeff had
more than his own birth certificate and pass-
port to store in it. He'd slipped the file with
his guardianship papers inside the portfolio
when they'd left Seattle and kept it in a small
carton behind the passenger seat. If Carson
didn't want to answer the counselor's questions about his mother's death, Jeff had men-
tally rehearsed a short version of the events
that brought them to Adelaide Creek.

The counselor, April Enright, a friendly
woman about Jeff's age, examined all the paperwork and nodded as Carson, with only a
little shyness showing, asked questions about
his classes. She pulled up the Seattle system's
site and said she was required to verify all the
information. "But that won't prevent me from
enrolling you today, Carson. I see that we have

classes that matched your schedule in your Seattle school."

Carson cleared his throat and sat up straighter in the chair. "I went online and saw that you have a basketball team."

"We do," Ms. Enright said as she tapped her keyboard and woke up the printer. "Tryouts for that come a little later this term. We're still rooting for the football team around here." She reached over and removed pages from the printer tray and pushed two copies across the desk. "That's a schedule I think will work, based on your previous classes and our requirements here."

Jeff glanced at pages and saw phys ed filling a time slot three days out of five. Was Carson going to mention his own limitations now or did he plan to wait to talk to the teacher? He'd worn a long-sleeved jersey and a hoodie that left only the lower part of the gash on his hand visible.

Almost as an afterthought, the counselor tapped the last page of the hard copy file and held it up so Carson could see what she was referring to. "I see that you were excused from phys ed because of an injury. I don't know how they had you spend that hour at your Seattle school, but here at Adams High School you're required to show up in the gym. Depending on what your doctor allows, you can use whatever athletic equipment you're able to or spend the time doing homework or reading."

"The pages I attached behind the transcripts explain why Carson still needs time to rehab from his injuries," Jeff said.

Ms. Enright frowned as she scanned the medical report. Then she glanced up at Jeff. "Have you found a physical therapist yet?"

"We have a referral and an appointment later this week," Jeff said.

Carson sat up a little straighter in the chair. "My rehab is going good. I couldn't play soccer this year, but my plan is to be ready to try out for the basketball team."

No wishy-washy attitude there. Jeff was impressed. The teenager had a plan.

"I see." She leaned forward on her forearms. "According to this medical report you're rehabbing from two major injuries."

"They were," Carson said, pushing up his sleeve and extending his arm. "But see? This is better now. My ankle is healing up, too." The counselor frowned as she studied the deep gash. "It's fading some now. And I'm still getting PT. The muscles and nerves are okay. No permanent damage." Carson recited that finding as if making his opening argument: *It may look bad, Coach, but watch what I can do.*

Seeing Carson's arm through the counselor's eyes, the length and depth of the cut shocked Jeff all over again.

Ms. Enright's businesslike expression softened. "It seems you're a determined young person. We admire that kind of gumption and commitment around here. Once you have medical clearance from your doctor, you'll have your choice of sports. Don't forget swimming and track." The counselor stood and her quick glance at Jeff sent the message that he was no longer needed. Carson got to his feet and grabbed his backpack.

"So, I'll pick you up out front at three," Jeff said before asking the counselor to put Carson on the bus route.

"We'll get the bus schedule in the works. You can pick the start date," Ms. Enright said. "If we get going, Carson, we can get you to your homeroom first, and then you're off to Practical Science."

Jeff followed the counselor to the door. "I'll see you later, then." This was it, his cue to leave. But someone put lead in Jeff's feet. He patted Carson on the shoulder, wishing once again the teen would let him replace his beat-up backpack. Between the pack and his shaggy hair, Carson didn't have a crisp first-day-of-school style. Jeff blamed himself, although Carson showed no interest in sharpening his image with newer and different clothes. When he saw some other boys in the hall, they were wearing long-sleeved tees and oversize sweatshirts—and baggy jeans and shaggy hair. No need to worry. Carson fit right in.

The counselor gave Jeff a pointed nod. "I'll be in touch."

Carson flashed a lopsided smile and fell in step with Ms. Enright. Jeff only saw the tiniest wince cross Carson's face as he walked down the hall. When Jeff exhaled, it seemed he'd been holding his breath since they'd parked the truck. Jumpy and jittery, he couldn't have explained why.

OLIVIA PULLED THE collar of her wool jacket around her neck to ward off the blustery air.

The sun had disappeared now and left behind a dreary gray sky. She blinked back tears as she walked to her car at the far end of the lot. What was with the tears? Must be she was weepy from a combination of happiness and relief. All along she'd dreamed of the day Jillian could go back to being a kid in a classroom.

Times like these sometimes brought on the pain of being alone to mark important milestones, and in a way, enrolling in a new school fit that description. This day was Jillian's graduation from homeschooling she'd never asked for. When she'd had to pull Jillian from her school, no doctor offered a one hundred percent guarantee that she'd survive to go back. But she'd just watched Jillian following the teacher down the hall wearing her new black boots. What a decision that had been for Jillian. New boots or new sneakers. Olivia believed the boots won out because they were shiny and matched her mood.

The faint sound of her name grabbed Olivia's attention, but flummoxed her, too. She hadn't met enough people in town to randomly run into someone she knew. Yet, when she looked behind her to identify the voice, Jeff Stanhope waved and broke into a jog and headed her way. He gave off a different vibe in a charcoal sport coat and black jeans. She was impressed by the hint of style he showed in something other than the typical cotton shirts and faded jeans almost all the men wore to the barbecue at the ranch. But some things were the same. Jeff's wide, friendly smile made his already handsome face even more appealing.

"I bet we were on the same mission," Jeff said, but then his smile disappeared and he touched her lightly on her upper arm. "Uh, are you okay?"

"I'm a little embarrassed." Olivia self-consciously touched her damp cheeks before she raised her head to meet his gaze. "Not to mention surprised to see you. I just left Jillian on her way to class."

"Are you concerned that she won't be happy at her new school or perhaps have trouble making friends?"

"Jillian has never had trouble making friends," she said, half laughing now. "No, no, it's so great to see her bouncing down the hall with the counselor. For her, this day is as exciting as it gets. She barely waved goodbye."

"I know this isn't the same thing," Jeff said

softly, "but I could tell Carson wanted me to clear out as fast as possible." He chuckled. "The counselor had to give me one of those you-can-leave-now looks to get my feet moving toward the door."

Olivia saw a touch of confusion in Jeff's eyes. "I'll turn the question back on you. Are you worried about him?"

Jeff stared into space, his expression thoughtful. He took her question seriously. "Hard to say. I watched him walk away with a counselor headed for homeroom. Stubborn kid didn't take his cane…" He shook his head. "I can't believe I said that. It's his choice, not mine."

"Maybe you haven't been a parent long," Olivia teased, "but you could have fooled me. You sound as if you've been one forever."

"Oh, yeah?" Jeff challenged. "Well, maybe I am getting a little obsessive about stuff." He grinned self-consciously. "On the other hand, he may be tall and athletic, but he's still a boy without a mom or a dad." Memories of Saturday's lightning storm prompted his next thought. "It even scares me sometimes to know that I'm all he's got." He took a deep breath and gazed into her eyes. "What are you up to now? Do you have time to grab a coffee?"

Flustered by the surprise invitation, Olivia managed to blurt a quick yes. "If you don't mind I can pick your brain about where to hunt for an apartment or a house to rent."

"Really? I thought you and Jillian were the newest Hoover bunkhouse tenants."

"Oh, we are, but not for long. At the ranch the other day it struck me that I need to find us a different home." She told him about over-hearing Stacey Burton talking to Jen Hoover about moving off the ranch now that Matt and Heather were married. "She's still going to be involved with the twins, so she wants to stay close."

"Oh, I get it." Jeff nodded as if a light bulb had come on. "The bunkhouse is a great location for Matt's mom. It's next door to Heather and Matt, or at least as close as a neighbor gets when it comes to the ranches around here."

"Exactly," Olivia said. Of course, Jeff would be familiar with the Hoover ranch and the converted bunkhouse. Heather had lived there with Bethany Hoover when she came back to town last spring. After Bethany's wedding to Charlie, Heather stayed on until she married

Matt last week. What a relief not to have to explain her dilemma. Jeff already knew the important players. "As generous and welcoming as the Hoovers have been, the bunkhouse is really a better fit for Stacey," Olivia explained. "And I'd prefer a place closer to the hospital, even though I won't be there every day."

"I was going to suggest getting coffee at the diner in Adelaide Creek," Jeff said, narrowing his eyes as he finished his thought, "but now I've got a much better idea. Why don't you follow me out to the lodge? It's possible I could help find a solution to your problem."

Instantly, a pleasant wave of anticipation shifted Olivia's mood. "I won't say no to an offer that good. Besides, I've heard about this mystery lodge and wouldn't mind checking it out."

"Not exactly exotic, as you'll see. So, follow me in your car. It's not far."

Olivia entered Jeff's phone number and address into her phone in case they got separated on the way, although Jeff assured her that was unlikely. He did the same with her information. Something struck her as special about that phone number exchange, as if they were marking a more than passing connection.

Jeff pointed toward the parking lot and onto Buffalo Street. "See you in a few minutes."

By the time Olivia got to her car, she was reeling from the unexpected way her morning was unfolding. Like so much of what had happened from the first moment she'd arrived in Adelaide Creek as a tourist back in August, nothing went quite how she thought it would.

Less than twenty minutes later, she was standing with Jeff in front of his still empty lodge. "You were right about the time," she said. "Nothing monotonous about the drive, either. It went from hilly woods to flat fields and now I'm on the edge of a deep forest."

"So you are. These woods go on up to trails on public land." Jeff pointed in the direction of Landrum. "You probably noticed we passed the hospital complex off Buffalo Street on the drive out of town," Jeff said.

She'd had a little ripple of excitement knowing that landing the job in the small hospital had been part of what had made all these life changes possible. Even better, she was set up to diagnose, report her findings and consult with colleagues mostly from home. She was working with the docs in the Landrum hospital and in other facilities that belonged to the major medical network in the county.

The lodge, smaller than she'd envisioned it, had large windows and a platform porch. Several other log buildings were part of the complex, which climbed up a slope to a craggy crest. From the clean, sharp appearance of the main building with its sparkling windows, Olivia immediately saw that this was no renovation project. The place was well maintained, but unlike Heather and Matt's ranch with its homey pumpkins and mums, the lodge needed some decorations and signs of life. A few people milling about would help the lonely lodge shake off its abandoned appearance. Even empty, though, the entire setup had a welcoming vibe.

"So, this is what brought you back home," Olivia said as she moved closer to Jeff's side. She gestured to the two log cabins, each set behind and to the side of the main building. Heather had said Jeff's reasons for coming back to Wyoming were complicated, but mostly bound up with making a home for Carson.

"Not this lodge specifically," Jeff mused. "When Carson's mom was killed, I had to solve several problems. For one thing, I couldn't see how to support us in Seattle, so I had to find something to do that suits the life I need to provide for Carson." He clicked his tongue in a classic sound of regret. "Ranching isn't an option, at least not right now. But then, shipping out on freighters and trawlers for months at a time wouldn't cut it, either. One year, I spent only six weeks ashore. Coming back home was a way to be around for him and, I hope, make a living."

Olivia motioned to what she assumed was the main building. "So, that's where you live?"

Jeff didn't waste a second correcting her. "No, no. This is the common building with the office and four fairly comfy suites upstairs, but it's closed up for now. There's a kitchen, too. This place used to serve breakfast and had a snack shop and small bar." He smiled when he added, "Everything, all the cabins and the lodge, will be operational by next summer. I hope to keep them filled. I'll show you the inside of the main building later, but first, come with me."

Narrow dirt roads and footpaths led in all

directions to the outbuildings and up to the smaller cabins. The two larger cabins close to the lodge were full-size log houses, and Jeff headed for them. He looked at nothing in particular in the distance, but the area had at least a dozen small log cabins spread out across the hill. "I'm opening two of those smaller cabins soon—first guests arrive on Friday."

He led her up a path to a log house with a front porch.

"So, are you saying…?" Olivia took in a breath. A log cabin in the woods less than twenty minutes from the hospital. Oh, my.

He pointed to the house. "It's yours for the taking. It's an answer to playing musical houses on the Hoover ranch. I know that bunkhouse. It's great, but…" He shrugged and pointed to the ground. "This lodge is still within the town of Adelaide Creek, but it's on the outer edge. It cuts about ten minutes off the drive into Landrum. That doesn't matter so much now, but come winter it could make a difference when you have to go to the hospital."

After her years of shoveling and snow-blowing in Minnesota, Olivia knew the truth of that statement. On the other hand, a white winter landscape was part of the appeal of Wyoming in the first place.

Jeff went up the steps and unlocked the cabin door. "Let's get some fresh air in here. I was in the other day to have a closer look and do some inventory of what it would need to rent it. Turns out, not much. It's furnished and pretty well supplied with kitchen stuff and linens." He kicked the door stopper into place and the chilly air followed them inside.

"It's so modern," Olivia said, pointing to the sleek granite breakfast bar with cheerful red-leather-and-chrome stools that separated the kitchen from the living space. A stairway with wrought iron railings led to a mezzanine-style second floor. "It's beautiful." Small, but cozy. Olivia's gaze settled on an alcove off to the side of the kitchen. It was probably meant to be a dining area, but she could use it to set up the computers and screens for her shifts, most of which she'd work from home.

"As I said, it's yours if you want it." Jeff spoke without a trace of hesitation in his voice. "I was going to try to find a tenant for the winter, or some kind of longer-term arrangement. It might as well be you and Jillian."

Olivia's first impulse was to shout yes and move in, but something puzzled her. "If you don't live in the lodge, why is it you and Carson didn't move in here?"

Jeff lightly took her elbow and led her to the window. He pointed to the log home on the other side of the lodge. "Because we live in that one. I chose it and showed it to Carson online when my offer on this place was accepted."

"Ah, I see. It's a single-story building."

"Right. We were still in Seattle when I closed on the lodge, and Carson was struggling to move around the apartment. He was graduating from a walker to a cane," Jeff explained. "We didn't know when he'd be racing up and down stairs again, like he did when he and Karen lived on the third floor of their apartment building. He's healed up faster than predicted…but still."

"The advantages of youth. I see that quick healing often with kids' orthopedic injuries." Choosing the single-level cabin was logical, but something about Jeff buying the lodge and the rental cabins in the first place puzzled her. "And you really bought all this sight unseen?"

Jeff opened and closed the indoor shutters on the three windows. "I'm checking the hinges for squeaks."

"Can't hear a thing." Olivia looked out at the dense woods and the paths crisscrossing through the trees and narrow dirt roads for cars to get up to the cabins built deep in the woods.

"Let's leave the shutters open to let in what morning light there is." He led them back to the middle of the room. "It must seem kind of strange to you that I'd make a deal this big from Seattle."

With a laugh in her voice, she was honest about her reaction. "It seems either incredibly risky or truly gutsy. I'm not sure which."

His friendly, almost flirtatious smile sent a warm sensation through her.

"Maybe a little of both," he said, "but, you can see for yourself, this isn't a dilapidated old lodge I'm bringing back from the dead. The owners added the modern touches in these larger cabins. They kept up the outbuildings and the stables—more or less—even after they buttoned it all up for the last time. It took them a couple of years to finally decide to sell the whole thing, plus the pasture beyond the corral."

"It's in great condition," Olivia said. "It's the first thing I noticed." As she studied the details, she admired the wooden beams across the ceiling and the brick fireplace with a sturdy wooden mantel.

"And it wasn't as if I didn't know the place," Jeff said, explaining that a couple of different families ran it when he and Heather were growing up. "For right now, I hope I can attract some fall and winter tourists for one- or two-night stays in the small cabins. Adelaide Creek has always had folks coming and going from Yellowstone and the ski resorts north of us. At this point I'm offering a no-frills, very affordable place for a quick stop or a weekend getaway." Jeff looked away and stared into space, lost in his own thoughts.

"Are you seriously offering this to me?" Olivia asked, somehow unable to match the friendly face in front of her to the man she'd so harshly judged as self-centered and uncaring.

"I am," Jeff said. "You seem surprised. I'm sure we can figure out a fair rent. You'll want to buy your own house eventually, but in the meantime, the cabin is available and in move-in condition."

Olivia laughed in surprise. "I can't believe my luck." She paused. "Although I might have known to expect good things. Meeting your sister was only the beginning of my charmed life—at least it seems like that."

Jeff nodded. "Heather told me a lot about her time living with you through Jillian's treatment. She mentioned both of you often in her emails."

"Well, at least you read them, anyway." Those sharp words were made worse by the sarcastic tone that went with them. As she had at Saturday's party, Olivia covered her mouth with her hand. "I'm so sorry. I did it again."

"Yeah, you sure did," Jeff said, his face turning red. "We've already covered this ground and nothing's changed. What goes on between me and my sister is none of your concern." Jeff walked away from her and toward the kitchen.

Embarrassed, Olivia started to follow him, but changed her mind and stayed put near the fireplace. "I apologize—sincerely. I'm not usually so judgmental."

"We can only hope," Jeff said dryly. He

turned the light switches on and off in the kitchen. "I'm just trying to help you save some time and solve a problem." He went to the cabinets next to the stove and opened and closed the first one in the row. "But feel free to read the apartment listings in the paper or talk to a rental agent in Landrum."

"I'm very grateful. Trust me on that." Thoughts of house hunting and tramping around the county had no appeal at all. She might speak lightly about her charmed life, but here was one more piece of evidence that proved her point. She and Jillian were being offered more than a roof over their heads. Like the bunkhouse, this was a lovely home nestled in the woods. Before she had a chance to accept his offer, though, Jeff hurried to the door.

"You look around," he said. "Go upstairs. Let me know what you think. I'll repeat what I said before. It's yours if you want it. I'll be in the lodge." He left and closed the door behind him.

Nice move, Olivia. She had no right to confront him about his sister. Besides, no one else treated him like a pariah, so why would she? Heather hadn't been nasty to him at Saturday's party. No, Olivia had appointed herself as judge and jury. On the other hand, for all his friendly ways and fabulous offer, one she fully intended to accept, she had vivid memories of Heather's hurt feelings. The two had lost their parents first, followed quickly by the foreclosure on the Stanhope ranch. These were serious blows, but Heather had been bewildered by Jeff's lack of communication. She'd told Olivia that she couldn't understand why she and Jeff had to lose each other as well as their parents and their ranch. With Heather becoming such a close friend, it was hard to see past her heartbreak.

Olivia didn't need to tour the whole house to know she was thrilled with it. To gather her thoughts, she sank into the soft cushions on the couch in front of the fireplace and enjoyed visions of building a crackling fire on a cold winter night. She so easily saw herself curled up with Jillian watching a movie and sipping hot chocolate.

With light coming through the cathedral-style windows over the fireplace, Olivia went upstairs and opened the first door and stepped into the room with twin beds and white curtains. Just right for Jillian. Two quilts with floral designs in white and various shades of purple lay folded in the middle of the unmade bed. Another door led to the larger bedroom with a double bed and its own bath. It had a view of the woods behind the house, where cottonwoods mixed with pines of various sizes. A smattering of yellow leaves still hung from branches, giving the landscape splashes of color. This room also had a quilt at the end of the bed, this one made from fabric in brilliant autumn reds and golds.

Everything in the house was perfect for her life now. It was furnished and after selling or giving away most of her furniture, Olivia had no desire to rush out and begin replacing it. Jeff had talked about working out a fair rent, and now Olivia hoped she could afford the price tag this kind of terrific house would likely command. She'd never know until she went to find Jeff and tell him that if the offer was still open, she accepted.

She cupped her face in her palms. Her cheeks were warm already and she hadn't yet faced him again. She groaned and hurried to the door to go to the lodge and apologize one more time. Despite her thoughtless jabs at him, she liked Jeff. If she was completely honest with herself, it had been years since she'd paid much attention to a man's eyes, let alone ones that were such a lovely warm brown. Jeff threw her off center. She couldn't deny it.

CHAPTER THREE

JEFF STAYED IN motion while he muttered under his breath about Olivia's latest dig. He'd be justified in taking back his offer of the cabin, but that thought brought a laugh. As if he'd do that for real. He huffed as he attempted to focus on the main room of the lodge, his thoughts flitting back and forth between his lofty visions for the lodge and talking to himself about Olivia's awful manners. He'd already beat himself up over the same things Olivia had pointed out. A couple of times by now. The last thing he needed was another lecture.

Rather than bringing himself down, Jeff began to funnel his angry energy into slashing through the jobs on a to-do list at least as long as his arm. He started by pulling the cover off the Ping-Pong table and casting it aside while he gave it the once-over. Not brand-new, but in good shape and ready to go.

With the paddles and balls protected in the storage box they'd probably arrived in years before, Jeff could challenge Carson to a game that very afternoon. That would get his mind off Olivia and her sharp tongue.

Jeff wandered to the dartboard cabinet and opened it up. He'd played darts with guys on a tanker, and hadn't been bad at it in college, either. The rustic pine cabinet was a little dusty and dull, but some furniture polish would bring back its shine. The cabinet held everything needed to begin using it immediately. Looking at the pool table, he predicted it would also be in good condition. He closed his eyes and imagined next summer, with cabins in the lodge fully occupied and families playing Ping-Pong, friends challenging each other at darts and pool. He couldn't compete with the relatively new Tall Tale Lodge, a high-end operation that bragged about its pool and spa. That was okay. He wasn't going for high-end.

He picked up a couple of darts and threw one. Oops, five points, but at least he managed to hit a ring. It was a start.

Hand poised, he set up for the second shot

and almost released it when the bell on the door jingled, followed by, "Wow, darts!"

The melodic voice. He'd know it anywhere now. He lowered his hand and turned to see her coming toward him and smiling broadly. "I'm rusty. It's been a while since I've played," he told her.

"Me, too," Olivia said coming alongside him, "but you are talking to a two-time dorm champion, followed by the acknowledged best in my medical school class. And that was *tough* competition."

"No kidding? I'm impressed." She looked so proud of herself he had to laugh. "I wasn't too bad myself." He told her about the crew on the supertanker who played at every available opportunity. "They were serious about their darts."

Olivia rubbed her palms together. "I get it."

"Then have at it." He offered the darts he held in his hand.

"Hmm…it isn't my favorite type. I prefer aluminum and softer plastic."

As if in her own world, Olivia tried her hand, throwing with deliberation and hitting a share of red and greens. If they'd been playing a real game of 301, she'd be heading toward a win. He was sure of it. "You're not so rusty," he said, in an only slightly accusing tone.

"We definitely need to play. What's your game?"

"The guys I played with stuck to basic 301."

"Me, too. You're on—soon."

"If you decide to rent my log cabin, anything here in the lodge is yours to use. Ping-Pong, pool, whatever." Jeff pointed to the shelves of books and games on both sides of the fireplace. "Those books and the games and puzzles were left behind, but they might as well get some use." He moved a few feet to one of the tables and pulled out a chair.

"Oh, I want to live in the cabin. I thought the question might be if the offer is still open." She closed her eyes and shook her head as she sat across from Jeff. "I promise not to let another rude remark come out of my mouth. That's a promise you can count on. Pinky swear."

Why did she have to be so appealing? And Heather's good buddy to boot. Jeff would find this conversation much easier if he didn't already feel a connection. Whether they got along or not, she was as close as family as any of Heather's other old friends. "I accept your promise. I'll take you at your word. But I had no intention of withdrawing my offer of the cabin. Besides, renting it to you solves your problem and mine. Now I don't have to scare up a tenant. See? A classic win-win."

"It's a beautiful place for Jillian and me. I start work in a few days and it's great to have this taken care of and off my mind." She looked around, her mouth opening, as if she had more to say, but weighing her words.

"Was there something else?"

"You can tell, huh?" She twisted her mouth to one side. "I won't bore you with a sad tale of my history, but let's just say I know the pain of having people leave and more or less disappear."

The muscles in Jeff's neck and shoulders stiffened, as if waiting for a blow...or a broken promise.

She held up her hand. "I only said that to explain that because of the past and what I've just been through with Jillian, everything in my life is about her and my work now. My move to Adelaide Creek was to make part of this dream for Jillian and me a reality. The bunkhouse, now this gorgeous cabin, which even has the perfect place for my workstation, are all part of what I'm building for my daughter."

Same kind of attitude he had about building a life for Carson. He couldn't have explained it better himself. The lodge, the move and the demands of raising Carson took all his focus. With the life he wanted for Carson vivid in his mind, Jeff couldn't afford to fail. "When it comes to what we need to do for the kids, we have a lot in common."

Olivia nodded, but she smiled slyly. "Hmm… maybe I can be persuaded to carve out a few minutes here and there for some cutthroat darts. And a turn or two at the pool table. What do you think?"

She was dazzling him; that's what he thought. But he didn't have room in his life for women who had that effect on him. She obviously didn't want a guy around. On the other hand, no harm could come from an occasional dart match. "It's obvious I need the practice."

Olivia stood and planted her hands on her hips. "If I'm going to move, I better start packing."

Within minutes, they came to an agreement

on the rental terms and Jeff gave Olivia the key to her new front door.

"We have a deal," Olivia declared as they walked to the car.

"Yes, ma'am, we do."

She smiled as she climbed inside and after he closed her car door, she turned on the engine and buzzed the window down. "Thanks to you, I've added a charming cabin to my list of favorite things."

When Olivia shifted out of Park, Jeff stepped back and watched her maneuver down the drive, a little light-headed and wondering who charmed who. He went inside and before he did anything else, he grabbed the furniture polish and made that dart cabinet gleam.

JEFF STROKED THE smattering of markings on Night Magic's face. "You are such a beauty." The otherwise solid black horse raised her head as if nodding in agreement and then pushed against Jeff's hand. "You want *more* love?" Jeff asked, as if teasing the horse.

"I should have warned you," Heather said, amused. "When it comes to displays of affection, our horses are very demanding."

"I can see that," Jeff said with a laugh in his

voice. Giving Night Magic a final pat, he left her with Pebbles, the horse Heather said she usually rode, and joined his sister at the edge of the creek. Not just any creek, but the one he'd grown up calling Addie Creek. As a kid, he learned his little hometown had been named after his great-great-grandmother Adelaide. That had handed him an excuse to put a little swagger on display. The creek itself ran through their ranch and had been a touchstone his whole life, and Heather's, too. Her middle name was Adelaide, which she'd carried with pride.

Leaves and brush crunched under his feet, but the thunderstorm had replenished the creek. It announced its presence with noisy bubbling as it flowed over tiers of rocks and stones. "I haven't had a chance to show Carson the creek."

"You can always get a glimpse of a narrow strip running through town," Heather said, reasonably. "It even has some willows on the banks, same as down here."

"I know, I know, but it's not the same as coming through the woods on the back of a horse and ending up at this special spot." That section where the creek cut through town had been part of the original ranch. Adelaide's children later turned over some acres to the town to start a cemetery and expand Merchant Street, the main street in town. He'd thought of asking Heather if he could borrow one of their off-road vehicles to get him and Carson close to the thick woods and then walk the rest of the way. Not a practical idea for Carson, at least not yet.

"Maybe by next fall, or even summer, he'll be riding with me on the trails through the hills from the lodge." Jeff gave Heather a smile he hoped reflected some optimism. And why not? He had experience riding trails that linked the few remaining large-scale ranches in the county.

Heather extended her open hands and raised her eyebrows expectantly. "Real possibility or wishful thinking?"

Right now, wishful thinking, but he didn't care to admit it. "I'm not sure. I only know one thing at this point. I'm not as good with kids as you are." It was a confession, implying that he had to be forgiven for committing the crime of making blunders with Carson.

"Give yourself a break," Heather blurted impatiently. "From what I can tell, Carson is doing fine, especially when you think of everything the kid's been through."

Jeff picked up a random stone and gave it a quick side-armed throw. It sank without rewarding him with one lousy skip. "I've lost my touch."

Ignoring his lack of stone-throwing skills, Heather asked, "Does Carson talk much about his mom?"

Jeff kicked at the stones at his feet. "Not much. When I probe around, he usually stares at something else and gives me two- or three-word answers. Apparently, he's training me not to even try to get inside his head." Jeff understood Carson in that regard. At the same age, he didn't like people probing around in his thoughts, either. "I'm forced to admit I was the silent type, too. If I claimed nothing was going on inside my brain, I assumed Mom and Dad would believe me. That strikes me as kinda funny now, but I must have been a frustrating handful."

Heather chuckled. "I'm glad the twins are still at the stage when they tell us every little thought that pops into their adorable heads."

"You're enjoying every minute of being a mom." Jeff had always admired his sister's big heart. In their nearly five years apart her generous spirit had embraced even more new people. "You can't convince me otherwise."

"I'd never try to," Heather said. "I love Matt and the twins. Stacey is a wonderful mother-in-law. But it's more than that. I love my life. I have a job I enjoy…plus horses. How lucky can an Adelaide Creek woman be?"

"Luck gets a little credit, I suppose, but mostly it's your doing," Jeff said, his mind on horses, too.

Heather walked a few steps away from him and closer to the biggest of the cluster of enormous willow trees. Heather's favorite tree on the whole ranch continued to survive the elements decade after decade. "I doubt I'll ever understand why you didn't call me after the accident. If you hadn't decided to bring Carson here, would you have ever told me about the accident or him?"

Jeff sighed. Heather had been dancing around this confrontation from the time he arrived at the ranch for their midday ride. The questions he couldn't answer were finally on the table. "I wasn't thinking about what was next. I had a few other things on my mind, namely Carson with his arm ripped open and his broken bones. Karen was dead."

"You said you were driving when the accident happened." With the toe of her boot she brushed loose dirt off gnarled willow roots protruding from the ground. "How does Carson feel about that?"

Jeff's body went rigid at her flat tone. "Is that a professional question? Are you asking because you're a nurse who works with kids? Are you worried about Carson blaming me?"

"I'm asking as your *sister*." Heather's voice grew louder with each word. She threw her arms open to the sides, exaggerating her show of frustration. "You can't show up one afternoon with a young kid who's lost his mom without raising a few questions." She kicked at the root again. "You made him part of my new wonderful family. So don't act so surprised that my heart is a little mushy over him already."

Tension drained from Jeff's body. "I hoped you'd feel that way. You can rail at me all you want. Be mad for years. I don't care, as long as you accept Carson."

"You see right through me. You don't have to be smug about it," Heather said. "But I think you owe me some answers. I want you to tell me more about what happened that robbed this teenager of his mom."

"Come on, let's ride. I'll tell you on the way back." The ugly pictures he carried never strayed too far from his thoughts.

Silently, they mounted Night Magic and Pebbles and slow-walked side by side as he told Heather the whole story. Except for repeating a choppy version to the police and EMTs, and then to the ER doc, Jeff had never recounted the sequence of details out loud. But it all lived in his head. The facts were easy. A truck ran a red light and T-boned the passenger side. "I took one look at Karen and knew she was gone. I was woozy, in shock at first, but I heard Carson asking about his mom. He was still awake at that point. The back seat door was almost torn off, so he wasn't trapped. I tried not to tell him too much while I stayed with him until the ambulance transported both of us. I only had a couple of gashes. Nothing serious." As an afterthought, he added, "The driver didn't survive, but he'd had a heart attack at the wheel. A freakish accident in every sense."

"And I imagine you were the one who had to tell him about Karen."

He nodded as he said, "I was, but he already knew, although he hadn't accepted it yet. He was conscious, barely, the whole time, which is why he saw the blood and her body crushed under glass and metal in the passenger seat." The EMT climbed into the driver's seat Jeff had left in order to gain access to her. Seconds later, he glanced at Jeff and shook his head. "I'd never tell him he was lucky. But the truth is, given what happened to his mom, his injuries could have been a lot worse."

Jeff didn't have words to explain what the accident had done to him, except change everything forever, and in a matter of seconds. The sudden slam and screech of metal on metal. The sharp odor of fuel oil, and the more subtle smell of the blood on the crushed passenger seat—and Karen. Sirens screamed. Emergency lights flashed. The sound and the lights rushed back to him in dreams—waking ones as well the kind that startled him and brought him to full attention in the middle of the night.

Jeff had been conscious, able to get out of the car and move, but his memories were foggy about the ride to the hospital and the long wait to hear if Carson would survive. Jeff had feared internal injuries and he remembered the relief of knowing Carson would be okay— ultimately. The doctor warned Jeff that whatever remained buried deep in his brain could surface one day, an image here, another there, until the narrative was filled in. Just when he thought he'd made peace with the tragedy, he found himself mired in changing some detail in his mind that would give the story a new ending.

"Even knowing I wasn't at fault, I can't let go of feeling responsible. As if I'm to blame for Karen being there in the first place. It's not true, but that doesn't always matter."

Heather reined Pebbles to a halt. "I'm so sorry for what happened, but I can't stop thinking about what if Karen had been driving. You'd have been the one killed."

He leaned across the narrow space between them and squeezed her shoulder. "It was a fluke that I was there at all. I'd just come back from a stint on a tanker and she invited me along on a visit to a friend on Bainbridge Island. As we were getting into the car, she asked me to drive because she had early signs

of a headache coming on." They'd even de-
bated whether Carson should sit up front so
she could stretch out in the back. Then Carson would have been killed. And Karen's life
destroyed. Every scenario was wrenching.

"But it wasn't a date?" Heather asked. "You
said…"

"We were friends. Carson understood that
almost from the beginning. The arrangement
benefitted us both. I had no need of a place
of my own since I accepted every job that
came my way. I used work—physical work,
mostly—to cope with my shame and bit-
terness about losing the ranch. My rent for
that one room helped Karen out financially.
Over the nearly four years I got to know her
pretty well. And Carson. He was a skinny
little squirt who still dressed up as one of his
superheroes on Halloween."

"He's no squirt now," Heather said with a
laugh. "His voice is almost as low as yours."

"And he shot up this past year. Karen was
tall, and from what she said, so was his father," Jeff said. "He's built for basketball. Carson used to take his basketball to the park and
practice his shots all afternoon. I drove the
car there to get him one time when it started

pouring rain and found him on the court in his yellow rain poncho still making free throws."

They rode in silence for a while longer and then Jeff paused and pointed across the field at the mountains in the distance with their peaks poking through hazy clouds. "Look at that. Carson grew up in a place where on many days the mountains are barely visible behind the clouds. Then, when it clears it changes everything. I appreciated that about Seattle." Jeff leaned over and patted Night Magic's neck and she danced around a little and nickered softly. "I bet this horse gets a kick out of building up some speed."

"Oh, she does. Night Magic will be my horse, once we train Lucy on Pebbles. The Appaloosa was Susannah's horse and Matt and his mom always meant for Lucy to have her."

Jeff had heard about Matt losing his twin sister in Afghanistan, and becoming an instant guardian for the twins. According to Heather, he and his mom had teamed up to shower Lucy and Nick with love and security. But the two were toddlers when they'd first taken them in, not a young teen like Carson.

"Seems you and Matt have another thing in common," Heather said, slyly. "What do you think of that?"

"I'd have said it was unlikely," Jeff said, grinning. "What with the weather turning, I didn't have time to feel too out of place on the ranch. Matt and I didn't get much chance to talk. I'll set things right with him another time." Puzzled, he replayed Heather's earlier words in his head. "What did you mean by 'another thing'?"

"From what Matt told me, when the storm hit, the two of you teamed up to make sure the kids were safe in the barn with Olivia and the horses were in the stables." Heather laughed. "That was your man talk."

"Maybe," Jeff said, still puzzled.

"Seriously, Jeff?" Heather groaned in exasperation. "You haven't figured it out? You must see that you and my new husband have all-things-horses in common...and this kind of life we have out here and you've come back to."

"Well, when you put it like that..." Jeff guffawed. Yeah, he and Matt weren't really so different.

"I'm glad you told me about Karen and Carson," Heather said. "I feel better knowing you weren't completely alone in Seattle."

"Nah, I wasn't alone, but I wasn't connected, either," Jeff said, thinking back on the bouts of loneliness that he'd dealt with—coped with badly. Usually he denied any lack in his life. He drew deeper into himself and spent even more time alone. "Karen was the only real friend I made. When I crewed on the freighters I played a lot of cards, and darts on one ship." He smiled to himself about his match with Olivia. "I only got roped into showing up for poker games so I wouldn't get a reputation as standoffish."

"Cards?" Heather squealed. "You never liked cards. Or board games. I couldn't even coax you to play checkers."

"When you're with a bunch of guys on a ship," Jeff said with a laugh, "you play poker whether you want to or not." He had no regrets about those years of nonstop work and being tightfisted with his money. "I may have lost at the poker table, but I made good money on those jobs. I seemed aimless most of the time, but down deep I always knew that one day I'd do something major with the cash I'd stashed away."

"And here you are now, the owner of a lodge in prime condition."

"And providing a home for Carson," he added.

Heather chuckled. "With ready-made stables and a pasture for horses. No wonder the lodge was irresistible."

"I'm not going to get ahead of myself there." But before he'd even considered putting an offer on the lodge, he'd studied the series of online videos that showed the buildings and the pasture. In his imagination he dropped in grazing horses in that spot. He had plans, but he wasn't ready to elaborate on them yet.

Heather kept up a stream of questions as they rode along, including why he hadn't considered staying in Seattle with Carson. It had been a possibility. The landlord offered to extend the lease. But he couldn't work at jobs that took him away from home for weeks and months at a time. Besides, Jeff had thought about his life growing up in a small town and wanted to give the teenager a taste of Wyoming country. "Seattle will still be there if Carson wants to go back one day."

Heather offered a sad smile. "Despite the tragedy, it's Carson's good fortune to have you, Jeff. One day he'll know how lucky."

"I'm pretty lucky, too," Jeff said. Given the alternatives, Heather was right. But from the minute he told Carson's ailing grandma Tina that he wasn't only *willing* to be her grandson's guardian, but really *wanted* him, he'd been brimming over with determination— purpose. He'd been jolted out of a rut he'd been occupying for years. It might not have been obvious from the outside looking in, but it was a protective rut he fooled himself into thinking kept him content enough. It also allowed him to think mostly about himself. When his heart opened up to take in Carson, other parts of him also came out to look around. "Something's changed, Heather. About me. I don't know how to explain it."

"Maybe you don't have to," Heather said, patting Pebbles and picking up the pace. "I can't wait to see what happens next."

It didn't take much for Pebbles to respond to Heather's command and break into a full gallop to cover the flat stretch toward the ranch.

Night Magic also picked up speed and for the first time in years, he and Heather raced the mile or so to the ranch. Pebbles won, but not by much.

CHAPTER FOUR

With Jillian beside her, Olivia heard Carson's voice when she made the turn on the curve that led to the end of the drive. "You can leave now, Jeff. I don't need you standing here waiting for the bus with me."

Jeff had his hands up defensively and took a couple of steps back. "Okay, okay… See? I'm backing off now." His hands dropped to his sides when he saw Olivia and Jillian.

"Uh-oh, Jillian's bus stops here, too," Olivia said. She couldn't resist teasing Carson a little. "I hope that's okay with you."

Carson offered Jillian a lopsided smile. "No, I don't mind Jillian." He mocked a deep growl and aimed his thumb toward Jeff. "I don't need *him* watching over me like I'm a kid."

Jeff groaned. "So, I'm a little overprotective. Big deal. This is the first day you're taking the bus. Okay? I promise I'll disappear when we see it coming down the road."

Olivia frowned. "Do the middle school students and the high school kids ride the same bus?"

"Uh, yeah," Jeff said, "they do. The teens go to the back and the middle school kids sit up front and get off first."

"I missed that tidbit," Olivia said, glancing down at Jillian, who hadn't stopped bouncing around all morning. It wasn't only the new house and school that had her excited about everything. She'd thought her room in the bunkhouse was cool, too. But this cabin was down the path from the stables and a corral. Any minute now, she expected Jeff to fill out the scene with some horses. *Not yet, Jillian, not yet.*

"I've never been on a school bus before," Jillian said rising up on the balls of her feet and rocking back on her heels. "I used to walk to school at our old house. This is better."

"I used to walk, too, miles and miles," Carson said, "back in the big, busy city."

Jeff snorted. "I think we measured the distance in blocks, pal, not miles."

"Maybe," Carson conceded. "But it rained on me day after day."

Olivia got a kick out of Jillian hanging on

every word of Carson's stories. Despite listening to the kids' easy banter, Olivia felt her stomach stay knotted up. A familiar feeling. She had knots living in her gut through every step of Jillian's treatment. These stages of recovery had only loosened them a bit. For all the joy of seeing Jillian healthy and strong, Olivia couldn't purge the other memories of fear and nightmares. Being a doctor herself didn't matter, and might have even made it worse. When it came to *her* child, she had a difficult time trusting that making her child sick with chemotherapy was the path to making her whole again. Olivia the scientist argued mightily for the other side, which won out in the end.

Today that child sported brand-new white sneakers on feet that could barely stay still. Slung over one shoulder she carried her so-called Wyoming backpack, khaki green with enough pockets to carry supplies for a real hike in the woods. So long and good riddance, pink backpack, made for a little girl. Best of all, Jillian's red hair had grown back to the point that no one would ever imagine she'd lost it all. Now she vowed to let it grow to her waist. Maybe she'd never cut it again…ever.

"Uh, Olivia, you don't need to worry about Jillian. I'll keep an eye on her." Carson put on a gruff voice as he eyed Jillian and said, "I'll make sure she doesn't get too rowdy on the bus."

Carson's teasing brought a giggle from Jillian and an amused smile from Jeff.

"Uh-oh, Jillian, you better watch it." Olivia's tension lifted at least for the moment. "I've got a spy to check on you now."

"Hey," Carson said, flapping his hand at Jeff, "I see the bus."

"Get a load of him, Olivia," Jeff said, feigning shock. "He's shooing me away like I'm an annoying fly." Jeff gave Carson a friendly slap on the back. "See you."

"Later," Carson responded with a nod.

Olivia stayed put while Jeff disappeared up the drive. When the bus pulled up, she squeezed Jillian's shoulders and whispered, "Have a good day."

The doors opened. Carson stepped to the side and said, "You first, Jillian. I'll see you on the way home."

Jillian nodded and didn't look back.

Olivia was still watching the bus head down the road when the gravel and leaves on the drive behind her crunched. It jolted her, but then she gave Jeff a teasing grin.

Jeff snickered. "What? You're surprised? You didn't think I was really going back to the cabin, did you?"

"I suppose I did," Olivia said. "You sure stayed well hidden. As for me, I made no such foolish promise in the first place."

"It's different for you with Jillian. Carson's fourteen. He'd never forgive me." Jeff grimaced and shook his head. "I avoided my parents at all costs at the same age."

"You had your kid sister to look out for." Olivia smiled. "Nice to know he'll look out for Jillian. He's a really fine young man."

Jeff smiled. "I think so, too, but I can't get much out of him. You know, how he feels inside, I mean." He paused. "You want to come in for a cup of coffee?"

It would be pleasant to say yes and while away a morning. Maybe throw some darts again. "Thanks, I wish I could, but I have to leave for the hospital now. It's my first day, so I have to be on-site this morning. Getting an orientation and a tour." She patted her torso. "I've got butterflies dancing around in here."

"Oh, you'll do great. I'll give you a rain

check on the coffee. I've got something I want to show you, too. Another day." Jeff stared down the empty road, then cleared his throat. "It might sound strange, but waiting for the bus with you and the kids gives me a dad feeling, even if I'm an impostor."

"Well…you're not an impostor. You play the part very well." Olivia picked up the pace, not wanting to cut her arrival time too close on her first day. "No kidding. He calls you Jeff, but other than that, any stranger would think you were his dad."

"Carson never had a father." Jeff's quick click of his tongue left a sad expression behind. "I had such a great dad. Makes me sad for Carson to miss that."

"Yeah, well, Jillian didn't have one, either." Had Jeff forgotten that? Or maybe he never knew she'd been on her own with Jillian from the beginning. Like Carson's mom. "Jillian's father had the same anti-family gene as my dad. Undiscovered until he created one. I call them both runners. As it turned out, Jillian's father couldn't handle having the family he claimed he desperately wanted, so he walked away and never looked back. Sent checks the court ordered him to pay and never so much as wished our daughter a happy birthday."

"I see," Jeff said, wincing. "I didn't know the whole story."

She waved him off. "No problem. I really need to go." She hadn't heard herself deliver that diatribe with such venom in a long time. She hurried to get into her car. When she drove past the lodge, Jeff was standing on the porch and waved as she went by.

Jeff was a runner, too, she thought when she waved back. No, he hadn't abandoned a child, not like her ex-husband had. But Jeff had walked away from the sister who adored him. As she got closer to Landrum and turned onto Buffalo Street, she had to admit the butterflies weren't all about the job. Jeff had a way of leaving her feeling a little quivery. In a good way. It had been a long time since any man had had that kind of effect on her. Not one guy since meeting Jillian's dad for the first time. Right. Look how that turned out.

As she pulled into a parking space, she almost laughed out loud. What difference did it make how Jeff made her feel, when she'd already constructed a wall between them with harsh words and near accusations? She'd told the story about her ex-husband as if putting him on notice. If she kept up her negative attitude, she wouldn't have to worry about her effect, if any, on Jeff.

CHAPTER FIVE

OLIVIA'S FINGERS TOUCHED the end of the pool, the last stroke to finish her sixth lap. She straightened up and looked around at her surroundings as she eased herself out of the typical meditative state that came over her when swimming laps. She'd needed that relaxed state. Reorienting herself to these surroundings filled her with happiness. The glass wall of the indoor pool offered a view of rolling fields with only patchy vegetation at the moment. The hills rose higher and higher until the morning sun brightened the mountain peaks.

She turned the other way and smiled at the sight of Heather sitting at a table flipping pages of the magazine. Ladies who lunch, Heather had jokingly called them when they'd come through the revolving door into the Tall Tale Lodge and Spa, emphasis on spa. Heather had planned their day to start with a swim, followed by a few minutes in the sauna, and when they were showered and dressed, they'd claim their reservation Heather made for lunch.

Olivia moved to the ladder and climbed out of the pool and grabbed the towel off her chair. "This sure is different from our time here during the summer with three kids in tow," she said, thinking back to the two pool days Heather organized when she and Jillian had visited in August. They'd been noisy days with the twins, who'd just turned seven, and Jillian, a mermaid, or Olivia teased, a real dolphin. The three kids had jumped into the pool and never wanted to leave, shouting "Marco Polo" every few seconds.

"I'm glad you enjoyed the pool portion of my not-so-secret plan," Heather said. "I'm not much of a swimmer, but you and I haven't had much time alone since you moved here. That has to change." She indicated the glass wall and rows of tables and chairs and poolside chaise longues. "This seemed to be the right place to spend some time and catch up."

Olivia had heard stories about this lodge, one of the newer attractions not far from Adelaide Creek. Heather's friends Bethany and Charlie had had their rehearsal dinner here the night before their wedding. Or were supposed to. Instead, Charlie had been stuck in a series of airports trying to get home from his work-site overseas and the Tall Tale's live music and dancing saved the event for those waiting for the groom to arrive. Olivia couldn't resist teasing her friend. "I think you fell in love with this place because it's where you and Matt committed yourselves to each other. And now you have a new place to dance."

"Maybe so. We do love to get out and waltz around the floor. We also get a kick out of showing off our Texas two-step." Heather frowned. "I suppose Jeff could do something similar with his lodge, but the main building is a little small for live music and not quite modern enough to attract a younger, single crowd."

Olivia bristled at Heather's tone, which she heard as edging close to critical. "Stanhope's Woodland Cabins isn't meant to be a spa. It's homey and affordable, not a luxury hotel with all these amenities. Where would he even put a pool?" She energetically rubbed the towel over her wet arms. "Don't get me wrong. I'm enjoying one of the Tall Tale's main amenities immensely right now."

Heather flashed an amused smile. "You and my brother are on the same page about the spa. I assume you're getting along okay. Maybe better than okay?"

Olivia returned her friend's smile with a pointed look. "Please, I'm just stating the facts."

"You found some common ground, anyway. You enjoy your new home, huh?"

An understatement. She'd never felt more at home in a new place, at least not so fast. "I do. We have everything we need, from bath towels to dishes. I haven't spent a dime on the place, and even the cat is content." Olivia laughed. "You know Tulip is hard to please."

Heather looked thoughtful when she said, "I hope Jeff can make a go of the old place. His life is so different now."

"I'm no expert, but near as I can tell he's off to a good start," Olivia said. "The weekend we moved in, he had guests in one cabin and last weekend, he'd opened cabin number three. Jillian gets a kick out of counting the cars and watching people come and go. Jeff works hard." She paused. "I don't know why I'm going on about it. I imagine he's told you all this."

"Not really," Heather said, "but my brother's work ethic has never been in question."

That didn't cover what Olivia was seeing and feeling when it came to Jeff. "I meant beyond that, Heather. He's putting a lot into making a home for Carson. More than once he's told me that to give the boy what he needs, he has to turn a profit with the lodge. But what I see is him trying so hard to fill the dad role."

"You're right," Heather said with a quick shrug. "I see it, too. I'm actually thrilled he's back. We have new families at the same time. And then you and Jillian are making your home here. How cool is that?"

"Pretty cool. So what's the problem?"

Heather bit the corner of her lower lip as she stared at nothing in particular. "It doesn't make any sense, but I can't help myself from being a little resentful. Jeff sort of breezed in here with Carson. I didn't hear about the boy's mother dying or about becoming Carson's guardian until after he'd bought the lodge and said he was coming. His big announcement."

Heather had slammed on the brake that stopped Olivia from letting down her guard and relaxing into an easy friendship with Jeff. He'd been honest with her about his past mistakes, though, while she was the one who made the snide remarks. "He couldn't have been more welcoming to Jillian and me."

"So I've noticed."

"Being friends with you was good enough for him." How quickly she'd judged him and insulted him with harsh words. With regret in her voice she added, "I didn't make a good first impression, either. To be honest, it was awful."

"All I can say is, don't listen to me." Heather pointed to herself. "My shaky feelings toward Jeff are my problem. He's apologized all he can." With that, she got to her feet and grinned. "So, Dr. Donoghue, how about we hit the sauna and sweat away all our toxins. So good for our health, right?"

An hour later, they were showered and changed and in the restaurant eating green salads and waiting for their platters of baked chicken. Their conversation had moved away from Jeff and on to the status of Carson's injuries.

"Jeff texted to tell me they have an appointment with Tom Azar this afternoon at his office in Landrum," Heather said. "He wondered if I was going to be working there today.

But this week, I'll be in Tom's satellite office in Butternut Springs."

"Carson is seeing Tom today?"

"That's what Jeff said. He's picking up Carson at school. You sound surprised."

"Well, no, it's just that I'm picking up Jillian and *we're* heading to see Tom for our initial appointment," Olivia said. "He can refer me to a local oncologist for follow-ups. It has to be done. No sense putting it off."

Heather nodded. "You're a little nervous about it, I'll bet. You may be a doctor, but that doesn't mean you're blasé about finding a new medical team for Jillian."

"Even Jillian knows enough to be a *little* nervous." Olivia's mind raced ahead at the prospect of running into Jeff. Maybe they could order takeout for dinner, a treat that would please both kids. Or, she'd offer to make burgers, or…

"Olivia? Where did you go?"

Heather's voice pulled her out of her reverie. "Oh, sorry. I was thinking ahead to the appointment details." Close enough.

"That could be a good thing, that you and Jeff have appointments on the same day. I picked up a little apprehension in his text."

Heather wrinkled her forehead in thought. "I *almost* offered to meet him there, but that could backfire. You know, make Carson think Jeff's making too big a deal out of it and then he'd wonder why."

Olivia agreed. "Especially since Carson insists he's on the mend."

"Carson's appointment likely has the same purpose as Jillian's." Heather sighed. "Tom can refer Carson to a counselor. Has Jeff mentioned anything to you about that?"

Olivia shook her head. "Jeff is probably more prone to sharing that sort of concern with you than with me."

"I wouldn't be too sure about that," Heather said, curling her lips up into an amused grin.

"Okay, what are you implying?"

"Oh, nothing." Heather stared off into space. "I don't have any special sense of Jeff and his feelings anymore, but it seems he's extra curious about you. Hmm…let's say he's appreciative of how special you are."

Olivia chuckled. "Says you…one of my all-time closest friends in the world."

"That doesn't make me wrong."

No sense arguing with Heather. Olivia gave her friend a teasing smile. As for her feelings for Jeff, they were completely irrational. Definitely not worth sharing.

THE MORE DR. TOM AZAR talked the more Jeff understood why Heather sang his praises. In sneakers, jeans and a red T-shirt under his white coat, the pediatrician greeted them at the door and motioned for them to sit in the cluster of three comfy chairs. Rather than separating himself behind an imposing desk, he took a seat with them. After a minute of chitchat about how lucky he was to hire Heather, Dr. Tom got down to business.

"So, here's how this works, Carson. Before I do the physical exam, I want a chance to get acquainted," Dr. Tom explained. "You're old enough to speak for yourself." He glanced down at the tablet in his lap. "You're already off to a good start. I've got a report from the PT clinic here. They've seen you twice already, based on the referral from the Seattle clinic. Correct?"

Carson sat up a little straighter in the chair. "The third appointment was yesterday."

"I see. Impressive progress, I'd say, at least on paper." With eyebrows raised in curiosity, Dr. Tom said, "What do you have to say about that?"

Carson's mouth twitched a little until he finally allowed himself to smile. "It's too slow."

Dr. Tom tapped his temple. "Since I knew you were going to say that, I'm guessing that you can fill in *my* response."

"Be…patient," Carson said, dragging out the words.

"Exactly. Go talk to every doc in the state and they'll tell you the same thing. So, when I do the exam I'll take a close look at your ankle and your arm and follow your therapy from here on. The PT clinic you're going to is the best there is, not only here, but anywhere. Okay?" Dr. Tom glanced from Carson to Jeff.

"Sounds fine to me," Jeff said, noting Carson's eager nod.

"Could you two walk me through your situation?" Dr. Tom asked Carson. "It says here Jeff is your legal guardian."

Carson clenched his fists in his lap. He looked down for a second, but then he raised his head. "That's 'cause my mom died." He shifted in the chair. "In, uh, an accident." He kept his gaze squarely on Dr. Tom.

"I made the legal arrangements while Carson was still in the hospital recovering from the surgery. Given all that happened, I thought it best to come back home to Wyoming."

"Why is that?" the doctor asked.

Jeff briefly described the long stretches of time he'd been away on trawlers and freighters, ending by adding that he was born and raised here. "As you know, Heather and the Burtons are in Adelaide Creek," Jeff said. "I bought the lodge, so I'm basically working from home. I'm close by for whatever Carson needs."

"And what about you, Carson? Are you okay with the move?"

Carson shrugged and glanced at Jeff. "It's okay. Different." He shifted in the chair. "I get why Jeff figured we had to leave Seattle. I don't have any family, except my grandma and she's really sick."

Dr. Tom didn't react, and Jeff held himself back from jumping in to explain his reasons all over again.

"A big change, though. You've only been in school a few days." Dr. Tom caught Jeff's eye. Jeff took it as a gentle warning not to jump into their exchange. "Freshman year can be tough for kids who haven't been through what you have. So, it's okay, expected, if you have mixed feelings about it."

"I might be ready to try out for the basket-ball team." Carson thrust out his injured arm and pulled up the sleeve to reveal the long curved scar and the puckered skin around the deeper edge of the wound. "I talked to the coach and he knows I'm still rehabbing my arm. My ankle, too."

"Okay if I see for myself?" the doctor asked, his arm poised in the air, but not touching Carson's arm.

"Sure."

Dr. Tom leaned closer and peered at what Jeff still found painful to see under the bright light in the office. He smiled when he looked up. "Great work. Whoever took care of you in the hospital was thinking about your future, Carson, and knew how important your arm is no matter what's ahead for you."

The tone of his voice, the careful manner in which he spoke touched Jeff in surprising ways. Karen seemed to expand her presence in Jeff's mind and fill the room. He'd have given anything for her to hear how this doctor was focused on Carson and his healing. When Dr. Tom asked Carson what other things he did with his time, Carson didn't need to think about his answer.

"I make videos of stuff I do and the people around me, maybe the twins playing and Jeff and Matt bringing the horses to the stable in the storm," Carson said. "I made a video journal for school," Carson said. "It was cool, so I kept doing it."

Dr. Tom let go of Carson's arm and pulled back. "That's a good project. You're making a record of your life." He fell silent for a few seconds, before he said, "So, how about your spirit, Carson?" He tapped his chest. "What's going on in here? Your arm and your ankle are doing great, but what about inside you?"

In an instant, tears pooled in Carson's eyes. Rare tears. At least from what he let Jeff see. Now Jeff felt pressure behind his own eyes. Man, the way the doc asked the question left no room to brush him off, especially because he kept his gaze fixed on Carson. In the stillness of the room, Jeff put the heel of a hand over one eye and then the other. He wasn't hurting for himself, not really. But his heart was broken for Carson.

"I miss my mom." Carson's voice was shaky.

"I'll bet," Dr. Tom said.

Jeff nodded. "I miss her, too. Karen was a great mother, and a good friend to me." With his elbow on the arm of the chair, Jeff made a loose fist and rested his cheek against it.

"She never got to do all the stuff she wanted to do," Carson said, "after I grew up and was on my own."

"What did she have in mind?" Dr. Tom asked in a soft voice.

"She wanted to go to school and become a nurse. But she waitressed during the day while I was in school, and then sometimes worked again at night. That's how she supported us." Tears spilled down his cheeks, but he had his voice back. "I was going to get a job next summer to help out."

"Good for you. You were aware of how hard your mom worked to make a life for you. I bet she knew you appreciated that."

"She did." Jeff felt propelled into the conversation. He explained how he happened to rent a room in their apartment, which was how he got to know Carson in the first place. "I wasn't around a lot, but I saw him help his mom. I used to look forward to seeing Carson when I got off a ship."

"I'll bet you did," Dr. Tom said as he reached

into his pocket and took out a business card and started writing on the back. "I'm putting my cell number on the back of this card, Carson. This isn't the office number, but a way you can reach me directly. Okay?" He held out the card and Carson took it and stared at it. "If you ever want to talk to me about anything at all, call me."

Carson glanced at Jeff as if checking with him.

"I'm sure Jeff understands. Even if you two get along great, you might not want to tell him everything that's on your mind." Dr. Tom paused and took a breath. "And when and if you're ready, I can refer you to a counselor who can help you sort through your feelings."

"That would be fine," Jeff said, relieved it hadn't been left up to him to bring up counseling. "Some things are private, Carson. I get that."

"Okay, then, let's have a look at you. We'll draw some blood and go from there." Dr. Tom stood and opened the door to the exam room. "We won't be long."

Surprised and a little spacey from what had happened, Jeff let himself out the other door and went around the desk to the waiting area, at first shocked when he came face-to-face with Olivia. He didn't know why, but the instant wave of relief almost overwhelmed him.

"There's Jeff," Jillian said.

"So it is." Olivia smiled as Jeff approached. "I'm not surprised to see you here. I was with Heather earlier. Jillian's also seeing Dr. Tom for the first time."

Jeff took in a deep breath. His voice was strained when he responded. "Carson shouldn't be long. He's with the doctor now." He rubbed his forehead as if clearing his thoughts. "He's not quite what I expected." Jeff was quiet, frowning slightly, as he sat in the chair next to Olivia.

"You have things on your mind," she observed, keeping her voice low.

"I'm a little stunned. It isn't wearing off. I thought it was going to be sort of cut-and-dried, draw some blood, look him over. Done and done."

Apparently, Jeff was planning to leave it at that. But that left her hanging. She rolled her hand toward Jeff to encourage him to open up. "And…"

"Let's just say Dr. Tom delved into more than the facts of Carson's physical health." He glanced across to Jillian, whose nose was in a book. "I'll tell you more about it later."

"Okay. I can wait."

"What about you? How are *you* doing?" Jeff asked.

Reading between the lines, she understood he was asking if she was anxious about this appointment. "Being with your sister, having a swim and a sauna and then lunch was exactly what the doctor ordered, or in this case, the nurse practitioner."

"Good." Jeff glanced at the closed door to the office. "Being a doctor yourself, I think you'll especially find this guy a likable colleague."

"I met him briefly, so I'm a little prepared," Olivia said. "How about if the four of us get together for pizza when we're done here. I'll make a fire and we can relax." She cocked her head toward Jillian. "The kids always go for pizza."

Jillian immediately chimed in with, "Yes, we do."

"Sounds good." Jeff got out his phone. "Tell you what. I'll order and pay for it now—my treat—and you and Jillian can pick it up on your way home."

"Good plan—and the next take-out meal is on me." Amused, she realized she'd declared there would be a next time.

"It's a deal."

"Extra cheese and sausage," Jillian said.

Jeff typed the order in the text box. "You and Carson are pizza-topping twins. I hope you don't mind, but I added an order of their chocolate chip cookies." Adding a little flourish, Jeff raised his finger high in the air before clicking the send button. "The deed is done."

Once again, Olivia forgot why she was wary of Jeff, almost afraid of him. Or, as she finally admitted to herself, it was how she felt when she was with him that scared her.

With dinner arranged, Jeff glanced toward the door to Dr. Tom's office and tapped his fingers on the arm of the chair.

"It's only been a few minutes," Olivia said quietly.

"I can tell time," Jeff said impatiently, but then he quickly smiled and added, "Sorry. Don't mind me. I've been jumpy about this all day."

Olivia was about to come up with reassuring words, but changed her mind. Jeff wasn't one for platitudes, especially not meaningless words about everything being okay.

They sat side by side and soon settled into a companionable silence. Jillian had gone back to her book, and if she was nervous about the appointment, she wasn't letting on.

Another patient arrived to speak to the receptionist and reschedule an appointment. "Here comes Carson," Jillian said, getting up and rushing toward him. "We're having pizza tonight. It's all ordered and everything."

"Oh yeah?" Carson teased. "Who says?"

Jillian pointed to Olivia and moved her finger back and forth to include Jeff. "They did."

Carson grinned at Jillian. "Cool. Good news for us."

Tom stood in the doorway to his office watching what was unfolding with the kids. Smiling, Olivia noted. This was the first new doctor who would see Jillian as a well child, not a newly recovering one. As more time passed, the side effects of treatment would weaken and with any luck Jillian would be spared long-term repercussions.

Tom spoke with Jeff for a minute or two. Jeff listened and nodded, and his face broke into a smile as he walked back to the waiting room. The nurse at the desk nodded to Olivia and then to Tom. "He's ready for you."

"See you later," Carson said, waving to Jillian.

As Olivia expected, Jillian hung back a little when they went into the office and he pointed to the chairs. Understandable apprehension had come over her daughter. Olivia pressed her palm on her upper chest to consciously will the tension away. After a quick nod to Olivia, all the doctor's attention went to Jillian. From the way he spoke, it was clear he'd gone over the details of Jillian's records.

"When I look at all these files," he said, dramatically scrolling with his index finger, "all I see is good news. Nope, let me correct myself. It's *great* news."

"Do I have to see an oncologist ever again?"

The doctor answered with a simple yes.

She would need follow-up testing for years to come. Jillian didn't balk. She'd already known the answer to her question anyway. Maybe she'd been holding on to a tiny morsel of hope that this doctor would deliver a different message. The rest of the appointment went fast and they moved on to the exam and the blood draw.

"Lucky you, Jillian, that you've made friends here already."

"We're sharing a pizza with Carson and Jeff later. We live in one of Jeff cabins." It took Jillian only one more second to add, "He's going to have horses soon." Jillian tilted her head toward Olivia. "And I want to ride them."

Olivia rolled her eyes. "Jillian, we can talk—"

Tom's interruption was swift. "I want to see those growing bones of yours get a little stronger first. And I bet your mom agrees."

Jillian threw back her head and groaned.

"Do you know what revisit an issue means?" the doctor asked.

Jillian nodded. "It means we'll talk about it later."

"I knew you were smart," Tom said.

Olivia walked through the door Tom held

open. When they were outside, she felt lifted up, filled with joy. The girl skipping ahead to the car was already on to other things like sharing pizza with their new friends. Olivia followed Jillian to the parking lot, clinging to these special feelings that the part of her life she cherished most was protected.

JEFF CLEARED AWAY the plates and Olivia loaded them in the dishwasher, realizing how carefree they all seemed. He and Olivia ate their early dinner with the same enthusiasm as the kids gobbled their favorite pizza. Carson was exuberant and patiently listened to Jillian tell a long story about kids in her class debating which pet was best, a dog or a cat.

"Speaking of dogs, I need to take Winnie out," Carson said, bracing his good hand on the coffee table and maneuvering his good leg to help him stand.

"Can I come along?" Jillian asked.

Carson didn't answer, but looked to Olivia, who glanced out the window. It was dark, but Jeff didn't see how that could matter. Carson wouldn't go far.

"Okay." Olivia tilted her head and gave Jillian and Carson a fond look. "You can have cookies when you come back."

Jeff pointed to the alcove, where her computers and screens stretched across the desk. "Would it violate any rule if got a look at your setup?"

"Not at all. I'd have to bring an actual patient's images to the screen and I won't do that." She led him into the alcove, with its small space, but large screens.

"Nowadays, there's so much we can see with the files when they appear on our screens." She turned a screen on and two X-ray images appeared.

Jeff drew back. There was no mistaking he was staring at skull fractures, one a thin line across the top left of the skull. The other was a spidery fracture of smaller lines. "Aren't those your patients?"

"Oh, no, no. I'd never violate a patient's privacy," she said. "Those are training images I used when I worked with an intern the other day." She turned off the screen. "Those images are what spin around in my head when I think of Jillian riding a horse. Fortunately, Tom convinced Jillian she had to wait a while longer." She sighed. "He reinforced what I knew to be true."

Jeff wished he hadn't asked to see her workstation. "I had no idea that's what you feared. Riding isn't risk free, but that kind of injury is rare."

"So is childhood leukemia."

Wow, the melodic voice was icy.

"I'm sorry. I didn't put those two things together," Jeff said.

"I didn't mean to sound so harsh, but at least now you know why I'm so cautious about Jillian."

"But you do know that I'm not doing anything to put Jillian in danger," Jeff said. "I'm not encouraging her or getting involved at all."

"I think I insulted you again. I'm always doing that." Olivia cupped her hands over her mouth and nose. "Yikes."

"Oh, you're not *always* doing that," Jeff said. In some corner of his mind, he understood her. He picked up her hand. "Come on back to the couch."

Olivia put up no argument.

When they sat down again, he described Karen's condition when he saw her after the accident. "I don't need convincing, Olivia, about risk and tragedy."

Olivia nodded and lowered her head. "That's traumatic, Jeff. Really."

"I'm sure it's why I still dream about it. But I do need to be clear. By next summer, I'll have horses in the stable and out in the corral," Jeff said. "I can't change that part of the plan I have for the lodge to make it work."

"I know."

He brushed his finger across her hand and then covered it with his. "I hope you won't up and move at the first sight of a mane and a tail."

Olivia laughed softly. "Are you kidding? Jillian wouldn't allow it."

"It's fun having you here." Jeff hadn't realized how much. "The kids have a good time together, too. I might understand more than you know. I'm just not that skilled at explaining it."

"Don't sell yourself short. I think you might understand more than anyone."

"You better stick around," Jeff said. "Who will I beat at darts?"

"Ooh, fightin' words. I do love a challenge."

At the sound of the kids coming through

the door, Olivia pulled away and stood and walked into the kitchen. "Okay, you two, dessert time."

Jeff smiled to himself. Everything that happened in the last fifteen minutes puzzled him. Not necessarily in a bad way.

CHAPTER SIX

CASUAL, CARSON HAD SAID. Not a party. He wanted to invite a few kids from school to play Ping-Pong, maybe shoot pool. No big deal. "You don't have to do anything special. Not a thing."

Of course, Jeff had said yes. But he couldn't resist a little mild teasing. "There won't be anything special about the chips and dip we put out in bowls or the cookies we serve—we won't even bother with napkins and paper plates. I *promise*."

Despite his attempt to maintain his cool demeanor, Carson snorted a laugh. "Think you're real funny, huh?"

"Not particularly, but I am good at ribbing you," Jeff said.

Now, with the snacks ready to go, Carson ran a cloth across the sides of the pool table. He'd already checked the Ping-Pong table. More than once.

No matter now casual Carson wanted to be about his Halloween evening get-together, Jeff was impressed. After being at the school a mere two weeks, he'd become friendly with enough kids to invite them over to the lodge. Some kids at the school were going to house parties, costumes required, but Carson was clear that he wasn't interested in that. Costumes? Oh, no, not anymore. That was too much like trick-or-treating. End of discussion. But an evening of pool and Ping-Pong was a different story.

When Jeff had studied the particulars about the lodge before he bought it sight unseen, he'd not given much attention to what had been left behind in the reception area. When the detailed photos showed up in his inbox, he'd been pleasantly surprised that it resembled a typical lodge activity room, plus the counter for buffet-style food service and tables and chairs and a small bar. It had been so easy to picture the room filled with guests having morning coffee or drinks on summer evenings. He'd planned to use the office but keep this social part of the lodge closed up for winter and hadn't even anticipated using the fireplace.

Once he and Carson moved in, though, the possibilities for the lodge were obvious. He could invite Heather and Matt and the twins and other old family friends here to hang out or put the tables together for holiday meals. The board games and paperback books had been gathering dust for too long. That was about to change. Seeing Carson helping to set up the room reinforced the wisdom of buying the lodge and making it their home.

"Alex and Eddie think it's so cool I live in a lodge," Carson said when he started stacking logs in the fireplace.

"You want help with the fire?" Jeff asked.

"Nah, I got it." He grinned at Jeff. "I've been watching you in the cabin. I'm a quick learner."

"Yes, you are," Jeff agreed. The apartments in their building in Seattle hadn't had fireplaces, or porches. Carson hadn't been to overnight camp or any other place where building a fire had been a skill of any consequence. After watching Jeff, though, building fires at night turned out to be one of the things Carson took to most about living here. Never mind that at first the teenager described the road they lived on as Nowhere Lane. Got a big kick out of himself, too. At least until he found out that lots of kids lived on roads exactly like this one, real name Norton Road.

Earlier in the week when Carson had asked Jeff if it was okay if he invited some kids, three other guys and a couple of girls, Jeff had said an easy yes and then asked, "Are they also freshmen?"

"Eddie and Alex are sophomores. They're in one of my classes and I know them from phys ed. They were real friendly and weren't shy about asking about how I got so banged up." He had a couple of classes with the other three freshmen, Owen and the two girls, Mindy and Nina. "Those three have been hanging out since first grade. The girls are…" Carson looked away and stared into space, as if searching for the right word.

Jeff waited, curious what was coming next.

"They're smart. They ace all the math tests. Real pretty, too."

Like Olivia. What? That jolted him. She was the first woman to pop into his head. And she was pretty—and so much more. He stifled a laugh thinking that back in the day she'd no doubt aced all the math tests, too.

"I've been surrounded by smart, pretty

women all my life," Jeff said, grinning. "Starting with Heather and my mom."

"How come…?" Carson stared into space again. A couple of seconds ticked by.

"What? Go ahead, Carson, finish the sentence."

"I wonder why you aren't… I mean…you don't have a family of your own."

Taken aback by the question, Jeff managed to say, "Fair question. It's not that I don't want to meet the right woman and settle down." That was more or less a whopping piece of dishonesty.

"But aren't you around thirty something?"

"Thirty-six to be exact." Amused by the question, born of Carson's natural curiosity, he was also left without good answers. "I was busy with the ranch after college and working at different odd jobs to keep some money coming in. And then I wouldn't have been a good partner for anyone when I ran away from Adelaide Creek. And that's what it was. Running away." He explained that he'd isolated himself on trawlers and freighters, living with the crew, but still alone in important ways. He left out the part about not feeling alone as much as taking pride in being a loner. That had a positive ring to it, implying that he valued his precious freedom above all else. He'd told himself that for years.

Carson's expression still reflected confusion, but he turned his attention back to the fire while Jeff shook chips from the bag and filled a giant bowl on the counter. The silence wasn't easy, though, because Jeff knew his answer hadn't satisfied Carson's curiosity. The boy might as well have asked Jeff what had gone wrong in his life that he hadn't been ready to settle down.

Jeff cleared his throat. "I'm glad you invited friends. It's fun for you, but it also gives me a chance to see how we can set up the lodge next summer." He gestured around the room. "Just think, we'll have coffee and muffins and cookies available all day and people can play a little Ping-Pong or pool and then hang out at the tables. With snacks and drinks at hand, it will be fun to stop in here."

"Or, sit around on the couches," Carson added, pointing to the long leather couch and two shorter ones that formed a U in front of the fireplace. End tables and a pine coffee table added a homey feel.

"Uh, don't forget the younger kids will be

stopping in later," Jeff said. "They'll show off their costumes and get some treats."

Carson shrugged. "I figured."

The hum of an engine grew louder as it came up the drive and was followed by the sound of car doors opening and closing.

Trying not to intrude too much, Jeff stood back to let Carson welcome his friends. "Uh, Mindy said her dad was going to want to meet you before he left her—and Nina and Owen—here."

Why hadn't he thought of that? "Sure thing." Jeff followed Carson outside. Mindy's dad was walking around from the driver's side of the minivan while Carson greeted Nina and Owen.

"Bart Malone," the man said, holding out his hand. "Wanted to meet Carson's, uh, the boy's people."

"Of course." Jeff introduced himself to Bart, a guy around the same age as him. "I'm from Adelaide Creek, but I've been out in Seattle for a few years. Do you want to come in?"

"Would I like to? You bet," Bart said, "but I've got to get back to Landrum. My wife and Mindy's younger sister and brothers are trick-or-treating with a crowd of kids. I promised

I'd help." He smiled at Mindy and the other kids. "Used to take these kids out. Seems they think they're too old for all that now."

"Da…*ad*," Mindy said. "We *are* too old."

Jeff made no attempt hide his laugh over the long-suffering look Mindy aimed at Bart.

"We want to play Ping-Pong," Nina said. "It's so much cooler than getting candy from the neighbors."

With that, Bart snorted and shook his head in a good-natured way. "Nice to see the lodge lit up again. Used to be a busy place in the summer. Looks real nice, too."

"Thanks. I'm looking forward to tourists packing the place," Jeff said. "Come around anytime and I'll give you a tour."

The girls followed Carson inside and he took their jackets and hung them on hooks behind the door. Jeff's sense of satisfaction grew with every ooh and aah over Carson's cool lodge. About the time Carson got sodas distributed to the kids, Eddie and Alex showed up in a car. Jeff went out to introduce himself to Eddie's mom, who didn't linger, because she had a toddler with her.

Jeff and Carson had compromised on how scarce Jeff would make himself. Since the lodge office was behind the bar and kitchen, Carson agreed it was sufficiently out of the way and out of sight. In the spirit of "love me, love my dog," Winnie was allowed to mill about with the kids, although Carson's strict rule about begging food applied. Jeff knew exactly where that rule came from. The day Carson chose Winnie at the shelter and brought her home, Karen had produced a list of rules. Rule #1: No begging for food, no exceptions. The other three rules were all about Carson's responsibilities for Winnie, including walks, filling the food and water bowls, and all-around cleaning up after her. Rule #5: Read rule #1.

Jeff smiled at the memory. Karen had been easygoing with Carson in some ways, but he knew when to take his mom seriously, no wiggle room to be found.

Settling in his office to work on two ads he wanted to place in a winter edition of a county tourist paper, Jeff kept one ear on the noise coming from the main room, where the kids had settled around the fireplace. Carson took care of replenishing the bowls of salsa and chips. And pretzels, Owen's favorite. He was impressed by the easy way the five kids who'd grown up together shared their stories with Carson so he'd get their inside jokes.

As the first hour moved into the second, Jeff had a look at the main room. Eddie and Alex, being a full year older, were strutting around and trying a little too hard to impress the girls, who seemed more interested in Carson's life in Seattle than anything else. Nina had been to the city so she knew some of the sights and told the others nothing in Wyoming was anything like Pike Place Market—or the Space Needle.

When the noise died down a little, Jeff hit the pause button and got up to stick his head around the corner again. The girls were playing Ping-Pong, with Carson silently recording them with his video camera. Owen was giving them pointers, but from what Jeff saw, the girls didn't need much coaching and were doing fine on their own.

Eddie and Alex were fooling around at the pool table, but they didn't know much about playing. Seeing the two supposedly older teens playfully pushing and shoving each other, Jeff was glad he'd kept the dart cabinet closed. The two untrained and awkward pool players were louder than the other four kids combined. But, Jeff reasoned, they were still young enough to believe that being dolts was the best method to impress the girls.

Jeff ducked back in the office and started a movie, but within minutes a different kind of noise filled the room. He'd have recognized that cheery voice calling out a giggly hello to Carson anywhere.

OLIVIA OPENED THE door and let Jillian walk inside first before following behind her. She'd had reservations about crashing Carson's party, but Jeff had insisted they had to stop in on their way to their Halloween party for the little kids at the Adelaide Creek library.

Jillian called out, "Hi, Carson," and headed straight for the Ping-Pong table, where he and another boy were now facing off against Mindy and Nina. Both girls dropped their paddles and headed to Jillian, but their eyes were on Olivia.

Jeff came around the corner and stopped in his tracks. She waved, but the two teenagers rushed toward her and grabbed her attention.

"Wow, you look *amazing.*" The friendly girl grinned and introduced herself, Mindy, and the other girl, Nina. "Where did you find that flapper dress?"

"Well, girls, it's the best costume I've ever had. I found it in a vintage catalog." Olivia hadn't been able to resist the classic 1920s velvet dress the color of blueberries. She had long silver beads that matched the color of the fringe on the bottom of the dress. Pointy-toed beaded shoes added more inches to her height. Her longish auburn hair was concealed under a wig, solid black and cut in a short bob. The 1920s-era pearl-and-silver headband was her favorite part of the costume.

She glanced at Jeff. It was obvious he couldn't keep his eyes off of her. Maybe the dark blue eye shadow and her scarlet lips were responsible for his intense stare.

She looked beyond the girls to him. "Wait till you see Heather. We helped each other put our flapper getups together. She and the twins are on their way." She glanced at the girls. "We won't interrupt your party for long."

"Oh, that's okay. This is fun," Nina said, turning to Jillian, who'd made herself at home with Carson's friends. "And you are a terrific cat."

"My friend's twins and Jillian decided to

dress up as animals," Olivia explained. Jillian had chosen the mostly black cat costume from a collection that one of Heather's friends kept in her attic.

As if on cue, the door opened to the sound of squeals and the twins rushed in. Nick wore a convincing elephant costume and Lucy, equally cute, was dressed up as a giraffe. Olivia stepped closer to Jeff and Heather, who was stunning in her red-and-black flapper dress with rows of sequins sewed across the neckline. Carson and Owen joined the girls in fussing over all three kids. As he usually did, Carson lined them up for photos and video.

"I was a robot cowboy last year," Nick said to his receptive audience of older kids, "but I like being an elephant better."

"We're going to the party in town," Lucy explained, "and get tons of candy."

"Good for you. You both look real cute," Nina said to the twins before turning to Mindy. "Now I wish we'd dressed up. Next year for sure."

"I'm speechless," Jeff said, looking from Heather to Olivia. "You two are showstoppers. I had no idea you were going for such glamor."

"We tried," Olivia said flirtatiously.

"And it worked." Jeff lowered his voice. "Isn't it good to see this room filled with kids?"

Olivia agreed. Mostly. Eddie and Alex, still acting up at the pool table, were the exception. Apparently, Jeff was trying to ignore them and focus on Heather and her.

Heather, radiant and happy, talked about how much fun she was having this Halloween. Olivia nodded along, but her gaze kept drifting to Eddie and Alex, who were sword fighting with pool cues.

Did Jeff see these boys through a lens similar to hers? He didn't seem particularly concerned, but the boys were going beyond rude. Something else was happening.

"They're just showing off. Don't pay them any mind," Jeff said, apparently noticing her studying them. "Come on over to the bar. Carson is picking out the candy to give to the kids."

Olivia and Heather joined him in watching Carson and Owen make three piles of wrapped miniature candy bars, which Nick counted before dropping them in their shiny paper trick-or-treat bags.

"My little brothers and sister will be at the

party in town, too," Mindy said. "They're cute, like you guys."

A hoot from the corner got Jeff's attention. Olivia's, too.

"What's with those two?" Olivia said in a voice barely above a whisper. "I suspect they've been drinking."

Jeff straightened and threw his shoulders back. "I can assure you they aren't drinking. I've been here the whole time." His voice tinged with resentment at her words.

"Maybe so, but that doesn't—" Olivia bit her tongue and told herself to shut up.

"No, not *maybe*. They're a year older than Carson and Owen and the two girls. They're just horsing around."

Since he'd opened up the subject, she decided to tentatively take the bait. "Well, kids can be sneaky, Jeff."

"You think I'm not paying attention?"

"No, I didn't say that." Olivia heard her defensive tone. "It's easy to miss, that's all."

"There's no alcohol in this building." He gestured toward the kids. "They haven't been outside this room, not even for a second."

Clearly, she'd stumbled into tender territory and it was time to drop the subject. "I hear you. You don't have to be so feisty with me." She pivoted toward the counter and took a few steps to get closer to the kids. "We need to be going, anyway."

Carson was still filming the twins, who were kneeling on the bar stools and counting pieces of chocolate.

"Hey, kiddos, let's get your jackets on," she said. "Time to head to the party."

Heather, who was clustered with all the kids, except for the outliers, Eddie and Alex, glanced up, surprised by the way Olivia was hustling them to get into their jackets and out the door. Heather had her eye on Jeff, too, who'd moved to Carson's side.

Only the kids hadn't noticed the tension in the air. They happily said goodbye to the girls and Owen and Carson and hurried to Heather's SUV with Jeff watching from the door, puzzled.

Olivia joked around with the kids about costumes and candy during the five-minute drive to Merchant Street and the library. Only after the kids ran into the building did Heather pull her aside and ask, "What was that all about back at the lodge with Jeff?"

Olivia waved away her words. "Nothing. It was a big nothing."

"It didn't look like nothing."

"I got into something with him that wasn't any of my business. Really, it's not important."

That was one way to look at it, but when it came to teens and alcohol, those boys' antics looked too familiar. She'd diagnosed injuries and alcohol poisoning in ERs far too often.

Warning against risky behavior was her business. But she had to remember that Jeff and those boys weren't her patients.

CARSON WENT THROUGH the front door with Winnie at the same time Olivia came in alone, still in her knockout costume. The black wig brought a smile to Jeff's face, but her earlier nosiness still bothered him.

"So, how did everything go?" Olivia asked. She leaned against the wall inside the doorway and crossed both her arms and her ankles.

"It was a big success," Jeff said, smiling at her. It was hard to stay irritated with Olivia. She might blurt critical things on impulse, but that didn't make what she had to say thoughtless. Even if he didn't agree.

"Good for Carson—and you."

"You don't have to stand by the door." Jeff gestured for her to come closer.

"Can I offer you something? I can rustle up some chips and dip, maybe a couple of cookies. These kids can sure eat."

"No, no, I'm fine. I'm filled up with frosted pumpkin- and cat-shaped cookies from the party. I've had more sugar tonight than I have in years." She walked toward the bar, the fringe of her dress swaying back and forth.

Jeff laughed. "It's hard to have a completely serious conversation with you in that dress and wig. The fringe is dancing around, and that thing bobbing on your head has a life of its own."

"I'll have you know these are real pearls and genuine vintage trim." She added some attitude. "You better get used to it, because Heather is vowing to wear it at one of your family's holiday dinners."

That sounded like the new Heather. "Maybe so, but the wire-and-pearl thingies waving around are very distracting."

A couple of quick tugs later, the headband and the wig were gone and Olivia's reddish-brown hair tumbled down to her shoulders. "Is that better?"

She had no idea how much. "You bet. I'm talking to the real Olivia now and she's kinda grown on me."

She pulled her head back and gave him a long skeptical look. "I'm glad to hear you find the real me tolerable."

"As a matter of fact, I think you're quite intriguing." That word covered a lot of ground. He didn't want to scare her off by telling her that her criticism of him aside, every time he saw her, she won him over. And in a way no other woman ever had.

Olivia blushed and fumbled around for words. "Okay, it's time to really clear the air. It's true the unruly boys were none of my business, but my doctor hat doesn't leave my head easily. So, when I see children acting a certain way I can't unsee it." She cleared her throat and looked away.

Now that she put it like that, it was obvious why she spoke up. Little stabs of doubt got Jeff's attention, but only for a second. He was certain he was right about the boys. Since this conversation had nowhere to go now, except in a circular direction, it was time for a neutral question. "Is Jillian at home?"

"She's having a sleepover with the twins,"

Olivia said, as she shifted in her chair. "Heather is going to drop her off at school tomorrow. She hasn't had a sleepover in years, so she was excited about it. I'll be up all night working my shift in front of my computers." Suddenly, Olivia squinted as if studying the fireplace. "That painting you hung there. It's your mom's style."

Jeff nodded. "One of my favorites. Heather has all Mom's work stored carefully in the attic at the ranch now." He'd planned to offer Olivia a painting for her cabin another day, but it seemed as good a time as any to bring out the one he had in mind. He raised his index finger in the air. "Stay right there."

He went around the corner to the storage closet next to the office and sorted through a line of paintings propped against the wall. He picked up one of the large ones depicting two rows of uneven hills and the deep valley between them. He'd had a feeling she might admire this one.

When he came back, Olivia was standing behind the longest couch staring at his mother's pink-and-purple mountains at sunset. "Heather put two paintings in her bunkhouse. One is of the two of you on your horses."

"Heather and I are slowly going through all her work now. I'll hang a few more pictures in here, and I already have a couple in my cabin." Jeff held up the painting in his hand so she could get a close look at his mother's vision of craggy hills and outcroppings glistening under the sun. "If you want it, I'll come by one day this week and hang it wherever you'd like it."

Olivia's face lit up. "Really? It would be perfect over my fireplace."

"Seems made for that very spot." He started to give it to her, but it was unwieldy, even in his longer arms. "I'll carry it to your cabin for you. You can put it someplace safe for the time being."

"Okay. Thanks. I should get ready for my shift."

"I'm glad you stopped by," Jeff said. "The longer I know you the better I understand you."

"That's good, isn't it?"

"I hope so," he whispered.

It was a frosty Halloween night, with a thin cloud cover blocking out most of the light from the crescent moon. Jeff felt the energy between them as they walked along together. It was a familiar vibe now. When they got to her cabin, Olivia directed him to lean the painting against the wall behind her desk.

When she walked him back to the door, he couldn't resist saying, "One more thing, Olivia."

"Oh? Uh, what's that?"

"If you ever wear that fringy dress again, you might want to ditch the black wig."

Olivia's laugh was as melodic as her voice.

"Believe me, the real thing is so much better." Taking such pleasure in her smile, he leaned forward and gave her cheek a quick kiss. "Night." He hurried away, but he knew she was still standing by the door watching him leave. It had been a great night all around.

CHAPTER SEVEN

AFTER LEAVING HIM alone for almost two weeks, the nightmare was back. Jeff pulled himself up and sat on the edge of the bed holding his head in his hands. The clock read 4:30 a.m. If the sound of a semi and the images of grillwork heading toward them decided to taunt him, they usually visited around that time, too early to wake up, but too late to go back to sleep. The nightmares always included an image of Karen's injured body next to him. Every time, Jeff's eyes opened when the nightmare had him staring at blood staining his hands, and his eyes stung from memories of sharp smells that pierced his nostrils. Then, relieved to find himself safe in his room nearly one thousand miles from the site of the accident, his heart slowed down.

He got to his feet and forced himself to call up a good memory. This time it was an image of Carson greeting his friends with

Winnie wagging her tail and reveling in the extra attention. But that train of thought led to Olivia's concerns about Eddie and Alex. She'd backed off but hadn't backed down from her opinion. Then, when Eddie's mom came to pick them up, she'd looked at her son and frowned and asked if he was okay. The boy patted his stomach and volleyed a flip remark back to her about eating too much. Jeff had joked about resupplying his snack shelf.

Frustrated with these thoughts, Jeff threw on sweats and a hoodie and went into the kitchen and brewed a steaming mug of coffee and took it out to the porch in the dark. Faint light filtered through the slats of Olivia's closed blinds. She was probably working in the alcove. He shook his head. Somehow, he'd gone and done it. Didn't he have enough complications in his life? Not that a friendly kiss on the cheek should be labeled a complication. Since she hadn't pulled away, she'd probably taken it in the spirit he intended. It was a positive thing to have a friend and team up with the kids now and then.

Nice try. He and Karen had been friends for years. But they hadn't done any cheek kissing. After a year or so, she'd offer a friendly hug hello when he'd come home from a long stint at sea. Right. Jeff had never gone to sleep thinking about Karen's soft skin or special scent.

By the time Jeff was back inside the cabin, Carson was climbing the hill with Winnie at his side. The dog was better than any alarm clock. The only times the teenager ever complained about the job of having a dog were on these early mornings when he lumbered out of bed to take Winnie out.

With both of them up so early, Jeff had time to crack some eggs and mix in milk and cinnamon for French toast. One of their favorite breakfasts, or suppers when Jeff added thick slices of ham.

When Carson came in with the dog, he sniffed the air. "Smells good in here."

"I thought you'd enjoy French toast this morning." Jeff didn't want to ask, but he wanted to know how Carson thought the night went. Having kids come around was a first for both of them. Maybe inviting friends to the house was nothing to parents used to arranging playdates and birthday parties, but it was a big thing to Jeff.

Jeff got the butter sizzling in the pan while

Carson disappeared into his room. When he got to the table, he was in his jeans and a clean sweatshirt and eager to polish off breakfast.

"Uh, everyone seemed to have a good time last night," Jeff said, hoping he'd get more than a nod.

"They think this place is cool. The girls say all it needs is an indoor pool." He snorted. "And hot tubs."

"Is that so?" Jeff grinned. "Then they'll have to head to the Tall Tale Lodge. It already has a heated pool and a sauna. I don't think we'll be trying to copy them." Maybe not the spa atmosphere, but Jeff could envision an indoor pool—eventually. From what he'd read, off-season tourism was expanding statewide.

Carson held his fork in the air and looked down at his plate. "I wish Alex and Eddie hadn't acted stupid. They're okay guys in school, but they were kinda rude."

Keeping his tone cool, Jeff asked, "How do you mean?"

"They hung out with each other, you know, ignoring the rest of us. They acted dumb around the girls. They were showing off to get their attention. Mindy said it's what peacocks do." He paused long enough to offer a priceless self-satisfied grin. "They weren't impressed."

Jeff stifled a laugh over the peacock comparison, as old as the hills out his window. "Well, if you ever do bring them around again, I can give them a few pointers on playing pool," Jeff said dryly.

Carson shrugged and helped himself to more food. "Sword fighting with the pool cues? That's something Lucy and Nick would do." He snickered. "Maybe."

In the interest of keeping lines of communication going, a phrase Dr. Tom had used came to mind. If he asked about the two boys sneaking alcohol into the lodge, Carson might shut down. Glancing at the clock, Jeff assessed the time they had left before the bus pulled up. The escape route from uncomfortable questions was rolling along on its route now. "Next time you can bring some other kids around. Good for you for already making friends. You've only been here a couple of weeks."

Carson's face lit up in surprise. "I can do it again? You know, have kids here at the lodge?"

"Absolutely. I never expected last night to

be a one-time thing. At least through the winter and early spring," Jeff said. "With any luck we'll be busy here in the summer, so things will change some."

"I'll video the place then. It'll be a sort of vacation movie," Carson said. "You can use it on your website."

"Good point. And you have a good voice, so you can add narration." Jeff gave him a pointed look. "Hmm... I'm thinking that taking care of the food bar might be a good summer job for you."

"Beats cleaning cabins, I guess." Carson smiled at that idea before he pushed away from the table and carried his plate to the sink. "Meanwhile, what are you going to do today?"

Jeff planted his hand on his hip and cocked his head. "You ask that most every day. You think Winnie and I laze around watching game shows or something. I am working my fingers to the bone."

"I guess so," Carson said, frowning. "What you do is different, though, not like my mom. She was always rushing around trying to make sure she got to work on time."

"Well, as soon as you're on your way, I'm

going to rush up the path to open up another cabin."

"That's good, right? Didn't you think it would be dead around here until spring?"

"Turns out I was wrong. The old place is coming alive." He paused. "Seems the ads and the flyers are working. If I open another cabin, we'll have next weekend's reservations covered, plus two extra for drive-ups. We'll never turn anyone away."

Jeff couldn't expect Carson to understand his daily routine involved more than cleaning the cabins and changing the linens. Getting a cabin ready to open meant more than making sure it was tidy. He checked every lamp and appliance and made sure the smoke alarms worked. He tested the fireplace to make sure the chimney was clear. "After school you can earn a little cash restocking wood in the crates on the porches. How about that?"

Carson nodded—eagerly. The only money the teenager had was what Jeff supplied, but he didn't ask for extra things. Finding ways to earn some spending money would give Carson independence.

Picking up on the usual signals that Carson was getting ready to leave, Winnie sat by the door and lifted her head for Carson's goodbye scratches and pats on her neck and jowls. "Yes, I'll miss you, Winnie," Carson said, his tone going right up to the edge of baby talk. "It won't be long. Be good for Jeff. You can help me stack wood when I get home from school."

Then he was gone. Winnie raced to the window and lifted her front paws to rest on the windowsill to watch him head down the drive. Next stop, her second bed, which Carson had put in the space between the living room and the kitchen. As Jeff poured himself another cup of coffee, it struck him that seeing Carson off to school in the morning, giving him a pat on his shoulder, was one of the best parts of his day. The most uncomplicated.

Carson took care of getting himself ready and ate everything put in front of him. It meant a lot to Jeff to fix him good food and keep the fridge stocked.

It was paying off, too, because even the physical therapist remarked about his growth spurt. Every time he observed a change in Carson, his mind took him to the cruelty of that freak accident. It had taken away the one person who loved Carson so completely. And Jeff was the only acceptable option to take over. He wasn't a criminal like the teenager's dad, who had died in prison, but Jeff knew next to nothing about raising a kid. Still, the boy had a room of his own, everything he needed, and a decent school. "And you, Winnie," he whispered.

Jeff drained his coffee cup and redirected his attention to the work ahead. He opened his tablet to scan his to-do list for the day, which included ordering supplies and making changes to his website. He'd barely pulled up his website when his phone rang. He checked the screen and recognized the last name, Ames.

"Jeff Stanhope," he said into the phone.

"Rolf Ames here, Alex's dad," the gruff voice said. "Alex was out at your place last night. That lodge."

"Yes, of course." Rolf's tone set Jeff's teeth on edge. This was no thanks-for-inviting-my-son call.

"As I recall, there's a bar in the lodge. Right."

"Not really. There's a setup for a small bar, but it's not stocked and open." Jeff waited for a response, but not getting any, he added, "Why do you ask?"

"There must be some alcohol somewhere. Wherever you're keeping your stash, that boy you have living with you must have found it."

Jeff's temples pulsated, but he willed himself to ignore it. "And why do you say that, Rolf?"

"Because when my son got home, it was obvious he'd been drinking."

Olivia's observations rushed back and hit him in the face. "Did Alex own up to it?"

"Uh, not exactly. He's fifteen," Rolf said. "Not an age when they willingly admit to breaking a rule."

Jeff had never handled a situation like this, but there had to be a first time and today was it. It felt like a test. Would he pass or fail? "Maybe so, but I want to make something clear." He took a couple of steps and opened the fridge. Two bottles of Jadestone beer sat in the door, right where they'd been for days. His heartbeat slowed down and his confidence went up. "I don't keep alcohol in the lodge. There was no alcohol in the lodge for Carson to find, even if he had gone looking for it, which I'm certain he didn't."

Rolf started to say something, stopped and then stumbled over his words. "Yeah, well, the parents around here, you know we don't like our young kids drinking."

"Put me in that camp," Jeff said. "Here's how I see it. I had five kids I'd never met before here at the lodge last night. New friends of Carson's, who has been at the high school all of two weeks. Now Alex and Eddie are a little older than the other boy and the two girls and they separated themselves off from the younger three."

Jeff left out Olivia's speculation about the drinking or the boys' behavior. He'd sort that out later. "I was in my office in the lodge the whole time. I never left the building. I never would knowingly allow any teenagers to drink in my house. It's out of the question."

"I don't want you to think I'm getting personal or anything," Rolf said, "but it's my understanding you, uh, aren't Carson's father. Alex said he's sort of like your foster kid...child." Speaking fast, he added, "What I mean is, you haven't been a parent of a teenager very long."

Jeff sighed. "That last part's true, which also makes me more cautious, Rolf. And this conversation *is* personal, but I don't mind. I became Carson's legal guardian after his mom was killed in a car accident. It's a permanent arrangement, not foster care." He paused, but then added, "This isn't information anyone is trying to hide. Carson told the kids what the deal is with the two of us."

"Okay… I see." Rolf had lowered his voice and his angry tone withered away.

"I'm asking all these questions because I need to be sure about what went on last night. Eddie and Alex…well, to be honest, they have a history of searching for trouble. I assumed they found it at your place."

Not hard to believe, that was for sure. "What I can do is ask Carson what he knows. This doesn't prove anything, but Alex and Eddie were loud and horsing around a lot," Jeff said. "More than the others. I saw it as a couple of boys showing off for the girls. But like I said, I'll ask Carson."

"You know, Alex is getting ready for varsity basketball," Rolf said, all trace of accusation gone from his voice. "He's not likely to be a big star or anything, but he's a solid player. The coach won't keep him on the team if he pulls stunts like this."

Jeff had no ready response other than, "I see."

"If you don't mind asking your, uh, Carson…what he knows, I'm curious to hear what he says." Rolf was quick to end the conversation with that and said he'd stay in touch.

Now Jeff was stuck in a dilemma he'd created. He hadn't believed Olivia when she'd tried to tell him something was off. His fallback position had been to stay on defense and believe Olivia was wrong. Even if he had smoothed things over with her last night, he owed her the truth. But not when she was working. Jeff sighed as he grabbed his jacket and headed out to start his workday up the hill in the empty cabin.

OLIVIA FINISHED HER note to Jillian and anchored it on the breakfast bar with the salt shaker. She glanced down at herself, checking her slim tan pants, matching blouse and tailored red blazer. She'd chosen simple hoop earrings, nothing too dangly and definitely not daring. It was ridiculous to be so nervous. Earlier when she sipped another cup of coffee, she'd written off the anxious flutter in her stomach as a case of newcomer jitters. Confident she'd relax once she got into the meeting and saw her colleagues, she closed the door behind her and went to her car.

At the sound of her name, she turned in the direction of the cabins up the path behind her.

"Hey there," Jeff said as he approached.

"I'm on my way to the hospital." Her voice strained, she managed to stop herself before she spilled the whole story. Instead, she kept it simple. "I need to show up in person for a meeting. Spur-of-the-moment kind of thing."

"You look real nice." Jeff chuckled. "That flapper style has a little extra flair, though."

She smiled back, wishing she had time for a little flirting.

"I won't keep you. But I wanted you to know you were right about those two boys," Jeff said. "The drinking, I mean. I got a call from one of the dads this morning."

As sheepish as Jeff looked, she could see he regretted treating her like she was off base last night. Nothing shocked her about his news. She was good at spotting kids who'd been drinking. Most were lucky. But not all. "I assume the dad called because he was suspicious?"

"The kid, Alex, denied it, but the dad is doing some investigating," Jeff said. "Turns out those two, Eddie and Alex, have a history of trouble."

"Is that so?"

"Funny how quick Rolf was to send the blame my way, though. Then he thought better of it." Jeff's expression turned grumpy. "Now I have to ask Carson about what he knew."

"Go easy." Olivia raised her hands defensively. "It's only a hunch, but I doubt Carson knew anything about it—or that the other boy was in on a plan. The only thing you know for sure is that the older two were rowdy."

"Unfortunately, the trouble Rolf is worried about happened in my home, so to speak. I didn't expect having parents accusing me of stuff. I'm so new at this and can't afford a mistake."

"Maybe lighten up on yourself, Jeff." Olivia backed up toward the car. "I have to run. This meeting is kind of looming over me." She opened her car door, but then turned back. "By the way, I left a note for Jillian. I don't know exactly how long I'll be, or if I'll need to stay after, but she knows there might be times now and then that I'll be gone when she comes home. She's old enough to take care of herself."

"No problem. I'm going to be here, and Carson, too," Jeff said. "If she needs anything, she can count on us."

Olivia nodded her thanks and then hurried down the drive to the road. Ticking off the miles, she mulled over the reason for the meeting, and by the time she pulled into the doctors' lot at the hospital, Olivia had come up with the answers to questions she expected about what appeared to be only a routine diagnostic disagreement. Nothing out of the ordinary. Differences of opinion were business as usual. The only unusual element in this scenario was her colleague's reaction. Apparently, the head of the department didn't like to be challenged.

Having been given a tour of the hospital on her first day, Olivia easily found the conference room, although she recognized very few people who passed her in the halls. When she opened the door she saw that both Clay Markson, the head of the department, and Sandra Brindell, the hospital administrator, were already seated at the table. She wasn't late, but the situation felt awkward anyway.

So far, Olivia's dealings with Sandra Brindell, also a woman in her thirties, had been positive and during their online interviews in September she'd developed a great deal of respect for this relatively young person taking on this tough job during a period of restructuring and expansion. Even without being briefed on all the details, Olivia was sure that Sandra inevitably stepped on toes and bruised a few egos in the process of doing her job.

"Have a seat," Sandra said. "We should be able to resolve this quickly. Dr. Newhouse will be joining us, too, but we can go ahead and get started."

What a lot of formality over a routine diagnosis. Olivia had a case of the jitters before, but now she was just annoyed. She'd worked a twelve-hour shift. Halloween night had a couple of injuries at house parties and a three-car crash, and several other situations that kept her busy.

Despite that, a case from a few days ago had led to this early-afternoon meeting. With the case in question, she'd been asked by the surgeon, Mary Newhouse, to review a patient's imaging tests and offer an opinion about the need for surgery. Not knowing what

Clay saw or recommended, Olivia had suggested surgery to repair the man's mangled shoulder. Olivia was certain her conclusion would be clear to any experienced radiologist.

Clay leaned across the table toward Sandra. "You're making this too complicated, Sandra. The fact is, Olivia, who has been working here less than two weeks, contradicted my diagnosis. Dr. Newhouse, also relatively new here, as…you…know, did the same."

Sandra frowned and glanced Olivia's way, which she took as an invitation to respond.

"It's true, I'm new here, but I'm not new to radiology—or to shoulder injuries, especially a common fracture, which caused additional damage to the surrounding tissue." Olivia spoke confidently about what she considered a no-brainer diagnosis. Clay must have seen hundreds of similar injuries in ranchers and guys working the rodeo circuit. The patient in question tumbled off a ladder in his barn.

Apparently, Olivia's point of view didn't sit well with Clay. Olivia had only seen Clay in person once, and that was on her first day. A pale man with a deeply lined face, he struck her as almost frail. He might have been eighty, not sixty something. He wasn't pale today. He couldn't conceal his anger behind his bright red face. Drumming his fingers on the table didn't help, either. He avoided meeting her eye. Clay had started out stand-offish on the day she'd met him, not as welcoming as Sandra or the other staff, including the trauma specialists in the emergency department and other colleagues. Together they worked across the network of clinics in the county and the main hospital in Landrum.

With a quick knock on the door, the surgeon entered the room and nodded to the others. Mary's presence lifted the energy, evidenced by Sandra's face, visibly more relaxed as she turned the floor over to Mary. The surgeon started with a positive report on the condition of the injured man. Then she put her surgical chops on display with her timeline, which included every step of the procedure.

"Mary could have waited," Clay insisted while staring at Sandra. "Olivia should have backed me up. I'm head of the department."

Like that had anything to do with it. Clay still hadn't given her so much as a passing glance. In the interest of keeping a professional stance, Olivia said, "My credentials are a matter of record, Clay."

"Your dozen or so years in practice to my thirty-five." His voice oozed contempt. Still red-faced, Clay stood.

Sandra, who simultaneously got to her feet, said, "We're done here, Clay."

Olivia waited for someone to tell her why she'd been required to be at an in-person meeting.

Clay was the first to leave, followed by Mary, who'd checked her watch a couple of times during the already short meeting. Sandra smiled at Olivia and mumbled something about staying in touch. That left no choice but to file out behind them.

Not a hint of this tension had been apparent during her lengthy phone and online interviews with Sandra and board members. If anything, Sandra and another radiologist were happy to have found someone as experienced as Olivia to fill the position in what would be considered a fairly remote area. Olivia agreed to an irregular schedule as long as she could work from home. She viewed that as adding one more plus to that column.

Once in the hall, Clay took long strides down the corridor. Olivia called out to him, but either he didn't hear her or he didn't consider her worth talking to. Instead, he hurried through the stairway exit door.

"Let him go," Sandra said from beside her. "It's done with. He'll get over it."

"Get over what?" Olivia demanded. She understood Sandra's exasperated expression. It mirrored her feelings. "That I disagreed with him?"

Sandra diverted her eyes. "All I can tell you is Clay sometimes acts like this. He's used to getting his way. I was certain he wouldn't let it go unless we had this meeting, face-to-face. A formality, really." She glanced behind her and to the side, as if making sure no one could hear her. "He's stuck in the past, where he thinks what he says goes, no questions asked. In the old days, his seniority and being department head used to mean more."

"But, Sandra, he was *wrong*. A gruff reputation is one thing. A couple of nurses hinted at that. But they also said that he's competent…usually. It scares me to think he would have delayed that man's surgery." She shook her head. "I'm left to hope others will step in to back Mary."

Sandra sighed. "Just remember, Olivia, it's not about you. And it's not for long."

"That sounds like a warning. Is there something I should be aware of?"

Sandra shifted her weight and her expression changed from annoyed to resigned. "Okay, here's the deal. Clay is due to retire early next year. Early January, to be exact. The board's decision, not his. He's unhappy about it…outraged is more like it. But these last couple of years he's become increasingly difficult to work with. He's gone from being a little cantankerous to intimidating nurses and techs. Most of the staff figured out how to work around him, because professionally, he's still sharp. You held your ground and didn't let him bully you. That's good."

"I know about hospital power plays and drama, but nothing triggered my radar to watch out for something like this." Olivia shrugged, hoping to send a message that she'd take this incident in stride. "Fortunately, I'm not easily intimidated." Since day one she'd consulted with Clay and turned in case updates and reports without incident. No friendly outreach or words of welcome had come from Clay, the department head, a notable break from the typical hospital courtesy to new staff. Whatever. She could live with that.

"Keep doing what you think is best for patients." Sandra paused. "Let me handle any needed intervention."

"Okay," Olivia said, realizing that she didn't want to leave the impression that she couldn't handle a difficult colleague. She smiled at Sandra. "For the record, I'm much better at collaboration." She kept her tone light. It was not only a true statement, but a political one as well. The employee handbook began with the hospital's recently revised mission statement and key principles, among them a collaborative approach to patient care at all levels.

Sandra nodded and turned away to step inside her office.

It's all smoothed over, then? Olivia supposed it was, at least in an unsatisfying sort of way. The message was clear. As much as Sandra disliked confrontations with Clay, they went with the territory, at least for now. Likewise, Mary had said her piece and didn't hang around. Well and good, but Olivia was left with the aftermath. Wow, lucky her.

If Clay was trouble but due to retire soon, she could be like everyone else and bide her time and put up with him, just as Mary was attempting to do. Maybe so, but had they missed Clay's rage? Possibly Sandra and Mary were used to hearing his harsh words or watching his face turn red, but she wasn't.

CHAPTER EIGHT

KNOWING THE SCHOOL bus was due in less than an hour, Jeff took to wielding the axe and splitting logs to burn off the stress that wouldn't let go of him. The talk with Rolf left him with the nervous energy to get a good supply of wood ready for the cold nights coming. Jeff had a sneaking suspicion he was blowing this escapade way out of proportion. Maybe so, but he couldn't avoid a talk with Carson.

By the time he heard the bus pull up, he'd moved on to the less taxing job of folding the last of the towels he washed for the rental cabins. Winnie had been snoozing nearby, but she perked up in anticipation of Carson's homecoming.

When Carson came inside, he returned Winnie's affectionate greeting, but the first thing he said was, "Seems Alex is in trouble."

"Yeah, I got that idea."

"How?" Carson challenged.

"Because his dad called me this morning." Jeff tossed the towel on the table. "He was upset and was ready to blame me for allowing kids to drink here—that was his accusation."

Carson tilted his head back and closed his eyes. "I didn't know Alex was...you know, up to something like that."

Jeff believed him, but he felt the need to add challenge to his tone when he asked, "What about Eddie?"

Carson went from staring at the ceiling to staring at the floor. "He was part of it."

"And you didn't want them to get into trouble, so you didn't say anything to me."

"I didn't know for sure they'd brought alcohol until today. Alex said his dad texted him this morning. Told him he knew what he'd done."

"So, how did they get alcohol in here?" Jeff asked. "What was the trick?"

Carson groaned. "They mixed vodka in water bottles they brought with them in their backpacks."

The kids carried those packs around no matter where they went. Jeff hadn't given that a thought. "And you didn't know?"

"I didn't think about it," Carson said. "But

today Nina told me Alex and Eddie have done this stuff before."

"Well, they got caught this time," Jeff said. "And Rolf, Alex's dad, thought I might have pretended not to notice. He asked me if the boys would have gotten the alcohol from me."

Carson rolled his eyes. "Oh, no."

"It's clear that they cooked this up on their own," Jeff said. "I don't blame you. Olivia spotted it, though. She's seen more than her share of teenagers in the ER. They drink, get into fights, have accidents—they fall down and hit their heads."

Carson nodded.

"I was upset with her at first. But I apologized when I saw her later on." Jeff shrugged. "It was my mistake, not hers."

"I'll pay more attention. I wasn't thinking about it." Carson's words sounded genuine.

"No, you have other things on your mind. I get it."

Carson moved to the door, where Winnie sat waiting. "Okay, Win, off we go."

"Take the leash, just in case," Jeff said. He liked watching Winnie off the leash and enjoying the freedom to romp around on the paths, nose to the ground and following scents. But there was always a chance they'd need to keep her from running into danger.

"I got it," Carson said, already halfway out the door.

"I was going to make burgers and invite Olivia and Jillian to join us. That okay with you?"

"Absolutely. I'll eat two—at least."

Jeff soon heard the sound of Carson's voice talking to Winnie, telling her to stay close. He sent an invitation to Olivia via text. As he waited for a reply, he thought about what he'd done that day, satisfied in a way.

Olivia wasted no time saying yes to his invitation. So, after stowing the clean linens in the storage room, Jeff locked up the lodge and went back to the cabin. As he walked on the short path, he scanned the landscape of bare trees and spotted Carson trekking uphill to the level ridge behind one of the cabins farthest from the lodge. He made steady progress walking along with not even a hint of effort. His limp was finally history.

Once Jeff showered and changed into fresh clothes, he noticed the temperature in the cabin had dropped. The sky had been blue all day, but it was rapidly turning gray. He built a fire and straightened up the main room and on his way back to the kitchen he gave the globe in the corner a quick spin. He'd always liked Karen's globe and Carson never considered leaving it behind. It had a home in their cozy living room, but it would always represent freedom to Jeff. When he'd first moved into the room in Karen's apartment, Carson had pointed to the Panama Canal, his chest puffed out a little because he knew where it was. He asked Jeff if he'd ever been there on a ship. He was happy to tell Carson about his adventures on a ship in the canal and explain the system of locks and the tugboats that took ships through the ditch that cut a whole country in half.

Winnie's barking drew him to the kitchen window behind the breakfast bar. It was spittin' snow, as his dad had liked to call sparse snowflakes swirling in the air. They weren't landing, though, so nothing was coated in white, not yet. Heavier snow was expected later, but not enough to keep the school bus from running. There was Carson, with Winnie barking as she came down the path, leaping in the air, her long ears flopping. She was on the leash now and Carson had to be quick on his feet to keep up. Winnie was taking Carson out for his walk, not the other way around.

Every once in a while, like now, the moment went hazy, not quite real. Never once in the years he'd come and gone from Karen's house had he imagined she'd be gone in an instant, leaving Carson's fate in Jeff's hands. These moments that seemed to come from nowhere hadn't been rare the previous months. It was as if Jeff lost track of how he ended up here in this lodge watching a teenager coming out of the woods with the dog.

"Why is Winnie on the leash?" Jeff asked when the two came inside.

"She saw something moving in the low branches and shrubs and took off." Carson made a disapproving face at the dog. "She climbed into a heap of broken debris but her legs are too short and she fell through." He stooped down and rubbed the dog's jowls. "Besides, Winnie, you don't need to be hunting down rabbits or birds or big guys like raccoons. It's not like you have to hunt for food."

"Hmm…she might have started out a dyed-in-the-wool city dog, but her instincts make this country living quite an adventure."

Carson chuckled. "No kidding. It's fun to

see her running through the woods and checking every scent and thing that moves."

Winnie had no idea what a lifesaver she'd been. And not just for Carson. Jeff found her good company during the day. Sometimes he wondered what the boy said to Winnie when she hopped up on his bed to sleep at night. Maybe he talked out his feelings to the dog.

Carson took the two chocolate doughnuts from the plate Jeff put out for him. "I'll do my homework and then fill the woodboxes. I see you split a big pile of logs. These doughnuts ought to hold me over until our burgers." He pointed out the window at the snow. "My science teacher told us this storm wasn't supposed to be a big deal, but it got stalled and the conditions changed. So we probably won't have school tomorrow. But an even bigger blizzard will probably hit around Thanksgiving. She showed us on the map how rain in the Pacific is heading our way, but by the time it gets here it will be snow."

Jeff's phone pinged and he glanced at the screen. "Well, well, as if on cue, I got a weather alert. Like your science teacher predicted, it's a revised forecast."

"I'm thinking about becoming a meteorologist." Carson had a dreamy expression as he bit the sprinkles off the top of the frosted doughnut. "We're studying weather now and the different ways to predict it."

"Okay, then, weather guy, what changed? Why did light snow turn into this?" Jeff pointed out the window. In only a few minutes the snow had starting coming down harder, blocking the view of the woods.

Without hesitating, Carson gave a coherent explanation of changing wind and moisture in the air, and shift in temperatures. "That's what Ms. Ambrose said."

"You used to give your mom weather updates first thing in the morning," Jeff said. "When I was around you kept me posted on weather here in Wyoming. You taught yourself a lot when you started searching weather sites on your computer."

"Yep, I used to give you and Mom fourteen-day predictions." Carson grinned and added, "Whether you wanted them or not."

"We'll call it training for your future career."

"Maybe. You never know." Carson polished off the last of the second doughnut and headed to his room with Winnie at his heels. "By the way, it's raining in Seattle right now. I still check the weather there."

Jeff might have known. Seattle was still every bit his homeplace as Wyoming was Jeff's. Carson had ties there, too, and still texted with some friends.

Jeff started a fire and rather than asking Carson, he replenished the log crate on Olivia's porch and theirs. The other cabins could wait. He didn't want Carson out in heavy snow maneuvering around on the uneven ground. He enjoyed knowing the four of them were snug inside and not navigating the road.

Olivia brought a salad and chocolate cream pie for dessert. She joined Jeff in the kitchen while the kids and dog stayed in the living room. Olivia was quieter than usual, and not as quick to jump into the conversation. Jeff concluded it had something to do with her meeting, but didn't want to pry, either.

Olivia waited to open up until after they finished dinner and the kids went into the living room and turned on the TV. *Weird.* Olivia's word to describe her day. As far as Jeff could tell, the head of her department turned a routine conflict into an issue that put Olivia on the spot.

"He treated me like a kid who acted up in school, but I'm not supposed to worry about it, because he's retiring soon."

Something about the details of the story stirred Jeff, especially the background she filled in. This wasn't the guy's first fight. It was like an early-warning light coming up in his truck. This sounded like more than a guy being rude over a disagreement, or even the boss throwing his weight around. "To be blunt, Olivia, this guy sounds like he may have a problem. Telling you to ignore the man isn't so easy when you work with. *For* him, since he's the boss."

"That's why I walked out of the meeting unsettled. I've been advised to do nothing. Bide my time until Clay retires."

"And he never softened? Didn't offer an apology?"

"No, he never acknowledged doing anything wrong, or even odd," Olivia said, her face scrunched in thought. "Good thing I like the administrator and the surgeon. Right now I don't have much choice but to keep going. The next regular staff meeting isn't until next week. They treat this guy like a thorn that's going to disappear in a few months, so they just go along."

"It's none of my business," Jeff said, "but the guy doesn't sound like a good doctor."

"Oh, yeah." Olivia paused. "Apparently, he's still regarded as an excellent doctor. I only have the one case to go on, but fortunately, the surgeon and orthopedic staff agreed with me. The patient had the surgery and is on the mend." Frowning, she added, "I feel like I've been through an initiation. I'm one of the inner circle now because I survived a clash with Clay Markson."

Jeff didn't have much to say to that, but Olivia changed the subject quickly enough when she leaned across the table and whispered, "Are those two really watching weather reports? Still?"

Jeff listened and heard a distinctive reporter's voice. "Sounds like it." He shrugged and added, "Maybe they're waiting to hear about school."

Sure enough, Jillian raised her arms over her head and shouted, "Yay, no school tomorrow."

Carson shot her a disapproving glance. "It's not cool to be so obvious about it, Jillian."

He glanced at his phone. "Says here it's supposed to keep snowing all night and not stop until morning."

"You aren't thrilled about missing school, Carson?" Olivia teased.

"I'm not. There's a cool coach and I like Practical Science. The teacher's really smart."

Olivia got off the stool and took a few steps toward the living room. "Well, school or no school, we should be going, Jillian. I've got another shift tonight. I have a feeling I'll be dealing with cases from all over the county. Bad weather, bad roads, lots of cars run off the highway. I've seen…" Olivia stopped talking but her words hung in the air. She lowered her voice when she said, "I'm so sorry. That was really insensitive."

Jeff shook his head, as if to brush off what she said. "It's okay. It's the reality." He expected Carson to do the same.

"It doesn't have to be bad weather to have a really bad crash," Carson said, getting to his feet. "Come on Win…one last quick trip out tonight. But not in the woods. We'll stay out front."

Jillian hurried to put her jacket on. "See you at home," she said, following Carson out the door. Olivia thanked Jeff again for inviting them, but her expression was full of regret.

"Seriously, Olivia, the warm, sunny day will always be part of the story, along with the driver's heart attack. That was the real cause of the guy missing the red light."

Jeff thought back on those first hours in the hospital. "Carson also has memories of doctors like you evaluating his injuries and others treating them, and listening while he wondered what was going to happen next. He gained a lot of respect for doctors and nurses—I can say that for sure."

Olivia lightly touched his arm. "Tough days, though."

"They were."

When the phone beeped, he picked up the call and heard a woman say she and her family were pulled over on Merchant Street in Adelaide Creek, and wondered if he had a cabin available for the night. He smiled as he said, "Oh, yes, we have rooms available, and you're only a few minutes away."

Olivia gave him a thumbs-up.

"We're two adults and two kids," the woman added.

"That's fine—I have a cabin ready for four."

"And our dog…we can't leave him in the car."

Jeff smiled at Olivia. "Your dog is welcome here."

The woman already had directions on her phone and ended the call.

"Stanhope's Woodland Cabins will be one family's shelter from the storm."

"For the second time," she said softly. "Not literally, I suppose, but it feels that way every time I open the door and step inside."

Olivia hurried away and Jeff grabbed his jacket, touched by Olivia's words. He'd never thought of himself as anyone's shelter. Not him, Mr. Freedom. But here he was with a cabin to offer for a family stranded in the snow.

THROUGHOUT THE NIGHT, Olivia had watched the snow pile up and form drifts as the wind picked up. Now, from her workstation in the alcove, the sun was coming up and turning the mountain peaks in the distance reddish orange. Jillian was still sleeping, but that wouldn't last long, not with Gordy, a shaggy English sheepdog, bounding through the snow and barking at Winnie, who was joining him. Carson and Elaine, Gordy's owner, were deep in conversation. Carson pointed back to the lodge. Without hearing his exact words, Olivia knew for sure that the boy was inviting them in for coffee.

The couple with two little kids had no idea how much Olivia had enjoyed being part of the welcoming committee. Jeff had taken off up the hill and turned on the heat and the lights in the cabin, while Carson and Jillian lit up the lodge. Jeff was still opening up the cabin when the car pulled in. Olivia had been prepared to be the greeter, but Carson stepped in and by the time Jeff came back all four guests were in the lodge. With her shift starting, she and Jillian had come home right away.

When Carson saw her in the window, she went to open her door and say hello.

"The whole family is coming down for pancakes in the lodge," Carson said. "You and Jillian are invited, too."

"That sounds like fun," Olivia said, surprising herself with how much she wanted to be included. "I'll get Jillian up."

"Jeff says to come as soon as your shift is over."

She should be planning to sleep, especially after the busy night, but this was a much better option. "We'll be there."

Elaine and Gordy went back up the hill, and by the time Olivia finished her shift report, Jillian was up and ready to go.

She and Jillian got to the lodge when the couple and the kids and the dog were halfway down the hill. When she went inside, the aroma of sausage and bacon mixed with the smell of the wood fire. Carson was pulling tables together and arranging chairs.

"I see there's a party going on," Olivia said.

"There is," Jeff called from the kitchen. "Elaine and Ron are staying for breakfast. No one is going anywhere for the next couple of hours."

Olivia took over Carson's job while he helped heap the platters and pour glasses of juice. But they were soon gathered around the table with the little kids perched on their parents' knees. The couple lived in Colorado but were headed to Utah to visit family, but like Carson's weather alert indicated, light snow had quickly morphed into blizzard conditions. They'd been prepared to stay in their SUV overnight. Jeff's new listing on the area's lodging sites had given them a much better choice.

"Can your kids build a snowman with me and Carson?" Jillian asked.

Carson snickered. This snowman plan was obviously news to him.

"Sure, they can," Ron said. "I'll bet our Gordy and your Winnie would like that, too."

Both dogs raised their heads at the sound of their names, but then went back to lazing around the fireplace. The adults lingered over coffee and talked about weather and cattle and the wind farm managed by the company Ron worked for. A teacher herself, Elaine spoke to Carson about his Practical Science class.

Soon everyone trooped outside to keep Jeff company while he plowed up the long drive from the freshly cleared road. After one snowman and many snow angels later, they trekked back inside and Jillian entertained the kids as Elaine and Carson played Ping-Pong, and Ron took Jeff on at the pool table.

Olivia curled up in the couch and watched the weather reports until she drifted off to sleep. She didn't know how long she'd been sleeping, but a hand lightly shaking her shoulder roused her. Groggy, she sat up and stretched her stiff neck. Someone had put a blanket over her.

"I didn't want to wake you," Jeff said. "You were sleeping so soundly."

Olivia looked around the nearly empty room. "Where are the guests?"

"The snow is melting already, so they'll make it to Utah in a few hours. They said to say goodbye."

"I had so much fun," Olivia said.

"Me, too," Jeff said. "I liked being a port in a storm."

"You're very good at it. I can't believe you were able to come up with all that food."

"The bacon-and-sausage larder is bare." Jeff sounded content and confirmed it with a satisfied smile. "But with Carson around, I can always throw together a stack or two of pancakes."

"Speaking of Carson, where is Jillian?" She rubbed her eyes and took Jeff's hand when he offered it to pull her up off the couch.

"They're watching a movie in the cabin. She can stay here."

Olivia glanced at the dartboard. "How about I sleep a little longer and get my wits about me. And then, if you're up for it, I'll challenge you to a round of darts."

Jeff laughed. "You are a pro, aren't you?"

"As Carson might say, I've got game."

"As I know all too well." He grinned and put his arms around her in a lovely hug. "Go home, sleep and then you're on."

Olivia slipped into her coat and waved goodbye, still thinking about Jeff's touch on her shoulder, holding her hand and the feel of his arms around her. She had a date for darts that was about a lot more than a game.

CHAPTER NINE

CARSON MEANDERED INTO the kitchen and plunked his elbows on the counter and held his chin in his palm. "This is so lame."

Impatience rising in his chest, Jeff swallowed back a chastising remark. Instead, he asked, "What's lame? You tell me, Carson."

The boy didn't meet his eye. Instead, he lifted one shoulder in a half-hearted shrug. "This whole thing. Making a big deal out of Thanksgiving at the ranch. Why do *we* have to bake pies?"

"Pies? This is all about making a couple of pumpkin pies?" Jeff gave him a pointed look. "Want to tell me what's really going on?"

While Carson stared at the granite counter, Jeff forced himself to wait for an answer rather than filling one in. Carson had been out of sorts over the last week or so leading up to Thanksgiving. Now it was Wednesday night, pie-baking night at Olivia's. Without the TV on or music playing, the occasional crackle of the wood burning in the fireplace provided the only sound in the quiet house. Even Winnie lay stretched out, her head raised now as if she was waiting for something to happen. The dog went into full alert when Carson grabbed his jacket and stood by the door, as if waiting for Jeff.

With no answer forthcoming, Jeff handed Carson one of the two shopping bags, one with ingredients, the other with bowls and the pie plates. Jeff slipped on his own jacket and picked up the second bag.

The snow after Halloween had melted, but had been replaced by another inch or two a few days ago. Now it was snowing lightly again and covering what had become muddy ground on the mild day. "We'll have to wipe off Winnie's paws at the door," Jeff said.

Carson patted his pocket. His voice was flat when he responded, "I stuffed a towel in my pocket earlier."

Jillian opened the door to let them in. Jeff sighed in relief. No need to make conversation with the sullen teenager. On the other hand, when they put the bags of supplies inside the door and kicked off their boots, Carson gently cleaned Winnie's paws with one of their new, thick, light gray towels. He answered his own question about why Carson hadn't used one of the cleaning rags. *Because he's fourteen.*

"We're ready for you guys," Olivia said.

Jillian took Carson's jacket out of his hands. "I'm the cohost, so I hang up the coats." She brushed off snowflakes. "I was watching the snow come down from my window."

"Me, too," Carson said, smiling now. "I don't remember much snow in Seattle on Thanksgiving."

Jillian hurried to the fireplace and sat back on her heels next to Winnie, who'd already found her spot. The dog extended her stretch, which Jillian took as an invitation to scratch the dog under her chin.

"We have a ton of blueberries and we already sliced up apples," Olivia said. "All we have to do is roll the crust and dump the rest inside it." She held up wrapped hunks of dough. "We have four bottom crusts and two for the top of the fruit pies. We'll be done in no time."

Jeff gave a rundown of what he brought as he unloaded the bags and lined up what he guessed they'd need and put the extra mixing bowls in the middle of her counter. His voice carried a note of enthusiasm he wished was real but wasn't. His forced tone was meant to cover the tension that was an invisible barrier separating him from Carson.

At least there would be a crowd for Thanksgiving at the ranch. More people for Carson to talk with. He'd hoped being at the big gatherings would make this first holiday without his mom easier for Carson to face. In the run up to the day, Jeff had seen that for what it was. Wishful thinking. As Jeff knew firsthand, big holidays only magnified losses, especially the first year they came around again.

Even with his attempt to be sensitive to Carson, though, Jeff looked forward to celebrating holidays again. Heather had been glowing with excitement when she'd told him about plans to throw a traditional dinner to mark their first Thanksgiving as a new family of four.

Holidays could be small, somewhat lonely occasions in Carson's house. Karen often had to work part of the day, and a couple of times Carson went to the restaurant with her and had a meal with the waitstaff. Jeff was with them one Thanksgiving and had helped Karen put a meal together before she went to work later on. Maybe the prospect of a big holiday at the ranch was a little overwhelming for the teenager, who spurned all of Jeff's attempts to talk with him about it.

At the moment, Carson was standing across the room with his hands on his hips observing Jillian try to teach Winnie to roll over on command. Unless Winnie understood the point to these commands, she wasn't likely to think much of Jillian's coaxing. Sensing someone's eyes on him, Jeff glanced at Olivia, who'd been watching him watching the scene. She immediately turned her attention to the empty mixing bowl, as if searching for something. Then she called the kids over to the counter.

"This isn't anything like last year," Jeff said, trying to make conversation, but he quickly regretted focusing on the past. Seeing Carson's quizzical expression, he had no choice but to explain. "I was on my way to an oil port in Mexico on a tanker."

"Oh, right," Carson said. "I remember that now. One of your cool trips."

"I was stuck at home," Jillian said, "yucky sick, wasn't I, Mom?"

Olivia stopped what she was doing and closed her eyes. Jeff guessed she was fighting a memory she'd just as soon hadn't been triggered. "Yes, sweetie."

"But look at you now," Carson said, a hint of pride in his voice. "You're baking the pies all by yourself." He chuckled. "You're not much of a dog trainer, though. If you want this dog to roll over, you have to tell her why."

Jillian glanced at him with a smug smile taking over her face. "You're right about the pies." She giggled. "And you're probably right about your dog. Oh, well. I'll be better with horses."

Jeff waited for a reaction from Olivia, but she didn't so much as glance Jillian's way. She pulled the step stool over for Jillian and then started rolling pie dough on the wooden pastry board. "This one is for your pumpkin pie. They take longer than ours."

"You can help me, Carson," Jeff said. "Then we'll share the blame if our pumpkin filling is a bust." He assessed the ingredients on the breakfast bar, unsure about the first steps.

Carson came alongside him and glanced at

the recipe Jeff printed from an internet site. He pulled a bowl toward him and cracked the first egg into it. "Gotta start somewhere."

Amused at Carson's take-charge attitude, Jeff said, "Since you've got the eggs. I'll measure the milk." The whirring of the mixer nixed the need to make conversation, other than to add the ingredients Jeff read from the page.

"We did it," Carson said when they'd finished mixing in the pumpkin.

Olivia delivered two piecrusts and Jeff divided the pumpkin mix between them. Then he slid the two pies into the oven and set the timer. Jeff watched Olivia role out top and bottom crusts and fill, one with the apple-and-cinnamon mix and the other with blueberries. Olivia covered them with the top crust and gave them decorative cuts in the shape of a flower and petals.

"Hey, Mom, let's put out some snacks," Jillian said. "I bet Carson would like to watch *The Wizard of Oz* while the pumpkin pies bake."

"Is that one of your favorites?" Carson asked.

"It's *everybody's* favorite, Carson," Jillian

said, leaving no room for doubt. "It starts in ten minutes."

"Well, then, sure, turn it on. Let's see what Toto is up to."

Jillian went to the cabinet with the large deep shelves. She pulled out a bag of pretzels and another of caramel corn and held them up. "These okay, Carson?"

Carson made a silly face at Jillian. "I like to *inhale* caramel corn. You know what I mean?"

"It's one of my favorites," Jillian said.

Jeff leaned against the counter and watched Carson help Jillian pour glasses of soda and ferry bowls of snacks to the coffee table.

"It's on," Jillian called out when the movie started. "Are you two going to come watch with us?"

"Maybe in a bit," Olivia said. "I'm going to rope Jeff into cleanup duty."

Jeff studied Carson from a distance. He seemed content to tilt his head back and drop kernels of caramel corn in his mouth, stopping for a couple of seconds to chew and swallow. Winnie had jumped up on the couch and had her paws on the back of it long enough to assess her surroundings. Then she dropped and apparently settled herself between the two kids because both of them scooched to the side to make room. Not to be left out, Jillian's cat, Tulip, who'd been snoozing by the fireplace, jumped into Jillian's lap.

"You're hogging the couch, Winnie," Carson said, frowning down at her.

Jillian only laughed at the dog and then pointed at the screen. "Pay attention, Carson. Dorothy's house is going to start flying around any minute now."

Jeff glanced at Olivia, who also watched the kids as if in a trance. At the same moment, they caught each other's eye and laughed.

"Are you thinking what I'm thinking?" Jeff said.

Olivia laughed lightly. "I think so, if you're thinking what I think you are."

He held her gaze and for an instant he'd have sworn he'd known Olivia for a very long time. Finally, he shifted his sights back to the kids. "I'm thinking they're acting like kids who've grown up together. This *feels* like something familiar, as if we've done it before." He gestured toward Olivia. "Am I close?"

"Very." She looked down and took a couple of steps to the sink and focused on washing the mixing bowls like they were precious objects.

Jeff opened the dishwasher and without words, they loaded everything into it. Jeff put aside the items from his cabin they hadn't used and set the bag down by the door. Then he kept his voice low when he said, "I'd forgotten that he and his mom used to watch this movie the night before Thanksgiving. It was a tradition for them, more than a certain kind of dinner. He'd tell me about it, even when I wasn't around for the holiday." Karen had also remarked that their days of fun kid-rituals were numbered. Sooner or later, watching Dorothy and her pals with Mom was going to stop being cool.

"I got that feeling," Olivia said. "He's showing a lot of something in being so accommodating with Jillian. More than kindness. Maybe *grit* is the word I'm searching for."

Could be, Jeff thought, but *good-hearted* was the simpler explanation. He liked to see Jillian happy.

"I'd understand if he wanted to avoid the holiday altogether." Olivia's thoughtful expression deepened. "As for me, this is shaping up to be one of the best Thanksgivings I've had in—" she stared into space "—a long, long time. Maybe ever. I used to force a cheery attitude for Jillian. There's nothing quite as powerful as a holiday to bring home the reality that Jillian and I don't have much family."

"With Jillian sick last year, I suppose you and Heather skipped the traditional dinner?" Now that Olivia and Jillian were like old friends, he no longer had trouble picturing Heather in their lives.

"I was on call, and had a couple of long stints at the hospital. Heather and I got one of those premade dinner packages from the supermarket. Jillian was feverish and slept most of the day." Olivia got a faraway look in her eye. "I practically put a banner in the window when she swallowed a few bites of pumpkin pie."

"No wonder this year seems much better."

"The other day I said we're living a charmed life right now. We have everything, from a cozy home to great friends." Olivia smiled. "My good luck started when I found your sister."

"Speaking of charmed lives, huh?" He'd never seen his sister happier, not even when she was Carson's age and riding Velvet all over the ranch. That alone chipped away at reservations he'd had about Matt. Jeff had been ready to swallow his pride and make amends, but he'd never expected to like his brother-in-law.

"From the minute Heather met the twins, she started telling Jillian cute stories about them," Olivia reflected. "I think she fell in love with those two before Matt had a chance to settle in her heart." She gave the counter one more swipe with the sponge and tossed it in the sink. "Done."

As if on cue, Winnie jumped off the couch and padded over to the door and stared back at Carson, who started to get up, but Jeff said, "You stay put. I'll take her out."

"I'll go with you," Olivia said. "I can use some air. The pies still need more time."

Once they'd bundled up against the cold and the light snow, they took off on the uphill path with the moon showing the way. "The longer we live here the more the woods lure Winnie to explore farther up the hill and deeper into the trees," Jeff said.

"No telling where that nose of hers will take her," Olivia said. "We'll keep an eye on her.

And on Carson. He was glum when he first arrived. Out of sorts. But then he perked up."

"You noticed his earlier mood, then?" Jeff asked.

"Sure, but it doesn't surprise me. It's only natural that he'd have some shaky moments this time of year."

The light snowfall and the smell of smoke from the fire added to the closeness he was feeling with Olivia. They were sharing experiences that were new to both of them, hers here in Adelaide Creek and his with Carson.

"Maybe with so many people at the ranch tomorrow, he'll be pulled into the festive mood," Olivia said.

"I hope so," Jeff said. "I tend to fret over him. Sometimes I'm so focused on Carson I forget that *I* lost a really good friend."

"No…hmm…romance?" Olivia asked. "Nothing like that developed?"

Jeff vigorously shook his head no. "Not at all. We were only good friends—and I was barely in the mind space to make friends, let alone have a woman in my life."

"So much can change in a year," Olivia said. "I give your Carson a lot of credit to jump in and cheerfully keep Jillian company, like a brother or a cousin."

"She gets him out of his down moods. He's been moping around a little for the past few days."

"Grief is tricky," Olivia said. "Carson lost his anchor. Nothing could have prepared him for how he'd feel six months later. Six years from now, it might hit him hard all over again. One day, he'll be a grown man trying to establish himself, but perhaps without the company of a family of his own."

No words could have rankled Jeff more. "That's *not* true. He'll have me. That was the whole point of being his guardian. I'm not going to *abandon* him when he turns eighteen."

"Does *he* know that?"

"I'm certain he does."

"Good." Olivia raised her gloved hand as if holding a glass. "A toast to the life you've provided. More than the basics, he has school, friends—and above all else, his dog."

"*Dog.* Where's Winnie?" Jeff scanned the area around him. He'd been focused on Olivia and forgot why they were out for a walk in the first place. "Winnie," he called. "Come here, come on out. We have to go." Jeff's gut tightened more with each second. "How could I forget about Winnie? Carson trusted me—"

"Stop, stop. We'll find her." Olivia hurried up the rising path barely visible in the dark and repeated Winnie's name.

Jeff crossed a sideways path to get to one of the trails that took him to the cabins closer to the stable. He jogged along the corral fence. "Winnie? Come on now. Time to go back to Carson." He sped along the path, illuminating it with a small flashlight he always carried in his pocket.

Olivia's calls to Winnie rang out as she climbed to the next tier of three widely spaced cabins on sloping ground. He reached the end of the corral fence and flashed the beam into the woods on one side and the field on the other. But no sign of animal tracks. She wasn't in the corral, either. There wasn't even rustling in the brush surrounding him. Jeff's gut churned and he fought off panic. He couldn't lose Winnie. Carson needed his best pal.

A bark pierced the air behind him, and when he aimed the beam, the light caught Olivia.

She was bent over. "She's here—I've got her by her collar."

Leash in hand, Jeff retraced his steps as fast as he could and reached Olivia, who was holding on to the dog. He snapped on the leash. "Don't you ever run off again, Winnie. Carson would never forgive me if you'd been hurt."

"What a relief, huh?" Olivia came closer and put her arms around him. Even in the dark he could see her eyes shining as she pulled her head back to meet his gaze. "Whew... I can't believe how scared I was."

Still clutching the leash, Jeff tightened his arms around Olivia. "Thank you."

She gave him a final quick squeeze before stepping back and starting down the hill. "Anytime. But don't give me the credit. Winnie was just exploring. She had no intention of running away from her family."

Jeff crouched down and patted Winnie's back. "*I* love you, too, Winnie. I don't want you lost in the woods."

"Oops," Olivia said tapping the heel of her hand on her temple. "We forgot the pies." The woman he'd held in his arms mere seconds ago was navigating the twists and turns of the network of paths in record time.

"Careful," he called out, but got no response. He held on to Winnie's leash and coaxed her out of the clumps of bushes and ground cover.

Olivia got to the door first and when he followed her inside, he saw the two pumpkin pies cooling on the counter.

"What happened to you guys?" Carson asked. "The piecrust was getting really brown on the edges. I was afraid they'd burn. I stuck a knife in the middle. The recipe said if it came out clean, with no filling on it, then it's done."

"Exactly," Olivia said. "I remember that tidbit, too. The most important one. Thanks, Carson."

"No problem," he said, appearing pleased with himself. "Did you two get lost or something?"

"No, but Winnie did. Sort of. She disappeared for a minute. You didn't hear us calling her?"

"No—the TV is pretty loud." Carson playfully rubbed Winnie's jowls. "You wouldn't run away, would you, Winnie?" When he leaned down to pet her, she stretched on her hind legs and tried to lick his face.

Jillian giggled. "Ew… Winnie's been sniffing dirty stuff in the woods."

Behind Jeff, Olivia let out a soft snort at the same time he did. He turned and grinned. Still crouched next to the dog, Carson looked up at him with a puzzled expression. Then he smiled at the dog. "You had a very long walk… They let you run and run. What do you think of that?"

Jeff was glad his face was probably already reddened from the cold air, because his skin was warming. He felt as if he'd been caught at something.

"We had so much to talk about we lost track of time," Olivia said with a casual shrug.

"Right," Jeff said. If she hadn't remembered the pies, he could have spent another hour walking in the cold, snowy woods with Olivia.

OLIVIA COUNTED TWENTY-TWO people getting ready to squeeze around the two long tables. Jen and Dan had brought extra chairs with them and Stacey's friend Grey Murtagh added two from his house. She and Jeff brought extra dessert plates from the cabins. They had everything they'd need to have a Thanksgiving to remember.

Before the food was put out buffet style, Matt organized the group into a circle around the two tables in the warm dining room and joined hands. Matt said they should take turns naming something they were grateful for and he surprised no one in the room when he said, "I don't have enough words to describe how grateful I am Heather agreed to marry me."

When Olivia's throat started to close, she wished Matt had said a simple grace and left it at that. Her chest tightened the way it used to when she was a kid and had to give a presentation in school. It resembled stage fright, and it was impossible to explain in this environment where she'd been so quickly invited into this close-knit group of family and friends. Public declarations brought out a shy, awkward side few people saw, because she avoided most large social situations. It was ridiculous, really, to find it nearly impossible to take a deep breath.

From the day her husband left her holding an infant in her arms, Olivia had been satisfied with a world she now recognized as far too small. Other than Heather moving in to care for Jillian, she'd made few close friends, and other than working, everything she did was focused on Jillian. Standing in the circle in this expansive, generous world, she was determined to experience it, even the fears.

Listening to Bethany talk about being grateful that Charlie was home for a month and that his parents were visiting for the long weekend gave Olivia a new sense of being connected to Bethany and her family.

"I'm grateful for my new bunkhouse digs," Stacey said cheerfully.

Grey—clearly madly in love with Stacey— got a laugh when he agreed with her about the bunkhouse and the chance for them to spend a little time alone. Olivia never would have predicted that Grey would add, "I'm also grateful that Jillian and Carson are with us today. We need a few more kids around to keep us on our toes."

Olivia found herself envious of radiant Heather, who made an unselfconscious expression of gratitude for all that had happened, especially her new family and so many friends gathering to create a memorable Thanksgiving.

Touched by Heather's words, and her happiness, Olivia's heart pounded as they made their way around the circle. She glanced at Carson, who was amused as he listened to Nick give thanks for a whole list of things, including a new mom. But there was nothing sentimental about his glee over having his own room across the hall from Lucy.

Next, all eyes were focused on Carson. Matt's expression changed watching Carson, as if in pain himself. Out of the corner of her eye Olivia saw Jeff eyeing him but not being obvious about it. More than anyone, Carson had been put on the spot. The teenager shuffled around a little before clearing his throat. "I'm glad I can start playing basketball again soon. And I'm, uh, I'm thankful for Winnie and for the new people I've met since I've been here."

Olivia exhaled and put her own discomfort in perspective. When her turn came, she kept it simple, too. "I'm thankful for my daughter, of course. And for my new home. *And* I'm with Carson, I'm happy to have all of you in my life." That wasn't so hard. Everyone in the room knew about Jillian and her illness and recovery. Olivia felt an excited buzz ripple through her. For once, she hadn't led with that part of her story. It no longer defined her. Her excitement came from the realization she'd made room for the freedom to add new things to her life.

The gratitude circle ended on a great note with Jillian saying she was especially happy with her three new friends, Lucy, Nick and Carson.

When they broke the circle, Olivia helped Stacey fix plates of turkey and sweet potatoes and cranberry sauce for the twins, leaving Jillian and Carson to get in line with the adults. Bethany and her new mother-in-law stood behind the platters and bowls of food set up buffet style and ferried empty bowls back to the kitchen and returned with ones Matt and Jeff were refilling. Carson, more interested in making videos than food, got it all on the record. Olivia purposely left Jillian alone to talk with Bethany while they ate ham and turkey and second helpings of everything. Olivia was free to listen in on Stacey and Matt's conversation about the Christmas Market on Merchant Street. Olivia agreed to volunteer on a committee to help with Adelaide Creek's biggest event of the year, Spring Fling.

Olivia was almost shocked by her realization that her work and Jillian no longer needed to be all-consuming. When Heather once asked her what she'd wanted in her life now that Jillian was well, Olivia stumbled around and came up empty. She surprised herself when she'd admitted she'd always wanted more kids and expected to have at least two if not three or four. But she'd nixed that idea when she'd resolved never to risk her heart with any man again. Twice abandoned, forever shy.

In the midst of rinsing dishes with Bethany, Olivia noticed Carson taking Winnie and Scrambler outside. He hadn't gathered up Lucy and Nick, or Jillian, to go along. In fact, he was being stealthy, perhaps hoping to slip away out the side door unnoticed. Moving to the row of windows with a view of the porch and beyond, Olivia noted the boy's downcast expression. It was hard to miss. Now his back was to her while he hurried down the steps without a backward glance.

She doubted anyone else noticed Carson had left the house, not even Jeff, who was deep in conversation with Grey and Dan Hoover, Bethany's dad. With everyone preoccupied, Carson made a getaway, or at least that's what she suspected happened. She was tempted to follow him, but hung back to give him the time alone he'd probably sought. The dogs followed Carson across the yard to the line of trees at the edge of the drive. He picked up sticks and started a game of fetch, making dozens of tosses before he knelt on one knee and put an arm around each dog and hugged them close.

Deciding it was a good time to reach out, Olivia grabbed her jacket from the pile of coats heaped on the washer and dryer in the laundry room. It wasn't that others were insensitive, especially Jeff, who was always on the lookout for signs the boy was troubled. But troubled wasn't what Olivia was seeing.

She also left without anyone taking notice. At least not that she knew of. Carson turned around and smiled at her when she crossed the yard.

"Is it time to cut the pies?" he asked.

"No, no, I didn't come to get you." She resisted the urge to touch the boy, perhaps squeeze his shoulder or hand. If she got too close he might shut down. "Are you having a moment, Carson? You know, feeling overwhelmed or sinking in the midst of all the festivities."

His reaction was instant. Her heart went out to this young teen who struggled to hold back tears. He didn't try to deny what was happening, but lowered his gaze.

"Whatever it is going through your mind, it's okay. Jeff understands that you can't feel happy all the time, Carson."

"But I'm having a good time." He shrugged. "You know what I mean. People are good to me, the same way they're real nice to you and Jillian."

"That's true." She took a deep breath. "Do I hear a *but* coming?"

"But I miss my mom." He brushed away tears with the back of his hand.

"I thought you probably did." She twisted her body and pointed to the house behind her. "There's not a person here today that doesn't understand what you're feeling right now, even if they hardly know you.

"Or, like the twins, who didn't know their mom. No memories of her at all."

Carson opened his mouth as if to speak. But he frowned and then looked away.

Olivia waited, staying silent, but crossing her arms against the wind picking up. It was already chilly as the sky darkened in the late-November afternoon.

"You didn't know my mom," Carson said, "but she would have liked that circle thing Matt did. She was big on being thankful for what we had."

"Oh? Tell me more about her."

Carson stuffed his hands in his jacket pockets and drew a line in the patchy snow with the toe of his sneaker. He picked up two sticks and tossed them past Scrambler and Winnie, who raced off to get them. "I didn't know what to say, but I was thinking that she would have had fun at a big dinner with lots of people."

"Was it usually just the two of you for holidays? Kinda like Jillian and me."

"Jeff was with us once." Carson scoffed and shook his head. "It must have been hard for him not to be back here with all these people."

"Maybe." Olivia was skeptical, though. "But toward the end of their ranching days, their holidays weren't like this. Heather told me all about that."

Carson's eyebrows lifted a little. "I get that I wouldn't be here if Mom was alive, but then I keep wishing she could be here, too." He paused and frowned. "One year there was a huge neighborhood dinner—they called it a potluck. It was kind of like this, only mostly neighbors. It was fun. That's why I was thinking so much about her."

Olivia sighed. "Oh, Carson, I know what you mean. My mom would have enjoyed today, too. I haven't talked to Matt or Stacey about it, but we know they lost someone, too. The only difference between what you're feeling today and what's in their hearts is that more time has passed. Your loss is fresh."

"When I came home from the hospital, I felt real sad. I couldn't believe she'd never ever be there again." Carson lowered his head again. "I kinda crashed. Jeff said that sometimes we need to sit with stuff that hurts and not run away from it. That's how he put it."

Unlike him. Olivia's heart danced around that reality. A warning light had flipped on.

"He wished he'd done that himself instead of running away," Carson said.

"I guess we learn some things the hard way," Olivia said. "He wants to protect you from making that mistake."

Carson shrugged. "He told me it didn't work, anyway. All he did was hurt Heather and himself."

"Wise words." That must have been a big step for Jeff to admit, but his words stuck with Carson, and probably always would. She remembered Jeff's arms around her after they knew Winnie was safe. "The others are likely to notice we're missing. I should go in and help with dessert. Do you want to stay out here a little longer?"

Carson scrunched his face in thought. Then he smiled. "Nah, I'm okay now. I'll go with you."

The dogs ran ahead of them to the side door, where Jeff greeted them.

"I was searching for both of you, but Jen said you took the dogs out." He patted Carson on the shoulder. "Good thinking. And perfect timing. We're ready for dessert."

She and Carson followed Jeff into the kitchen to join Heather, who held a giant bowl of whipped cream. Olivia stood back while Jeff began slicing the pie and putting the pieces on plates, which Carson carried to the dining room table.

Then Carson took a couple of photos of the buffet table and went to get his video camera to capture more film of the crowd enjoying the pie. Some drifted back to the football game on TV in the living room, but not everyone.

If Olivia harbored doubts about speaking to Carson on such a personal level, they'd vanished. For a few minutes she'd been the teenager's sounding board. Eventually, Carson would understand that as much as he mourned his mother, his feelings for Jeff were also complicated.

"Hey, Olivia, come on into the dining room, so I can get you in my movie." Carson waved her into the room.

"Does your film have a title?" Olivia smiled for the camera as she moved to the table and picked up a plate with a slice of pumpkin pie.

"Hmm… I'm not sure yet, but starting today, I'm making a record of what goes on around town this time of year." Carson shrugged. "I'm using the newcomer angle."

"You've got plenty of material. Adelaide Creek loves its holidays. Today was only the beginning." Olivia couldn't speak for Jeff or Carson, but the launch of her first holiday season in Adelaide Creek had been everything she hoped for.

"Okay, okay, I get it, Jillian. I'm well aware you're too old for a trip to Santa Claus," Olivia said impatiently as they walked from the parking area in the fairgrounds to Merchant Street. They were on their way to the annual Christmas Market, held on the Saturday after Thanksgiving. "We're here to be with Lucy and Nick. And there are other things to do at the market."

From the time Jillian sat down at the table and took her first bite of toast that morning, she insisted she had no interest in their trip to the Christmas Market. Heather had hyped it as one of the best of Adelaide Creek's events of the holiday season. It was a beautiful sunny day, with the fresh Thanksgiving snow adding to the beauty without making the roads treacherous.

"I wanted to go with Carson. He was going to run Winnie way out across the pasture where she could play in the snow."

"Honey, he'll do that again and I'm sure he'll take you with him next time. Besides, Jeff and Carson are going to meet us at the diner later for lunch." She studied Jillian, who had hit an impasse. The twins, though cute and funny, were more like younger cousins than her close friends. Carson fascinated her, especially when she prodded him into talking about Seattle and playing pickup basketball games in the park. He'd told her about trips to the harbor where he watched car ferries traveling to and from the islands. He'd developed his passion for making videos in Seattle, too.

Jillian shrugged indifferently at the idea of the diner, but since she offered no new arguments, Olivia assumed acceptance of her fate.

Merchant Street was closed to traffic, so pedestrians wandered freely among the booths lining the sidewalks. Olivia didn't recognize many people, but at least she could wave to the owners of the grocery store and to a couple of nurses from the hospital standing in line with their kids at the cookie booth. The women were surprised to see her—in a good way—and sent her friendly smiles.

Olivia took a couple of steps toward them,

but Jillian pointed to Stacey and the twins and broke into a run. Shrugging helplessly, she called out to the women, "See you later."

"We were looking for you," Stacey said. "The twins didn't want to get in line until they knew for sure Jillian was coming." She switched her attention to Jillian. "I know, I know, you've outgrown Santa Claus visits, but the twins feel special when you're around." She winked at Jillian. "You're in *middle* school. No wonder they look up to you."

Given how cranky Jillian had been earlier, Olivia held her breath waiting for Jillian to respond. She exhaled when Jillian said, "Santa Claus is fun no matter how old you are. Right?"

Oh, so grown-up. Amused, Olivia watched Jillian moving to stand closer to the twins and being their protector. "I'll wait with you."

"Have you been here long?" Heather asked, coming into their circle.

"Only a few minutes," Olivia said, but lowered her voice to add, "She was a little crabby this morning. She's getting eager to skip over the next couple of years and turn into a teenager."

"Another stage to anticipate," Heather quipped, pretending to put on a glum face. "I'm trying to focus on this one holiday."

"One minute she's talking about riding from the cabin over to your ranch on the horse she envisions in her not so distant future," Olivia said. "The next thing I know she's re-arranging stuffed animals and dolls on her shelves."

Heather chuckled. "I identify with that. Bethany and I were still playing make-believe with our dolls when we were Jillian's age. But Jeff and I were doing grown-up chores on the ranch—Dad put the two of us in charge of looking after the horses."

Olivia enjoyed the dreamy look in her eyes when Heather talked about that part of her past, but her attention was drawn away by Santa waving at her. Then the man put his finger over his lips as if to shush her. She jolted. Was Santa Clay Markson in disguise? Santa shifted his attention to the mom and baby approaching, giving Olivia a chance to see him from another angle. Oh, yeah, it was him.

"What is it?" Heather asked. "What made you so jumpy?"

"It's Santa. Clay Markson," Olivia said. "Do you know him?"

"Hmm…well, yes, I know him, but not well," Heather said. "He consulted on my mom's cancer diagnosis years ago."

"He plays Santa at this Christmas Market," Stacey said. "At least we've seen him every year since we moved here with the twins."

Since she wouldn't be taking Jillian up to see him, Olivia relaxed a little. Heather and Stacey weren't fooled, though. "You're a ghost. The blood drained from your face," Stacey said. "What's wrong?"

"No, no, I'm just surprised." She glanced at Heather. "I had a bit of a run…well, a *disagreement* with him at work. Strictly professional." That's why she'd chosen not to mention it to Heather. "It was early in my first week. He's been mad about it ever since." Had she sounded convincing? Probably not, or Heather wouldn't still be scrutinizing her face.

"Did it get resolved?" Heather asked, in a low voice.

"Yes. Well, sort of," Olivia answered. "But when he complained that I disagreed with his diagnosis, there was no sign of a jovial

Santa. He was fierce, nasty. For no good reason, he demanded an in-person meeting. He was wrong, I was right, but he never backed down."

Heather gave her an accusing look. "You never said anything about this."

"I've been trying to be extraprofessional and keep it within the department."

"Didn't you meet him online before you were hired?" Heather asked. "He's the head of the radiology department."

Olivia explained that she'd interviewed with Sandra and board members. She hadn't met Clay until her first day. The dispute happened not long after.

"It must have been some disagreement because the expression on your face when you saw him was transparent," Stacey said.

Olivia forced a smile. "At the moment, I'm seeing another side to the same man. It threw me, that's all. I'm told he's retiring very soon, so none of it matters. And he didn't single me out. He's furious with the surgeon involved, too."

"Before she died, his wife used to come to the Christmas Market with him," Stacey said.

"She did a Mrs. Santa sort of thing and handed out candy. Even without her, he dons that Santa suit every year."

The line moved and they shuffled a few steps ahead. The bluegrass band started playing at the other end of the street and they ended their conversation. Olivia thought of walking away with Jillian, but better to appear sociable in public and on good terms with her colleague. At the moment he was classic Santa, full of smiles and jokes, murmuring comforting and understanding words when a toddler let out a piercing scream and refused to sit beside him. The baby stayed secure in his dad's arms while Santa wiggled his fingers at him. Still, she eyed Clay with suspicion the whole time. Olivia decided the toddler was a good judge of character.

When it was Lucy and Nick's turn to run up to Santa, Olivia and Jillian stepped out of the line and off to the side. Before Clay greeted the twins and Stacey could position her camera phone for her first picture, his voice boomed past the crowd surrounding his gilded chair. "Merry Christmas, Dr. Donoghue. Welcome to you and your daughter to your first Christmas Market, an Adelaide Creek tradition." Clay drew the attention of everyone in line. Even people at a nearby craft booth, where Jen sold her wool, turned their heads.

Thrown by Clay's cheery tone and noting people watching her, she faked a matching tone and called back, "Thanks. It's a lot of fun." The guy she thought of as her nemesis wasn't so fierce in that red suit and the white beard that ended at his black Santa belt.

"Have a good time." He waved before turning his attention to the twins and acknowledged Heather with a silent nod.

Olivia put her hands lightly on Jillian's shoulders and moved closer so they could listen to the kids chattering on to Santa, and not showing a hint of shyness. The two explained they had teamed up to ask for the same thing.

"We want either a brother or sister—or twins would be okay," Nick said.

"That's our *first* choice, Santa," Lucy said using the same we-mean-business-tone as Nick.

Taking a quick photo, Olivia caught Heather rolling her eyes.

Santa did a quick ho-ho-ho. "Okay, you two, what do have in mind as a *second* choice?"

"If there's not enough time to get us a baby, we'll take a puppy," Lucy added.

Jillian giggled.

"Did you hear that?" Santa Clay said to his helper elf, who was sitting in a red-and-white rocking chair writing the kids' requests on a long paper scroll. With a broad smile he winked at Heather before turning back to the kids. "Toys can be a little easier than babies or puppies, but I promise the elf gang and I will do our best."

The twins cheerfully thanked Santa and ran to Jillian. "I bet you get the puppy this year," Jillian said in a sage tone. "But you *could* have a baby around by *next* Christmas."

"Jillian, let's not spec…u…late," Olivia said in a light singsong voice. She hoped it carried enough of a warning to stop Jillian from going any further down the baby road.

Heather changed the subject fast. "Next stop, cookie booth."

After carrying away a bag of gingerbread cookies, Olivia stopped at Jen Hoover's booth to admire the baskets of raw wool and spun wool in skeins. She ran her fingers through the soft, crinkly wool from the Shetlands. "Maybe I need a hobby," she said to Heather. "I've never learned to knit or crochet—or weave."

"If you ever want to spin your own wool, you've come to the right place," Heather said. "Jen sells it and teaches, and takes her wheel to spinning groups. Some knit or make things from felted wool. Weaving is becoming popular, too."

Olivia ran her hand through raw Icelandic wool. "I hear this wool is good for rugs. Would be nice to have a rug in front of the fireplace. Something to consider." Olivia went from the baskets of wool to the shelves, where she picked up packages of Jen's herbs and tea blends to send to coworkers in Minnesota.

"I heard about Clay's upcoming retirement," Bethany said, coming alongside Olivia. "I think that's best for all concerned, including Clay himself."

Olivia met her eye and smiled. "I agree." It meant a lot to hear that from Heather's friend Bethany, an orthopedic nurse at the hospital.

"People talk, but not about you," Bethany

added in a low voice. "Lately, Clay's been having trouble with staff in every department."

"Thanks for passing that on. It helps knowing this problem didn't start with my arrival," Olivia said. "Now I'm not sure what is more disconcerting, the hostile doctor at work or the friendly, almost exuberant Santa."

"Me, neither," Bethany said. She abruptly changed the subject to her mother's upcoming participation at a winter art show for fiber artists in the county gallery in Landrum. "You'll want to come. Mom's doing spinning demonstrations."

"I'll do that," Olivia said.

Bethany ran Olivia's credit card and packed the shopping bag and then sidestepped to help a customer nearby.

Heather and the twins and Jillian were outside the next booth fixated on the jewelry made from Wyoming jade. Jillian was holding up a piece that from a distance was surely a necklace. She was talking to Heather, who admired it with her. They were deep in conversation and she was about to join them, but then she held back. With Heather at her side, Jillian took money out of the pocket of her jeans and paid for the piece. Heather spoke to the artist, who put the item in a velvet drawstring pouch and then gave it to her, not to Jillian. Heather looked behind her and slipped the bag into her backpack and gave it a pat.

Olivia smiled. The twins wouldn't give away Jillian's secret. They were distracted by a woman dressed as one of Santa's helpers passing out red reindeer noses. She had a feeling Jillian and Heather had conspired over her Christmas gift. Olivia pretended to stare across the street to the bakery booth and waited for Heather and Jillian to join her.

"When's lunch?" Jillian asked, sniffing the air. "Or we could just eat popcorn."

"Lunch is right about now," Heather said. "I spotted Carson and my brother going inside the diner a couple of minutes ago. Matt, along with Stacey and Grey, is already there and claimed the table."

"I've been sniffing that popcorn, too. We'll get a large bag of it to take home."

Later, lingering over blueberry pancakes, Olivia sensed peculiar tension in the air. At first she thought it must have built between Jeff and Matt, but on second look, the two men seemed okay with each other. The strain seemed to be between Carson and Jeff.

Olivia tried to pretend she didn't see Jeff's glum face, until Heather steered the conversation toward the Christmas Eve dinner Jeff and Carson were hosting at the lodge.

As they were filing out and heading down the street to their cars, Jeff came alongside her and asked if she was free the next day, Sunday.

"As it happens, I am. I'm on call at home overnight and have tomorrow off. What's up?"

"I'm taking a ride up toward Jackson tomorrow." He smiled. "I'll dub it a business trip, but I'm not going to say any more. I was hoping you and Jillian might agree to ride along. Where we're headed, you'll have a chance to take in a little more of the mountain scenery."

"I wouldn't miss it. Jillian will be thrilled. She never misses a chance to hang out with Carson."

A grimace replaced Jeff's smile. "Carson won't be coming along. He's got *other* plans."

Olivia nodded, but Jeff's manner didn't invite more questions. Between the look on Jeff's face and his tone, he was doing a bad job of hiding the rift between him and Carson. Maybe so. That wasn't her business, but she wouldn't miss a chance to spend the day with Jeff.

CHAPTER TEN

"ARE YOU *STILL* mad at me?" Carson asked, as he came into the kitchen after taking Winnie out.

Jeff's impatience came out as a low grunt. "I *told* you, I'm not mad. Any other time, I'd have been fine with you hanging out with Owen and his family. I wish I'd known the plan was in the works, that's all. I might have organized this trip for a different a day." Time was tight for this particular project, though, so he might have ended up going alone on a weekday.

"Did you tell Olivia and Jillian where you're going?" Carson asked.

"No, I thought it would be kind of a fun surprise." Jeff lightened his tone. He was hanging on to tension that was his fault in the first place. He'd planned a day trip out of town without thinking to ask Carson if he was okay with it. Now the teenager was heading for a day with Owen and his family. They had a cabin a couple of hours away and were making an overnight trip of it. They'd drop the kids off at school in the morning. "I'm just disappointed and this trip with Owen's family seems a little last-minute."

"I know." Carson shrugged and turned to walk away.

"Do you have everything you need?" He didn't want an itemized list, but Carson hadn't asked him about what to take or leave behind. Jeff had checked with Owen's parents and already had the information and phone numbers they needed.

"I remembered all the important stuff— my tablet and my toothbrush," Carson teased, slipping into his jacket. He held up his hat and gloves. "And hiking boots. Owen's mom knows some good trails up there."

His boots were on the worn side. A new pair might be a good Christmas present for him. Not that Carson had said he'd outgrown his old ones. But they were a gift from Karen last winter, so they wouldn't fit for long. He hoped the boots wouldn't become another irreplaceable item, like the tattered backpack.

"I'll walk out front with you to wait for

your ride," Jeff said, trying to breathe and ease the cramped muscles in his shoulders. *Cramped* was a less powerful word than *fear*. The cause of the ache in his body in the first place. Except for the school bus, this was the first time Carson was riding in a vehicle with someone other than him. That was the source of the dread rippling beneath the surface. He was afraid to let him go off with new people. He was aware of how completely irrational he was being, and not simply because he'd been driving Karen's car the night she was killed. He could shake that off more easily than the reality that a split second was all it took to change everything forever. He hadn't quite learned to live with that. Not yet.

On a scale of one to ten, Jeff scored himself a solid nine for managing to hide his anxiety as he chatted with Owen's mom and dad when they rolled up. He stowed Carson's backpack with the family's gear in the back. Carson helped Winnie jump into the back, where a brown boxer and a black Lab got to their feet and greeted her with nonstop bumps and sniffs. Winnie didn't seem to mind the other two sizing her up. At some point, they backed off, apparently deciding she was a playmate, not an interloper.

When the SUV disappeared down the drive, Jeff went back inside the cabin and leaned against the kitchen counter and rubbed his cheeks to loosen his jaw. He had to loosen the reins on Carson. Keeping Carson close guaranteed exactly nothing. He still had moments with fear so raw it grabbed control of his mind and took his thoughts to awful places. At these times, the weight of being Carson's guardian crushed him. What was a guardian, after all, if not a protector?

With these thoughts shuffling around his head, he took a deep breath and patted his pockets checking for keys and his phone and went outside. Jillian was already waiting by the truck, with Olivia coming to join her.

"Perfect timing," Olivia said.

"And I see you're ready for the cold." She wore a heavy wool jacket and had a bright red scarf wrapped around her neck. Red puffy gloves covered her hands.

"I've got a lot of experience staying warm." She glanced down at Jillian, dressed the same way. "I was telling Jillian it seems odd to be heading out without Carson, like we're missing the fourth member of the team."

Jeff nodded, but didn't elaborate. After the turmoil of watching Carson leave with Owen's family, he understood Olivia's concerns better. He needed to tell her that.

"When are you going to say where we're going?" Jillian asked when they climbed in the truck and she buckled herself into the seat in the back.

"Not just yet. It's going to be a surprise." He held up two fingers. "We could be going to two places today." He was climbing out on a limb. Making a second stop depended entirely on what happened at the first.

"Okay," Jillian said. "I'll wait."

Chuckling, Olivia reminded her that no matter where Jeff was taking them, they'd be seeing some country and towns they'd never been to before. "I told Jillian that next summer, we'll go all the way up to Yellowstone."

"I want to see the geysers," Jillian said.

"That's a worthwhile trip," Jeff said. "Carson has mentioned them a couple of times." He came close to suggesting the four of them make that trip together, but held back. Sometimes he slipped into talking about them as if they were one family, not two.

As if reading his mind, Jillian said, "We could all go to Yellowstone together."

A laugh escaped from Olivia at the same time Jeff chuckled softly. They'd had that same thought at the same time. He was sure of it. It was so easy to imagine the four of them on a summer adventure to explore the park.

Now, as they headed north they started to see more snow on the ground in the higher elevations. The sun peeked through and shadows shifted across the valleys sloping down the highway. As they reached a plateau they had a panoramic view of vast grazing land and cattle. When the GPS told him to take the next right turn, Jillian giggled. "I saw the sign. We're on Bumbly Road?"

"That's right. Bumbly it is."

"Better than Mumbly or Fumbly," Olivia quipped.

"Or how about Dumbly?" Jillian shifted the conversation when she asked, "But you still haven't said why you're taking us here. Oh, is that Mr. Bumbly?" She pointed with her chin to a white-haired man coming out of his house.

"No, no. There is no Mr. Bumbly. That's probably Bryce Henderson. No more mumbly-fumbly talk. We don't want him thinking we're making fun of his road."

"But we are," Jillian said. "I bet people make fun of it all the time."

"Jill…ian," Olivia said as a playful warning.

With a couple of waves, the presumed Mr. Henderson directed Jeff to a spot in front of a chain-link fence and gate that separated the gravel drive from some good-sized piles of metal and shells of old vehicles. A couple of friendly golden retrievers emerged from the house along with a white-haired woman who stayed on the porch and swayed side to side as if soothing the baby she held in her arms.

"Wow, dogs and a baby. And all the junky stuff behind the fence."

"Hmm…let's be careful about what we call it, Jillian," Olivia said. "We don't know what it's for."

Jeff laughed as he stepped out of the truck. "You know the old saying, Jillian? 'One person's junk is another person's treasure.' I think that's scrap metal for sale, maybe some old cars and tractors being stripped for parts.

And that's Mr. Henderson's treasure." No sign of what Jeff had come for, though.

Jillian and Olivia were alongside when he greeted Bryce.

Bryce extended his arms. "Welcome to our spread. Seems it's a good day to do a little business, huh?"

"I hope so," Jeff said. Then he introduced Olivia and Jillian. "They just moved to Adelaide Creek in October, so I'm showing them around the area."

"Bryce and I are babysitting our new granddaughter today," the older woman said as she approached with the baby on her hip. Then she turned to Jillian and said, "Everyone calls me Polly and this little girl is Erica."

Jillian curled her fingers down in a typical baby wave and was rewarded with a smile.

Bryce gestured for them to follow him. "I'll take you around back and show you the prize you came for."

The baby, snug in fleece pants and jacket and miniature boots, was still content in Polly's arms, so they were a group of six when Bryce led them through a gate behind the house and past piles of metal with sharp edges. Jeff's heart sank with every step. So far, he hadn't seen anything that didn't match Jillian's word, junk. Whatever parts had been harvested from this hodgepodge of old tractors and trucks were hauled away long ago.

"Over this way," Bryce said. "She's back here—we can pull the flatbed from the other direction and take her out on the road. If you decide she's right for you."

"She" was hidden behind a stand of trees, but the dark green paint came into view. Fresh paint, Jeff guessed, just as Bryce had said on the phone.

"It's a sleigh!" Jillian's voice was filled with surprise—and excitement.

"Yep, she's a sleigh, all right," Jeff said. "With room for all of us and quite a few more."

Olivia appeared puzzled, but Jeff didn't stop to explain. What he was up to would be clear in a couple of minutes.

"You see here," Bryce said, pointing to the boxy body of the painted sleigh with runners attached to an undercarriage. "This is set up for wagon rides, too. You just rig it up with wheels. I got 'em stored. Too bad, though. From what I've seen wagon rides aren't so much in demand anymore. I don't know why."

Jeff agreed. "That's why I'm thinking of

offering sleigh rides at the lodge—there's flat land and an old farm road adjacent to my pasture but beyond that is a barely used road." Out of the corner of his eye, he saw Jillian's face light up.

Polly came closer and stood next to Bryce. "We usually had ten, maybe twelve people— lots of kids."

Jillian took a few steps forward and, mimicking a stage performer, she swept her arm to take in the sleigh from front to back. "If there's a sleigh there must be horses."

Jeff guffawed. "You're onto me, Jillian."

"What?" Olivia said, her face reddening.

"Don't worry," Jeff said fast and loud. "They aren't horses we'll ride. They'll be Clydesdales. Draft horses trained to pull loads." They could ride them, but he'd made a decision to use them only for the purpose they'd been trained for, assuming he found the right source for them.

"But you'll keep them in your stable, right?"

Remembering the eruption of his earlier fears, Jeff kept his voice low and conciliatory when he answered. "They'll be kept in the stable and the corrals, Olivia. I know how to tend to them. They won't be horses I'd use in my riding school next year or raise for leasing."

"Wow, I love horses," Jillian said, clasping her hands in front of her chest and studying the area around her. "Do you have them here?"

"Nope. Used to have some fine horses, but not anymore. Jeff has to get his Clydesdales from someone else."

"I've got that lined up, Jillian," Jeff said, "but remember, we won't be saddling them. We'll harness them and ride in the sleigh across the snow." He assumed Olivia would be okay with that. "For holiday rides, and special occasions. Valentine's Day would be a romantic night for a sleigh ride, or winter weddings or anniversaries."

"Keep the flowers and champagne. Nothing's quite as romantic as a sleigh ride," Polly said. "We had loads of good times with this girl." Speaking directly to Olivia in a reassuring tone, Polly gave the sleigh a friendly tap.

"I'll bet." Olivia's face and voice were more relaxed now.

"We rejuvenated the sleigh to sell," Bryce explained. "We're not in that business anymore."

"That's because there's a high-end resort a couple of miles north. They book solid for holiday ski trips and they feature sleigh rides in their ads," Polly explained. "There wasn't room for a family operation like ours. We catered to locals and some church groups that hosted rides for the young teens."

"I get it," Jeff said, thinking that in a way the former owners of his lodge closed because of the more luxury oriented lodges opened not far from him. But he'd checked. The managers of that hotel had no plans to offer sleigh rides. Jeff believed a market still existed for the kind of affordable service he offered. The horses and riding school would make the difference in the long run, but even now, he could scare up some sleigh-ride business.

"I can see Carson inviting his friends over for a ride," Olivia said.

"And me," Jillian insisted. "I've got new friends, too. And don't forget the twins."

"Possibilities for sure." Carson came to mind as he mulled over his vision for the future. It had been a while since Jeff had mentioned anything about buying horses and Carson never asked. Jeff had *almost* resigned himself that Carson would never develop a passion for horses, not even close to what had been nurtured in Heather and him. Meanwhile, Jeff let the subject drop and developed an interest in basketball.

"Let me show you the specs on the wagon, and then you can inspect it as we go down the list," Bryce said.

"Why don't you two come with me?" Polly suggested to Olivia and Jillian. "I think you might have time for a mug of hot chocolate."

"If it's not too much trouble," Olivia said.

"Not at all. Come on with me inside where it's warm."

Jillian's expression told Jeff she was torn between going with her mom and staying behind with him. "You go ahead," Jeff said, amused by Jillian's enthusiasm. "I won't be long here. You won't miss anything important. I promise."

It took fifteen minutes to examine the solid wagon structure with its sturdy attached seat and back closures, and a harness easy to rig. Bryce's handcrafted wooden steps went with the deal.

"We'll throw in the plaid lap robes, red and green for the season. Polly used to decorate the sides with wreaths and big bows. Made it real festive."

"I'll bet," Jeff said, playing with that homey image. A few days ago when he'd made up his mind to do this, it hadn't taken long to learn that the Hendersons had built a solid reputation for sleigh and wagon rides, a side business for them, as it would be for him.

"You've got yourself a deal, Bryce. I'm not exactly sure which part of my low-key lodge will keep us in business, but I've got to try everything."

As he and Bryce walked back to the house to take care of the paperwork, Jeff told him he had a source for Clydesdales.

"Are you planning to buy 'em outright or maybe rent them for a season?"

"I'll get a lease on them and hope to buy them." He told Bryce a little about his plans for a riding school. "You'd think the market in Adams County, with all its ranches and lodges and big estates popping up, would have its fill of riding schools, but it doesn't. So, maybe next spring. Meanwhile, the lodge is already carrying its weight."

"Sounds like a plan for a man with a young family and all."

"Well, we don't exactly fit that description," Jeff said, throwing himself off-kilter by almost adding *yet* to his explanation of who was who.

"Seems to be a nice lady," Bryce said.

"She is that," Jeff said. "She and her daughter are new to town. She's a radiologist."

"Impressive." Bryce grinned. "So, who are you seeing about those Clydesdales?"

"Trey Ford. My brother-in-law recommended him. We're actually headed there from here. I had thought I'd keep it a secret, but once Jillian knew I'd come here for a sleigh, the surprise is over." He laughed, aware of how that sounded. "Jillian's tough to keep up with."

Bryce was quick with his comment. "Polly would call her a spirited girl. Now, Trey is exactly who I'd have recommended if you'd asked me. He's the best guy around here for those specialty types of horses."

"It must seem odd to you that I didn't tell Jillian or Olivia where we were going, but they're new to Wyoming, so everything is an adventure," Jeff said. "Jillian isn't riding yet, but she will be and she's excited to be around horses."

Bryce narrowed his eyes and gave him a long look. "Would you be one of the ranching Stanhopes? Raised sheep over in Addie Creek?"

"Born and raised there," Jeff said. He swallowed hard. "It's the Burton place now. My sister married Matt Burton, so I get over to the ranch now and then." That wasn't so bad. Maybe it was because walking side by side with Bryce took him back twenty-plus years when he was a younger boy than Carson and out and about with his dad. Dad would do a little business, maybe some buying and selling old tools from the shed or tack for the horses. Everybody had to find ways to make it in sheep-and-cattle country, where the weather and the markets were predictably unforgiving. Jeff was carrying on that tradition for sure.

When they went inside, Olivia and Jillian were sitting at the kitchen table with Polly. The baby was in a high chair next to Jillian.

"What's the story?" Polly said, her eyes sparkling. "Are you taking that old sleigh off our hands?"

Jeff couldn't help but laugh at the woman's jovial, but practical attitude. "Yes, ma'am, that's what I'm doing. I'll arrange for her transport this week."

"It's late in the year to be starting a new venture," Bryce said, frowning.

"That's true. I bought the lodge and then moved back to Adelaide Creek only about six weeks ago, so I'm thinking long-term. When I do get horses, they'll probably know more than I do about pulling a wagon, so I'll learn from them."

When he was in the midst of transferring funds from his account to Bryce's, his phone alerted him to a text coming in. For no particular reason he assumed the text was from Carson, but he was wrong. He read the message and then glanced at Olivia. "Change of plans. The person we're supposed to see next has a family emergency, so I have to reschedule for early next week."

"Don't rush off," Polly said, pulling a chair out at the table for him. "Not before you have hot chocolate and some of these cookies. You need fortification for the ride back toward Landrum."

"She means business, son," Bryce said, smirking.

Jeff sent Trey a message and then joined

the others at the table in the warm kitchen Bryce and Polly had built, where he relaxed into the familiar scene. Jeff wasn't deceived, though, by the homeyness of the place. A lot of effort went into creating that kind of atmosphere. He'd been around people like the Hendersons all his life. Hard workers, but without the broken spirits that could come from struggle and hardship. Bryce and Polly reminded him of his parents during their best days, when he and Heather were growing up and the ranch was holding its own.

By the time they'd said their goodbyes and were on the road, Jillian smiled and exclaimed, "Woohoo, horses are coming!" Jillian didn't waste a second before firing questions about the Clydesdales.

"They're the kind farmers used in the old days," Jeff explained. "That's why we won't be riding them on the trails."

Jillian shrugged. "I can't ride yet, *any... way.*"

"I bet Jeff will take us for a sleigh ride, though," Olivia said.

Jeff grinned. "I might be persuaded. When the sleigh arrives, I can clear a place for it near the stable and decorate it."

"So the horses will live in your stable at home?" Jillian asked.

"Yep, I've spent some time getting the stalls ready, and I've arranged for hay and other feed as soon as I'm ready. Clydesdales can be outside some of the time. These horses are used to cold and snow."

"Polly's cookies were so good," Jillian said. "I remember the gingerbread ones Heather made for us last year. Maybe we could make our own now."

"What do you say we ask Heather for a few tips?" Olivia chuckled and turned to Jeff. "Last year when your sister was with us, she was shocked, truly shocked, that I'd never baked holiday cookies, or any other kind. I'm a true fan of bakeries."

"I felt awful most of the time," Jillian mused. "Some days, Heather's gingerbread cookies were all I ate."

Jeff caught Jillian's eye in the rearview mirror and smiled. "I'm so glad you're well. Carson is glad, too. He said so after we came back from the Christmas Market."

Jillian smiled. "Some kids in my class thought he was my brother. That's 'cause we get on the bus at the same place. I always wave to him when I get off first at my school."

"I hope he waves back," Jeff said in a teasing tone.

"Uh-huh. Carson is always nice to me."

The way Karen wanted him to be. Jeff remembered her specific words, almost a mantra. "It's never a bad thing to be known as the kind kid, Carson." Sometimes she'd add, "You can stand up for yourself and still treat others well." She'd been especially adamant about being nice to the younger kids. A buzz went through Jeff as more memories of Karen flooded.

"Are we going home?" Jillian asked.

"We can," Jeff said, "but I think we should head back to Landrum and check out the holiday display in the town square. It's pretty special. You'll see."

"Sounds fine to me," Olivia said, and Jillian readily agreed.

While they rode along in comfortable silence, Jeff was struck by how glad he was that Olivia, and Jillian, too, had been up for spending the day with him. His first holidays back in Adelaide Creek were turning out so much better than he'd anticipated. Jeff had imagined himself laser focused on the lodge, while also helping Carson to get through the holidays. But he'd set his sights too low.

He glanced at Olivia, looking relaxed as she stared out the window at the long stretches of grazing land and the mountain peaks in the distance. Jeff had never expected to feel so deeply about her. Every minute they spent together left him wanting more. It had surprised him, too. He couldn't even remember the last time he'd felt that way about a woman.

He parked close to the square, and before he could open the driver's side door, Olivia put her hand on his arm. "Thanks for this… this fun day."

Jeff caught her hand and gave it a squeeze. "*You* make it fun."

When Jillian hopped down from the truck she ran ahead to the displays in the park. The multicolor lights hung in the trees were turned on and brightened the overcast afternoon.

As they had every year since Jeff was a child, the county gallery and the downtown merchants had teamed up to turn the park surrounding the square into a miniature fenced-in ranch, with its own collection of carved cattle, sheep and a few cowboys and cowgirls on horses, all painted in detail from the green of the pastures to the ranchers' red-and-blue bandannas.

"They even have the border collies," Jeff said, pointing to the dogs interspersed with the sheep and cattle.

"And a Santa's workshop." Jillian ran toward a lean-to style building with a glass front to protect the vintage ornaments and various-size painted elves and Santas arranged on tiered shelving. Labels marked a few pieces as dating back to the nineteenth century, including a trio of delicate angels.

"Look at the reindeer and sleigh—it's made of wire and cloth," Olivia said. It hung from the ceiling like a mobile.

"Cool," Jillian said. "It's almost one hundred years old."

After being gone for so long, Jeff had more or less forgotten about the reindeer and sleigh, reminders of his childhood. "Not too much has changed," Jeff said. "There's just more of it. The wooden ranch is a lot bigger now." He nodded to a tent. "The hot pretzels and mustard are definitely a snack update for the better."

"Yes to the pretzel, no to the mustard," Jillian announced as she hurried to the tent.

"I'll take mine with loads of mustard," Olivia said.

After Jeff bought the pretzels, they sat at a table near one of the space heaters.

Jillian took a few bites of her pretzel before turning to Jeff. "Is it okay if I ask Carson about his mom?"

Before Jeff could answer, Olivia jumped in. "That came out of the blue."

True, but that was okay. "What do you want to know, Jillian?"

Jillian shrugged. "I wonder what she was like, that's all. Carson says he thinks of Seattle a lot. He says it's okay here, but he misses his mom."

Good sign, Jeff thought, Carson's ability to talk about it. "Of course, you can ask him about Karen. I'll leave it to Carson to fill you in on some things, but I can tell you he was his mother's whole world. Her parents were gone, and she didn't have any brothers or sisters, so she was raising Carson alone." The instant the words left his mouth he second-guessed being so blunt. Olivia and Jillian's story was practically identical, at least in that way. He glanced at Olivia for a reaction, but she was watching Jillian.

"What about his father?" Jillian asked.

"Well, he went away, and so Carson never knew him. But his grandma is his dad's mother. He talks to her on the phone and sends her video clips and photos. She's not well, but she loves Carson very much."

Jillian glanced up at her mom. "Carson's dad must be kinda like mine, huh?"

"Seems so, sweetie." She looked like she had more to say, but apparently changed her mind.

Jeff wished he could make the sadness in Olivia's eyes, more gray than blue that day, disappear. One of the things he found the most alluring about her was the way her eyes could change, thoughtful one minute, full of fun the next.

"Karen was a loving person, who adored kids, Jillian," Jeff said. "She would have liked you and your mom."

"From little things Carson has said, she sounds a lot like Heather," Olivia said.

Jeff nodded, as a sweet image of Heather interacting with Carson and Jillian on Thanksgiving drifted into Jeff's mind. It was no surprise that she took a career path into pediatrics or had the heart to easily embrace Lucy and Nick.

It was his sister's brand-new husband who'd surprised him. Jeff's doubts—and resentment—about him started to erode the day he met Matt. Then, seeing the man's soft gaze when he looked at Heather broke through barriers of Jeff's own making. Watching his sister offer the same deep love back to Matt turned Jeff's knee-jerk suspicion of the guy and the marriage into a joke on him.

Heather and her new family had given Carson a warm welcome. That was great, but now Jeff wanted more for Carson—and for himself. The parts of him that he'd shut down with a vengeance were opening up again and he wasn't fighting it.

"You might have left Adelaide Creek thinking that you lost a lot," Olivia said, her eyes soft now, "but you came back to a whole new family."

He gave Olivia a quick glance. "Funny, I was just thinking the same thing."

CHAPTER ELEVEN

JEFF'S PHONE RANG when he was doing a last-minute check of the stalls for the horses arriving soon. He recognized the name on his screen. Brandon Voorhees, the basketball coach. "Hey, Coach." Jeff couldn't resist adding, "I always knew you'd make good. I'm not surprised you took up working with kids."

"You mean because I'm the oldest of six?" Brandon said with a laugh in his voice. "I had a lot of practice, huh?"

"Carson thinks you're very cool, and not just because we went to school together." For a minute Jeff wondered how much Brandon knew about Carson's situation, but he'd let that unfold and fill in the blanks if necessary.

"Well, as you can guess, I'm calling to talk with you about Carson."

"Should I be worried?"

"No, no, nothing to fear here," Brandon said. "When Carson first showed up in the gym, he was a little reserved and reluctant to talk about himself much. I got the lowdown on his injury, though. Wow, a terrible thing. Then he told me a little about his Seattle school. Turns out he's quite a hoops guy."

"I know. He and the physical therapist think he's almost ready for phys ed, and then later, to try out for the team. I don't know. His arm is still taking a little time. The ankle is good, though." Jeff found he was proud—even excited—to be talking about Carson to someone he knew when he was a teenager himself. The reports he'd received from the counselor at the school were okay, but sort of impersonal. "What do you think?"

Brandon cleared his throat. "Yeah, yeah, he's come a long way. I was, well, curious if you were aware of how he's been spending his time in the gym for his alternate phys ed. Has he said anything?"

"Not really," Jeff answered, perplexed but listening. "He said he's free to study or read, and mentioned shooting some baskets with his good arm."

Brandon scoffed. "Some baskets, huh? More like one after another for forty-five minutes. I have to shoo him away from the hoop to get him to his next class."

Jeff frowned, puzzled by Brandon's tone, as if Carson was creating a problem. "He hasn't gone into that much detail. It tells me a little about his dedication, though. For as long as I've known him…and I assume you know he's not actually my son…he's had razor-sharp focus for things that matter to him. Basketball is one of them."

"Are you kidding? Of course, I see it. As messed up as his body was when he started, he practiced any way he could. He's going after those shots with his injured arm now."

That all sounded good. "So, you think he'll be able to play junior varsity?"

"It depends on how he does in the tryouts, but the kid's good. We might boost him up to varsity."

Even better.

"Here's the thing. He told me he lives at the old lodge on the edge of town. That place that's sat empty for a couple of years. You bought it?"

"Right," Jeff said. "I wrapped that up before bringing him here to live. I named it Stanhope's Woodland Cabins."

"I see. Well, I asked him if he had a hoop at home. When he said no, I suggested he talk to you about getting him one."

Odd, Carson had never said anything about that. "Sure, I suppose I could. Although, it's kind of late in the year." He took a mental trip around the sides and rear of the building to locate a spot for it. He'd level the ground and maybe pave it for one-on-one pickup games. He had enough room at the back there. "Carson didn't mention it to me."

"A lot of the players have them—we encourage it. Shooting baskets outside on a decent day is good for the kids, even in the cold weather." Brandon sighed loud enough to cause static in the phone. "Here's the thing. When I followed up with him about whether or not he'd talked to you about the hoop, he was honest and said no. That seemed odd, so I probed a little. In an offhanded sort of way, Carson reminded me that he's not your kid— his words. It seemed as if he isn't comfortable asking you for things."

A wave of sadness pounded him. He took a deep breath and leaned against the stable wall. "I didn't know he felt that way. And it's not the message I've been trying to send. Not even close."

"Don't get me wrong. I'm not being critical." Brandon's voice revealed understanding. "Matter of fact, Carson seems well adjusted for a kid who's lost so much."

"Well, as low as this conversation has brought me," Jeff admitted, "it could help me to unravel a couple of things." He paused. "I assume this conversation won't go beyond the two of us."

"Absolutely," Brandon said. "Consider this a conversation between friends."

Trying to keep it short and to the point, Jeff told the story about how he knew Carson in the first place before explaining the circumstances around Karen's death and their move to town.

"You mean, you weren't his mom's boyfriend?" Brandon asked.

"No. We were strictly friends. Did something Carson say leave that impression?"

"No, that was my assumption."

"Good, I'm glad to clarify that. And I will see to it Carson has a practice hoop," Jeff said, "but I also need to figure out why he didn't think he could ask. But it's true, he hasn't asked for much. I try to see what he needs and offer it."

"He told me about having some kids over to the lodge on Halloween for pool and Ping-Pong." Brandon chuckled. "You ready to have the lodge become an old-fashioned clubhouse?"

"The place should make it easier to keep track of him." Bantering with Brandon was okay, but Jeff's mind was drifting to the curious situation with the video camera and the backpack. Maybe even the hiking boots. It all wove together in his mind.

Jeff ended the call and for the rest of the day his thoughts kept coming back to what Brandon had revealed. He waited to bring it up until he and Carson had finished dinner and cleared the table and Carson started to head to his room to make a couple of calls.

"Wait a second, Carson," Jeff said. "I need to talk to you about something that came up." Carson didn't come back to sit down. Instead he stood in the doorway next to the fireplace.

"What's up?"

"I got a call from Coach Voorhees today." Carson's eyebrows lifted in surprise. "Good.

It's about time. Are they letting me into regular phys ed?"

"You'll be cleared soon. I hear you've been practicing a lot. He told me that you've been shooting baskets all along, starting with your good arm and now working with the other. Getting ready for tryouts."

Carson held up his injured arm and mimed a hook shot. "Yep, I'm getting pretty good."

"Sounds as if you have a better than even chance of making the team."

Carson responded with an eager nod. "That's what Coach told me." He stared at the floor. "I was going to tell you about it."

"You were?"

"Uh, yeah, sure."

"Was that the same time you were going to ask me about putting up a hoop?"

Carson shifted around. Jeff wanted to let the teenager off the hook, but something much too important was at stake. Even if Jeff wasn't precisely sure what it was. "I can't explain it, Carson, but is it possible you didn't ask me about a hoop for the same reason you don't use the camera I gave you, and why you wouldn't let me get you a new backpack?"

"My *mom* gave me that backpack," Carson

shot back, his voice loud, "*and* the first video camera I ever had."

"I know, Carson, which is why I dropped the idea of getting you a new pack." The camera seemed different, so he'd leave that alone for now. "But that doesn't answer my question."

Carson lowered his head and stared at the floor. "My mom gave me those things because she loved me. I was…like…important to her." He took a deep breath, but it caught in his throat and he gulped. "You gave me a cool camera. I know that. But it's not the same. You don't love me. And you didn't love my mom."

Jeff reeled. The boy's words weren't completely wrong, but still way off base. Not the whole story. Jeff swallowed hard in the hush that had fallen over the room. He gripped the breakfast bar counter and spoke. "You were the most important person in your mother's life, Carson. That wasn't going to change. *Ever.* You'll *always* know you had a mom who'd have moved mountains for you." He crossed his arms over his chest. "That's how she lived. For you."

"I miss her." Carson raised his head, tears

filling his eyes. "*You* don't miss her. You took me because there was no one else. You're not my dad. *I* don't even have a dad."

Jeff winced. Man, the truth could hurt. Partial truth. But the true pieces of the story made it even harder to hear. "I do miss your mom," he said, keeping his voice low. Karen was never far from his thoughts, especially at times when Jeff was afraid he wasn't doing right by Carson. "Those guys I knew on the ships were casual buddies, but your mom was a great friend."

Carson didn't meet Jeff's eye as he said, "Back when I was younger I thought maybe you were going to be, you know, more than Mom's friend."

Jeff remembered that about a younger Carson, who had regarded him with a little suspicion at first. He assumed the boy's mistaken idea about Jeff and his mom hadn't lasted for long. "I remember. When I first moved in, I sensed you thought I might be Karen's boyfriend. That wasn't what our friendship was meant to be. But families and love can be a tricky business."

Carson rubbed his eyes, but he seemed to be listening.

"Everything I learned about love came from my mom and dad. And Heather. I'm still learning from my little sister." The image of the twins with Heather flitted by in his mind. Then he shook his head. "You would have liked my parents. They would have done anything for me. Which is how your mom was with you. To be honest with you, I'll never stop missing my mom and dad."

Carson nodded and Jeff searched for words. Something nudged him to keep the channel open and not let Carson walk away without being frank. As Carson would say, being real. "I became your guardian because I wanted you to have the best chance to grieve this huge loss and then have a good life in the future. It was also my way to...to *honor* your mother, Carson."

He'd also hoped that would mean honoring what Karen wanted for her son. "But I know something else, too. Love takes time, Carson. You and I haven't been at this arrangement very long." He took a deep breath and in a lighter tone he added, "You liked having me around during those breaks when I was back from sea. But that's not the same as love, is it?"

Jeff held up his hand when Carson looked alarmed, as if Jeff had accused him of something. "You don't need to explain or agree or disagree. That's not the point, not at all. We've done okay so far, or at least I thought we had. Maybe we need to add a few ground rules."

Carson leaned over and patted Winnie's back. "I thought if I asked for things, I'd be a burden. You already agreed to let me live with you until I'm eighteen."

Did he think that was a cutoff date? *"At least* until you turn eighteen. All that means is that you have the choice to leave and be on your own. I thought it was clear that you have a home with me for as long as you want it. Until you're ready to move away on your own. Every young person eventually wants to leave home." Jeff snickered. "Until that time comes, you're stuck with me."

"You seem to prefer being alone. I mean, you didn't tell us much about your sister. And you never talked about visiting her." Carson's tone had taken an accusatory turn.

Guilty as charged.

"You never cared about basketball. It's always horses this and horses that."

Jeff nodded at the observation, more or less

true, but not relevant. The truth about how he'd treated Heather smacked him awake. His biggest mistake, biggest regret. Since he'd been back and involved with Heather and her family, he'd let the past slip to the back of his mind, but Carson remembered.

The trickier task was explaining that Carson wasn't a burden at all, but instead, he'd been more of a catalyst for Jeff to change his life. That was complicated, though, a conversation for another day. "I care that you get a chance to do what you love—and what you're good at. It's what prompted me to give you the new camera. As for basketball, when the season starts and you're on the team, nothing will keep me away from your games. *Nothing.* I want to be there to see you play."

"Really?"

"Absolutely. I thought you understood that. I'll always be your biggest fan." Tension drained from the muscles in Jeff's neck and arms. The awkward moment was easing and he saw no reason to prolong it. "Get your tablet. Let's go online and find you a hoop."

IT CAME TO Olivia in a flash. Jeff had been waiting for years for the moment he'd lead horses off a trailer and into his own pasture. Even she knew the lodge hadn't yet been a complete home until he got back this part of his life in Wyoming he'd missed the most. Until today.

"Did you ever think the first horses you'd be taking care of would be a couple of Clydesdales?" Heather asked.

"Nope. But it's good to be around these creatures again." The way Jeff gazed at Heather was unlike the way he was with anyone else. Olivia had seen that from the first day she met him at the ranch. It was a kind of softness in his eyes that acknowledged their understanding of each other.

Olivia was pleased when he offered a warm smile to her. "I keep telling you. No better way to see the world around you than from the back of a horse."

"I'm convinced that's true for you." She pointed to Heather and Matt. "And them. Jillian, too. But…" She chuckled. They'd had this conversation before. No need to finish the sentence.

"I know, you're sticking to darts," Jeff said, giving her a pointed look.

Olivia watched as Jeff, along with Heather

and Matt, got acquainted with the Clydesdales, Sassafras and Bonnet. He stroked Bonnet's shoulders and neck, but she did a nervous little dance as she moved away from him. Then she raised her head high and gave it a quick shake. Olivia stepped aside to put more ground between herself and the horse, all the while wishing she wasn't afraid of its power.

"She's not sure what's going on," Matt said, calming the other Clydesdale, "but they'll catch on quick."

"You'll settle them in no time, Jeff." Heather patted Bonnet's face. "Hey, girl," she whispered. "You're going to love it here."

"Your voices and touch match," Olivia said, watching Jeff approach Sassafras in the same quiet way.

"That's how they get to know us," Heather said, joining Jeff. "Right, Sassafras?"

"Having draft horses around is a new adventure, that's for sure," Matt said. "But these two know how to do their job."

"Yep, I've sure gotten myself into it now," Jeff said. "A six-month lease to take me through the snow season, assuming I can get enough people interested in sleigh rides down Rock Curve Road."

Olivia understood Jeff a little better when she heard him pose the question, "What's the worst that can happen?" He took the question to its logical end and confirmed his hunch that even if his sleigh-ride business ended up a flop it wouldn't be catastrophic. A calculated risk was worth taking.

The only time Olivia had ever asked that question was when she'd followed her hunch and kick-started her move from Minnesota to Wyoming by giving notice on her job. It had been an easy choice because the worst-case scenario wasn't so bad. It had been unlikely, but possible that she wouldn't take to Adelaide Creek after all. Or her job. With the exception of her dealings with Clay Markson, no downside had appeared.

The ground in the corral and the pasture had patchy snow, which according to Jeff was good for the moment. The two new horses wouldn't be confined to the stable while they got used to their new surroundings. When the snow came, they'd be familiar with him when he harnessed them to the sleigh and took them out for some practice runs.

Watching Heather with the horses now brought to mind her skepticism about Jeff's plan. To Heather, the Clydesdales and sleigh rides seemed an odd way to start if opening a riding school was his real goal. Matt and Jeff pointed out the slowly expanding winter tourist season. Having seen the growing number of weekend guests at the lodge, Olivia agreed with the two men. If anyone could pull off this venture, Jeff could.

When Jeff and Heather started walking the horses to the stable, Olivia quietly fell into step next to Matt. It was the first time she'd been in Jeff's stables. When she'd first moved in, she'd tried to ignore the corral and stables, mostly because of her fears for Jillian. She'd harbored the notion that Jillian would outgrow this thing she had for horses. Olivia had opened her eyes, though, and finally accepted that had been a foolish fantasy.

The horses were calm as Jeff and Heather led them inside and walked them down the space between the stables on both sides of the long building. "It took me a couple of days work to get the place cleaned up and the two stalls ready." He shook his head and gave Bonnet a pat. "Hey, girl, you and Sassy are my first, but you could have a dozen different kinds of pals once my riding school is underway."

Matt and Heather were obviously pleased for Jeff. Olivia was, too, but she didn't understand what it all meant in the same way the others did. At the same time, being in the stable, seeing these horses, listening to the neighing and nickering and the occasional snort, she finally got it. For all the reservations she had, she wanted Jillian to be part of this world. Maybe Olivia would never share this unique feeling that Jeff and Heather, and Matt, had in their bones, but now she wanted Jillian to have this world with its special bonds.

Olivia kept her thoughts to herself, but deep within her a celebration was underway. She had Heather and Jeff to thank for the shift in not only her thinking, but her feeling about life in the town she'd made a choice to call home. She was still enjoying that combination of excitement and peace when her phone vibrated in her jacket pocket.

She hurried away from Jeff and the others and saw Clay's name on the screen. Her boss. She answered the call.

"Olivia, hello. So nice to reach you."

Clay's disconcertingly cheery voice made her heart beat faster. "I'm not at home at the moment, Clay." Proud of her professional tone, she said, "Is there something you needed?"

"Not really. Just saying hello and checking in," Clay said, his tone not shifting in the least. "You haven't forgotten that I am head of the department, have you? It's my job to keep track of how everything's going."

"Well, nothing has changed since yesterday when I answered your text. I'm doing fine." Making conversation to get through this awkward exchange, she added, "My latest shifts have been busy. I'm sure you noticed that's true across the board." They were also understaffed, but that was a different story.

The sound of the horses clomping on the stable floor combined with some loud neighing made Olivia wince. The noise was hard to muffle.

"Where are you?" Clay asked.

None of your business. "Nowhere in particular. Out and about with a friend."

"I hear horses."

"That's because we're in his stable at the moment." She paused for a minute, a little startled by her need to explain herself. "Was there anything else?"

"No, no. I won't keep you from your *friend*."

His tone was sarcastic, implying he didn't believe her. He'd taken to texting almost every other day, and now a call. Most of the communication was not related to work. So far, she hadn't told anyone, not Jeff or Heather, or even Sandra. As long as Clay didn't draw her into another dispute over a patient, Olivia could cope with his odd behavior until he was gone. She counted down the days, even as she resolved not to let her first months on this new job be defined by Clay's behavior. If she came forward, she risked misunderstandings and gossip. She was certain she was right about those possibilities. But she couldn't say the texts, and now this out-of-the-blue call, didn't bother her.

"Everything okay?" Jeff asked when she rejoined the group.

"Everything's fine. I just had to answer a couple of questions from a colleague."

"Thanks for coming out to greet these newcomers with me," Jeff said. He glanced at Matt and Heather. "I thought better of being completely alone when I greeted these two. I'm a little out of practice."

"It's in your blood. You know what to do," Matt said. "How about Carson? Is he showing much interest in your new sleigh-ride venture?"

Jeff chuckled. "He thinks the sleigh ride is the same as stepping into a Christmas card, so that makes it an okay idea, but in terms of wanting to put himself on the back of a horse, no go."

"Ah, but Carson's mind is on basketball," Olivia said.

"And working on his videos." Jeff seemed to stand up a little straighter when he added, "He edits them and adds transitions. He's making real movies out of them."

Jeff's obvious pride pulled her out of lingering thoughts about Clay. "Jillian and I are counting on going to his basketball games after the winter break." She deliberately directed her next words to Jeff. "When it comes to his passions, Carson has amazing focus. It's one of the teenager's gifts." She shrugged. "Well, that's my opinion, anyway."

Jeff's soft smile melted her heart. "But you're right."

"I know one thing for sure," Matt said. "Carson is an all-around nice kid."

"Thanks," Jeff said. Then he looked at Olivia and chuckled. "I don't know why I said that. It's not like I had anything to do with it. His mom gets all the credit for that."

"Get real." Olivia's tone had gone from casual to firm. "You took on a badly injured boy who'd seen his mother take her last breath in front of him."

"That's a heavy load on your shoulders," Matt said.

Jeff nodded. "You should know. You've taken on a lot yourself."

Conscious that Heather had been turning her head, ping-ponging between her and Jeff and then Jeff and Matt, Olivia didn't want to leave. She wanted to stay with Jeff and listen to him talk about his plans for the new horses and the lodge. Most of all, she enjoyed seeing the affection in his eyes when he spoke about Carson. But… "I've gotta be online for my shift soon." She tilted her head toward her cabin. "Good thing it's not far."

Olivia backed out of the circle, ready to go, but not before telling them, "In my opinion, you're all amazing. I mean, who knew about all the ways you could put together good families?" She rushed out of the stable and started down the path.

She didn't want to think about Clay or even Heather and Matt right now. She stretched her imagination out many months to the summer and in her mind's eye, she saw Jillian and a horse. Jeff was in the picture, too, passing on riding tips to Jillian. She also fit somewhere in the picture of this almost family.

CHAPTER TWELVE

"WE NEED TWO TREES," Jeff explained as he propped up one of the fir trees in the group. He and Carson stood by one of a dozen or so clusters of cut trees leaning against a wooden stand with slots built to hold three or four trees each.

"Why two?" Carson asked.

"We need one of these tall ones for the lodge, and a smaller one for our cabin. We're doing the celebration on Christmas Eve—kind of an open house in the lodge, and then later, time with just the family."

Carson seemed pleased. "I didn't know you planned to have one in the cabin, too."

"Sure. The lodge has what we use as a big family room right now, but it's not where we live, our real home." Jeff wasn't quite ready to talk about the rest of his Christmas Eve plan, not until he knew for sure he could pull it off. "We have plenty of room in the lodge to have a tall showy tree for the shindig." He nodded toward Olivia, who was with Jillian down the row in a section displaying the smaller trees. "The tree for our cabin will be similar to the one they're getting."

"Right, right." Carson raised his eyebrows. "A lot going on at Christmas. The dinner at the lodge and brunch at the ranch on Christmas Day?"

"According to Heather, she's going for the kind of meal we grew up with. And other traditions, too." Might as well add one of Heather's favorite traditions. "If the snow isn't too deep and it's not too cold, Heather will organize a midday ride out on the trails for whoever wants to go. But that's optional."

Memories of Christmas poured in, specifically of the warm kitchen and when he was very young, grandparents joining them at the table for Christmas brunch.

Carson snorted. "That means you. You won't pass up that chance."

"You're right, I'll probably saddle up one of Heather and Matt's horses, but there will still be a houseful of folks for you to be with."

"Always lots of people hanging out with your sister and Matt." Carson pointed to Olivia, who had pulled out a tree and had it standing straight while Jillian circled around. "Maybe they found one they like."

Jeff smiled watching them. "If it passes Jillian's inspection."

Carson kept his gaze on Olivia and Jillian. "One day when we were waiting for the bus Jillian told me about being in the hospital last Christmas. She had a bad infection from being so weak." His voice was thoughtful when he added, "Heather stayed with her when her mom was working, but then Olivia slept in the hospital room with her at night."

"Olivia mentioned that, too. Look at them now." The two were all smiles and laughter as Olivia pulled out another tree and Jillian gave it a once-over. Jeff wished he could eavesdrop on their conversation and find out what was bringing on such hearty laughter. Olivia was never more beautiful than when she was chatting and laughing with Jillian—or Heather.

"Good thing you have the truck," Carson said. "I can haul the tree into their cabin and help them set it up."

"Olivia would appreciate that. I can lend a hand if you need it." Once again, Jeff noted Carson's strong streak of kindness. Earlier on the drive to this tree farm, he aimed his attention at Jillian and showed interest in everything she said. When Jeff thought about how he'd been at age fourteen, he remembered himself as a kid that adults said had good manners. Mom and Dad's doing, with no exceptions allowed. But he'd been less aware of other people and he avoided being around adults as much as possible. No one would have called him a mean kid, but when he was Carson's age he'd teased Heather a whole lot more than he'd listened to her.

Jeff drew his thoughts back to the present moment and that involved finding the right tree for the lodge. One after another, he pulled out each of the Fraser firs in a group of six or eight. Carson shook his head over the first few because the skimpy lower branches didn't pass his test. Finally, he pulled out one that towered over him. "Hey, I found one that's tall enough." He brushed his hand across the lower skirt of branches on the pretty tree. Full, too. "What do you think?"

"It'll work," Carson said, with almost too much enthusiasm. "Do you have stuff to put on it?"

"Uh, no. I thought we'd start with white

lights and go from there." Jeff had slipped so easily into including Carson in his language, *we* and *ours*. It was second nature to consider Carson or include him in this kind of talk. Not so for Carson, though, he noted. But he wouldn't dwell on that today. Jeff waved down the woman driving a vehicle pulling a wagon-style trailer. He and Carson each took an end and loaded it.

"I'm picking out a smaller tree in the next section over, and my friend and her little girl will pick one, too." He pointed to Jillian and Olivia, both bundled up in puffy coats and scarves. "They're with us. Not sure how long they'll need before they make their tough choice." As if confiding a secret, Jeff said, "The tree has to be perfect, you know."

The woman nodded and glanced at Carson. "Of course, it does. Give me your name, and I'll take this tree to the front until you're ready to go."

She rumbled down the narrow farm road.

Jeff and Carson navigated around the smaller trees and joined Olivia and Jillian. Carson put himself to work picking through the trees.

"We've narrowed our choice to these two

favorites," Olivia said, studying the trees they were considering. "We can't seem to settle on which to get."

"How about this? You choose the one you want," Jeff said, "and then Carson and I will take the other. That okay with you, Carson?"

"Sounds good to me," Carson said, glancing down at Jillian. "You know, the sooner we load the trees, the sooner we get the free hot chocolate in the building."

"Oh, good," Jillian said, hopping up and down. "Then whatever tree we *don't* get won't be far away. It will mean we have both of our favorites."

"Exactly." Olivia's eyes were bright and everything about her exuded happiness.

"Hey, you can have your cake and eat it, too," Carson said, making a funny face at Jillian. "So which will it be?"

Jeff almost laughed out loud. Carson's funny faces were making a comeback. The two trees were essentially identical. Finally, Jillian sighed and pointed at her choice. "That one. Is that okay with you, Carson?"

"You bet," Carson said. "We don't need that trailer, do we? We can carry these. It's not that far."

"Sure."

"Uh, were you planning to stop on the way home to pick up lights?" Carson asked.

"We need some, too," Jillian said. "Don't we, Mom?"

Olivia nodded and looked at Jeff expectantly.

Jeff shrugged. "Next stop, Landrum."

Jillian clapped her gloved hands. "Yay… this is so much better than last Christmas."

Same for me, Jeff thought. Last year he'd been one of a crew of sixteen on a tanker headed for Alaska.

The rest of the morning passed quickly. Olivia bought some new ornaments along with lights, but Jeff thought that for now he'd wait on everything but a slew of white fairy lights, which got Carson's vote. As they drove around and stopped for burgers and milkshakes, a nagging voice broke through. At some point during their time at the tree farm, Christmas started to weigh heavily on Jeff. He wanted to get Carson a special ornament that would travel with him over the coming years. When he'd packed up the apartment, he'd expected Carson to take some ornaments, maybe a couple he'd made in school.

But they were never mentioned, and Jeff hadn't found any. Strange to think the boy had never spent even one Christmas with his father. Then again, neither had Jillian.

After delivering Olivia's tree and helping her set it up in a stand, Jeff and Carson carried the bigger tree to the lodge and put it up, but left it bare while they took care of their small tree in the cabin. Daylight had faded and the late-afternoon darkness had taken over. Carson took charge of weaving strings of lights through the branches. "You bought enough lights to hang on the outside, didn't you? You've got lots of reservations between now and New Year's Day, so you want the place dressed up and cool."

"You got it. I got a kick out of booking so many couples and families coming to visit relatives over the next few weeks. I'm stringing lights on the porch and on the shrubs and trees in front."

"I can help with that," Carson said amicably. Then he abruptly turned and hurried into his room, leaving Jeff alone standing by the tree, now lit up with the white lights. It was awkward, but it wasn't the first time Carson either fell into silence or as he did just now: he walked away without explanation. Maybe he was changing his clothes or texting a friend. Whatever. Jeff shrugged it off and went into the kitchen and filled the soup pot with water to cook the spaghetti he planned for dinner.

A few minutes later, Carson came around the corner into the kitchen carrying a table-size artificial tree. A little old and faded, but it triggered a memory. "That's the tree from your apartment."

"Yeah, Mom got it for us."

Jeff recalled one year that he carried a battered card table out of Karen's storage locker in the basement of her building. It was a few days before Christmas and she'd covered it with a festive red-and-white cloth and put the table and the tree in front of her living room windows. She'd hung a star that Carson had made with Popsicle sticks and glitter when he was young. That star made the trip and was attached to the top. Later that same day Jeff shipped out for a four-month stint on a freighter. "It wasn't easy for your mom to get a live tree up three flights of stairs and into the apartment and then haul it out again."

"Except the year before last when you came back in time to have Christmas with us. Remember? You helped Mom get a real tree. I remember it smelled good, like being outside in the woods."

Jeff had clear memories of that year, because it had meant a lot to Karen to have a live tree. It made the holiday extra festive for her.

"I forgot all about that spruce tree. Now that you mention it, I recall having to lift that tree over my head to make it around the sharp corners on the narrow stairway."

Jeff had no recollection of packing up this artificial tree to move it to Wyoming, although he'd told Carson to take anything he wanted from his room. The teenager hadn't been attached to much and was kind of proud when Jeff suggested they donate the bulk of the furniture in the apartment to a local shelter. Most of his posters and sports gear and a model ship he'd built made the cut, along with boxes of books and photo albums and a couple of Karen's favorite framed prints from the dining room.

"I packed the tree myself in one of the bigger boxes," Carson said. "The branches come off and the lights are built in. The box isn't that big. When we unloaded the truck here,

I stuffed it in the back of my closet with the ornament I made in school." He frowned. "I forgot about it until Thanksgiving."

And hadn't thought to mention it. Ever. Or had he thought Jeff would discourage him from bringing it? Jeff shoved the question away. The answer didn't matter anymore. "No problem. Do you want to keep it in your room?"

Carson's shoulders drooped enough to be noticeable. Jeff took that as a subtle no. "Or, if we kept it out here, we could display it on the table in the corner near the door. Then we'll see it from outside." The live tree they'd just brought home was centered in the living room in front of a row of windows. The small table a few feet away had only a lamp that could easily be placed elsewhere.

Carson nodded and went to the corner and switched out the lamp for the tree and turned on the lights. "See? Perfect." Smiling, he took two bouncy steps back and stared at the tree on the table.

Finally, Jeff put his finger on what had been slightly off all day. The closer they got to the holiday, the more cheerful Carson became. He was overly cooperative, too. It was a facade, though, and Carson was trying to hide his real feelings behind it. He was coping and had a great ability to pretend he was doing fine. He probably was okay most of the time.

Jeff moved closer to Carson and put his hand on his back. "Christmas is another marker for the first time you do something without your mom. It's not your imagination, holidays can be tough."

"I hate it that she's gone." Carson leaned against the wall and slid down so he sat on the floor with his knees bent. "I hate it."

Jeff got down on the floor with him. "It's okay to hate it, and you don't have to pretend to be cheerful all the time." He sat next to the teenager, not touching him, but trying to be a presence.

"I didn't think it would feel so weird." His voice was strong as he kept going. "My mom made holidays fun. You weren't there, but she sometimes had an open house. She invited her friends and people from her job to the apartment. She made hot spiced wine."

The ache in Jeff's chest worsened by the second. "I remember she volunteered to organize the toy drive for the restaurant every year."

Carson nodded. "Yeah, it was important to her."

During those same years, Jeff tried to ignore the season, but memories of his childhood holidays on the ranch invariably showed up and messed with his moods, no matter where he was or how indifferent he pretended to be. He'd accepted those times as a consequence of choosing to be alone. Extolling his precious freedom. Here with Carson now, Jeff hardly recognized himself in those memories.

"When we were picking out the trees, I felt bad for her, because she was missing stuff she would have enjoyed," Carson said. "Same as Thanksgiving. Lots of people in a big house out in the country. She'd have had fun." Carson sighed. "And then it hits me. She won't *ever* do any of these new things."

"Sometimes it seems everyone is happy and carefree," Jeff said, Carson's grief weighing heavy on him, too. "Olivia and Jillian are excited about Christmas. My sister is over-the-moon happy, but last year was a whole different story."

Carson nodded. "You're happy, too. You're glad to be back here. For you, it's home."

"I hope one day you'll think of this state, this town as your home."

Carson shrugged. "It's okay here. The school is good. Owen is cool, and Mindy and Nina. Coach Voorhees, too. And basketball."

"Seattle has its cool side. The best part for me was meeting your mom and you." Jeff paused to consider what he wanted to say without patronizing Carson about how everyone agreed he'd adjusted to his losses remarkably well. Finally he said, "It's a good trait to have, Carson, to be okay wherever you happen to end up. But you can't be okay all the time."

"Did you ever feel bad when the holidays came around? I mean, you weren't with your family."

Jeff scoffed. "Only every year, and it was *always* my fault. And I never admitted how much I missed my old life." He took a deep breath. "If I had to do it over…" He didn't need to finish the sentence. Carson was no stranger to Jeff's regrets. Jeff puffed out his cheek and blew out the air. "I hope I've learned that lesson about connections once and for all."

They sat quietly side by side, okay if not

completely at ease in the silence, until a me-
tallic, burning smell filled the air. The screech
of the smoke alarm assaulted his ears. "The
pasta water!" Jeff scrambled to his feet and
raced to the kitchen. He grabbed a mitt and
dragged the pot off the burner, wincing
against the piercing sound.

Carson followed and opened the side door
into the kitchen to let the cold air in and smoke
out. He crouched down and held Winnie's
head close to his chest. A few seconds later,
relief. Quiet.

"That warning scream is the worst sound
in the whole world, isn't it, Winnie?" Carson
grinned at Jeff. "You forgot you turned on the
stove, huh?"

"Yep, that's what happened." Jeff dropped
the scorching pot in the sink and ran water
into it, sending steam billowing through the
air. "Keep the door open a minute more." He
shook his head and opened a bottom cabinet
where he kept his pots and pans. "Good thing
this cottage came with two soup pots."

Carson chuckled. "And I'm hungry." He
took out a jar of marinara from the cabinet.
"My mom used to say it was only newswor-
thy if I *wasn't* hungry."

"She was right about that." Jeff scanned the living room with their two lit-up trees. "You okay with where we put your tree?"

Carson didn't answer right away and Jeff didn't press. The teen nodded. "It's good." Then he opened the front door and ran outside in the cold, with Winnie close behind. A minute later he and the dog rushed back inside and into the kitchen. "It's like our windows are from a Christmas card photo. It will be even better when you get the lights up on the building."

Jeff smiled, glad Carson was satisfied with his tree—and the new, live one. "I need you to promise me something, Carson."

Carson's eyes opened wide in alarm. "What?"

"You can talk to me about your mom anytime you want to. If you'd rather talk to a counselor or someone else, all you need to do is say so and I'll make that happen." He paused and held Carson's gaze. "Promise you won't hold back?"

He didn't look at Jeff, when he said, "I, uh, talked to Olivia on Thanksgiving when we were out with the dogs. She asked if I was… you know…thinking about stuff in the past."

He quickly turned away and pulled out a loaf of crusty bread to heat up in the oven.

"I'm glad." Jeff filled the pot with water and turned on the burner. "Olivia has been through a thing or two in her own life. She understands." The smoke alarm had broken the flow of the conversation, but that didn't mean it was over. His mind drifted to Karen and he wished he could ask her what she'd want him to say or do to give her son the best shot to grow up okay. Without warning, his mom and dad joined his wishful thinking. What advice would they offer? Jeff wanted to do right by Carson. If only he knew how.

CHAPTER THIRTEEN

OLIVIA OPENED THE door and let Jeff in, surprised by his earlier text asking if he could talk to her. She embarrassed herself by how happy she was to say yes, come on over. Since Thanksgiving, things between them had been steadily warming up. And she wanted it. They'd hung several pictures in her cabin, competed at the dartboard a couple of afternoons, ordered in food to share. Even Heather, who'd run into the four of them at the diner on Merchant Street earlier in the week, thought they were like a typical family out for a spur-of-the-moment dinner. "Only happier than most," she'd added. And Heather should know.

It was undeniable, if scary, that riding around in Jeff's truck doing simple errands, even picking out Christmas trees, gave her an entirely new feeling. The fun of today's trip for the tree, hunting for the perfect lights and stopping for lunch were more than fresh experiences; they were firsts for her. In her marriage, she'd had only the faintest hint of the good side of being half of a couple. She'd been married barely two years and in that time her husband hadn't been interested in hanging out together as companions. As it turned out, he'd spent only enough time with her to woo her into marriage, but once the deed was done, she was on her own. In the weeks she'd known Jeff she'd felt more like part of a couple than she ever had before.

She quickly changed her clothes and took her hair out of the ponytail and let it hang loose. In the time it took to dump peanuts in a bowl and get out two bottles of Jeff's favorite dark beer, he was at her door and greeting her with a kiss her on the cheek. The first words out of his mouth were, "I know it's late—"

"Don't apologize. I was up and enjoying the fire and aimlessly clicking on movies to stream." And browsing sweaters she didn't need on a clothing site she rarely visited. But her mind was really on Jeff and the day they'd shared.

Now, studying Jeff's expression, she could see it matched the tone of his text, serious, maybe leaning toward worry. "You have things on your mind, don't you?"

Jeff offered a sad smile. "Yep, I suppose I do."

"And I bet they're all about Carson." She picked up the bottles on the counter and handed one to him. Leading him to the couch, she said, "Please, what's going on." She touched his arm. "Whatever you say is between us. You know that, right?"

"Not all my thoughts are on Carson." Jeff opened the bottle and took a gulp before he elaborated. "You take up a fair amount of space in my head."

"No kidding?" The same was true for her when it came to him, but she hesitated and then the moment was gone.

"But when it comes to Carson, I hope I'm not messing things up."

By the time he got done talking about Carson's completely reasonable, even expected show of grief, Olivia felt pressure behind her eyes, too. Only the hardest heart wouldn't be touched by Carson wrestling with his memories.

"Carson mentioned he'd talked to you about his mom on Thanksgiving."

She nodded and took a quick sip of beer. "I didn't tell you about it. I didn't want Carson to think I'd share things about him behind his back."

"No, of course not. I'm glad he talked to you. You have a good way with him...a rapport."

"From the outside, where I am, he's not that difficult to understand. And he's a strong kid. But even strong people crumble sometimes. He needs to know that."

Jeff nodded in a way that encouraged her to continue.

"I've just learned that lesson myself," Olivia said. "I'd bottle up my feelings and end up perplexed by the stress that caused."

With a deep frown wrinkling his forehead, Jeff said, "Carson hasn't said anything, but what if he'd rather not be part of the group here on Christmas Eve, or even at the ranch on Christmas Day?"

Surprised by Jeff's speculation, she responded quickly. "I seriously doubt that. He likes being with you. You're his rock. He's not going to stay home alone in his room, not when he can spend time with you—and the rest of us."

"I guess you're right. Even if he broods, he works it off shooting baskets." Jeff took a long swallow from the bottle. "He still gets twinges of pain in his ankle. He compared it to a hard pinch. But then he tells me his medical team assured him that's to be expected."

Olivia nodded toward the windows at the far side of the room. "Jillian and I see Carson out back at the hoop. He doesn't let a little snow stop him. If he makes the team, I promised Jillian we'll get to the games when I'm free to take her."

Jeff put the bottle on the coffee table and turned to face her. "Working here at home, you can't leave to take Jillian to Carson's games, but she can come with me. I set my own schedule and I plan to get to every single one."

Same as an attentive dad. That thought popped up and equally fast, she resisted Jeff's offer. He wasn't Jillian's dad. Carson wasn't her brother. She was presuming something she wasn't completely sure she was ready for. "I wouldn't want to impose. That's taking on a lot."

"Not really." Jeff frowned. "Think about it. It's like those two are growing up friends.

They're creating memories that include each other, right down to picking out Christmas trees."

"Yes," Olivia said, deliberately not adding the part about appearing to be siblings. Some days, this one in particular, a life with Jeff was so possible, so real, it left her shaky with doubt. She'd wonder if she was imagining things. But the extra beats of her heart when she'd seen his text were undeniably real.

Jeff spoke with a teasing smile, "Sharing good times… I admit it's surprised me a little. *You* surprised me." He leaned toward her and with a light touch ran his hand over her hair and let his fingertips rest on her cheek.

"Same here," she whispered. Her eyes closed at the sensation of his touch on her skin. She took in a breath and met him halfway.

The kiss was everything she'd ever hoped for. Gentle but without hesitation. He left no doubt and she let go and responded with an urgency she'd almost forgotten she could feel. They broke the kiss, but tightened their arms around each other and seconds later, Jeff found her mouth again.

Breathing hard, Olivia closed her eyes and

drew away long enough to press her cheek against his.

He covered her other cheek with his hand. "Your skin is silky and smooth. I always knew it would be. I've wanted to hold you in my arms for a very long time."

"Me, too." She pulled back and kissed him again, lightly this time, but he deepened the kiss. Olivia responded with a yearning for this passion to go on and on.

The trilling of the doorbell exploded the moment. She jumped to her feet. So did Jeff.

"It must be Carson." Jeff's voice was full of alarm as he took long strides to the front door and yanked it open. Then he took a quick backward step and held out his arm, as if warning her to stay where she was.

Too late. She was right behind him. Clay Markson was on her porch stomping snow off his boots. She moved forward and repositioned herself next to Jeff. "Uh, what's up, Clay? It's late."

Clay stared, shifting his gaze from her to Jeff and back again. "Aren't you on call tonight?"

Why would he think so? He was in charge of the schedule. Even if she were on call, she could still have a guest in her house. "No, I start my shift tomorrow at noon." She cleared her throat. "Was there something you needed, Clay?"

"Uh, no, Olivia. I haven't run into you at the hospital lately. Thought I'd stop by to say hello." His offered a tight smile.

"It's almost ten o'clock," Jeff said flatly. "Kind of late to ring someone's doorbell when they're not expecting you."

"My mistake." Clay shuffled back a few inches. "I saw your light on and assumed you were working. Maybe welcome a break for a chat." He craned his head and stared at the screens in the alcove as if he'd never seen the equipment before. "Everything working okay?"

"Yes, Clay, I'd report it if something was wrong." She took in a breath. "I have company right now." Fire blazing, beer on the coffee table. Oh, yeah, she had company. "This is my friend, Jeff Stanhope." She glanced at Jeff. "This is Dr. Clay Markson, the head of our radiology department." He'd better hear that as another way of saying he was her boss.

Jeff nodded. "I own this lodge, Dr. Markson. I live in the cabin on the other side of the main building." Jeff's tone was measured, respectful. But in case Clay missed the point, Jeff jabbed his thumb sideways.

"I see." Clay gave Jeff a look Olivia couldn't interpret. It wasn't hostile, but it fell short of friendly. In fact, for a split second, Clay's eyes were blank and suddenly a tiny frown appeared. "Well, sorry to bother you." He abruptly turned away and hurried down the steps. "Night."

Olivia closed the door and locked it as she let out the breath she'd been holding.

"I'm not buying this, Olivia. Who drops in at this time at night for a friendly chat? Without any warning. No call or text." Jeff glanced out the window.

She said nothing, but watched the taillights of Clay's car disappear around the curve of the drive.

"And what was the bit about driving by. I don't believe that for one second."

"I don't either, but there's something off…"

"There's plenty that's off here." Jeff's voice was full of emotion. "He was nasty and angry with you in a meeting with colleagues, and then he's a ho-ho-ho Santa at the Christmas Market," Jeff said. "Right?"

"The shift in his attitude was weird." She replayed each of the handful of times she'd seen him since the Christmas Market. "We had two staff meetings, and he was okay then. We had one disagreement on a scan, but he withdrew his objection."

"So he's erratic," Jeff said, widening his stance and crossing his arms over his chest.

"He texts me now and again for no particular reason. Then he called the other day when I was in the stable with you and Heather and Matt."

"Was there a professional reason for the call?"

She shook her head. "Not really."

"If he ever shows up here uninvited again, don't answer the door—you call me first. Or punch 911 and then call me." He grunted. "You need a dog over here, one to scare people off if need be." Jeff's tone wasn't light, so she knew he wasn't joking.

A dog was one thing. But no way could she call 911. "Let's not overreact, Jeff. For one thing, I can't get the police involved. I'm still the newcomer, and with the online shifts and the distances between medical systems, my colleagues don't know me very well." She caught his gaze. "That's why I haven't told anyone about his texts or calls. Besides, my boss knocking on my door isn't against the law."

Jeff stared into the room with worried eyes. "Well, according to him he happened to be driving past and saw your light on. And he decided to drop in? Doesn't make sense. The cabin is a long way from the road. Besides, this is not one of the busiest routes around here. What would you have done if I hadn't been here?" Jeff asked.

Olivia took a minute to think. But her answer was undeniable. "I'd have let him in. Like I said, he's my boss."

"Which is precisely why you should report him. The man could be dangerous. Even if he isn't, he has no business acting like this." With a huff, Jeff added, "I get your concerns. And can understand not calling the police, but at least promise me you'll tell the administrator about this. Or the surgeon you're friendly with. If you won't leave a paper trail, at least create a verbal one."

As if stuck, they hadn't moved away from the door and back to the living room. She didn't want their lovely evening to end on this sour note. Not after…after the best kisses of her life. No exaggeration. She wasn't worried about Clay, but she understood why Jeff was. It was her boss messing with her job that grabbed her attention. Not to mention what was happening to Clay himself. The empty eyes, the weird texts. These were symptoms. Something was seriously wrong with her colleague.

"Yes, you're right. I'll definitely tell the administrator." Olivia thought about her coworkers. "I also have to consider people I work with. What if he's dropping in on other docs and nurses? I'll call Sandra in the morning."

She couldn't leave it at that. She linked her arm through Jeff's and started back to the couch. "*A couple of coworkers have told me* he wasn't always like this. Especially being so argumentative, but then acting like nothing happened. From what I hear, most people blamed the death of his wife for the changes. But maybe he's never recovered. He's become so hard to work with, everyone is happy he's agreed to retire without a fight. But no one seems to think he's dangerous." When they got to the couch, she gave Jeff's sleeve a tug. "C'mon, let's finish our beer. Maybe pick up where we left off?"

Jeff frowned, but then he smiled. "Okay. But I'm sleeping on your couch tonight. Don't try to talk me out of it."

"Really? That's not necessary."

He stirred the fire, and then rested his elbow on the mantel. "Yeah, it is. If I went back to my cabin, I'd be awake all night anyway. I'd be listening for a car to come up the drive."

With Jillian asleep upstairs, she had to admit she was relieved.

"I'd bet that Sandra will have to take some action now," Jeff said. "She'll have no choice."

The longer she mulled it over, the more she agreed. Clay's long career was going to come to an end before his scheduled retirement, less than a month away.

"I still think you need a dog." Jeff left the fireplace and sat down next to her. "I'm serious. What do you think?"

Olivia didn't have an answer for that, but she'd had another kind of animal on her mind all day. Now was as good a time as any to talk about it. "I have an idea I'd like to run by you." She smiled. "In fact it's something I really can't do without you."

With a flirtatious smile, Jeff said, "Tell me more."

OLIVIA PULLED THE last sheet of goodies out of the oven, immersed in the cookie bake. The best part was being with friends. On the other side of the counter, though, the measuring, mixing, rolling and cutting only reminded her of the reasons she preferred bakeries to baking. She'd been on call from midnight to noon, and unlike other nights, it had been busy with only a chance for a couple of cat-naps on her couch between cases.

With dozens of cookies cooling on racks and others set aside and ready to be divided and packed into containers, Jen and Stacey had taken over supervising the kids' decorating job, leaving the final cleanup to Heather and Olivia. That was fine. She liked having her hands in warm, soapy water. Besides, she had something to talk over with Heather. No, two things.

"Is there a way you could make an excuse to come outside with me?" Olivia whispered to Heather, keeping her voice low. "Could we walk the dog or something?"

"Sure. You sound serious. Grab your jacket and mine." Heather peeked into the dining room, where the kids were busy turning tree-shaped sugar cookies into works of art with green-and-red frosting and sprinkles. "Hey kids, Olivia and I are going to get rid of all this trash and then let Scrambler run around."

They responded in unison with "Okay."

Olivia slipped into her jacket and she and Heather each picked up a bag of trash. Scrambler was already at the door, ready to bolt.

"Okay, what's wrong?" Heather asked as soon as she'd closed the door behind her.

Olivia immediately regretted making her friend worry. "Oh, no, it's not that kind of serious—you know, like bad news." She laughed nervously. "It's actually about happy stuff. It's an odd request, especially for me, but could you take me to see that horse you ride. I can't remember her name."

"You mean Pebbles. She's Matt's sister's horse, and officially belongs to Lucy. Matt has a horse designated for Nick, too, but he's not as eager to learn as Lucy is. They'll both be riding this spring." After they disposed of the trash, she led the way to the stable and corral. "So, tell me, why the sudden curiosity about Pebbles?"

"It's not specifically about that horse. We were together in the stable the day of the welcome party for Bonnet and Sassafras. That was fine. But I stayed away from the two horses. I was afraid to get close."

"I didn't expect you to," Heather said. "Why is this important now?"

Olivia stopped walking and folded her hands over her chest. "I've wrapped Jillian in an invisible safety cloak—you know, like the protection suits we have handy for chemical emergencies. That's what I've done." Impatience bled into her voice. No surprise, since she was frustrated with herself. "And it has to stop."

"You've been resistant to loosening the ties," Heather said, "but who can blame you? You've had to protect your daughter."

"That's not as true anymore." Olivia pointed in the direction of the stable. "Jillian used to talk about going to riding camp, but now we live next to a stable. A couple of Clydesdales are already part of the landscape. By next summer, Jeff will have new horses and a school to go with them. All of that became clear like a photograph of the future." She took a deep breath. "And I'm going with it."

Heather bowed and applauded. "This is great! When I was first getting to know Jillian, all she wanted to talk about was what it was like to be a kid in Wyoming. She thought I spent most of my time horseback riding. Nothing else aroused her curiosity, not even the sheep."

"I remember her grilling you," Olivia said. "At the time, seeing her interested and engaged, your talks were music to my ears."

Heather spread her arms wide. "And oh, her questions ran the range…my saddle, the trails, cleaning stalls and taking care of Velvet's coat."

"I made promises, Heather. I told her once she was in remission, a horse would be in her future."

"Ah, I get it. The time is coming to make good on your promise," Heather said as they turned the corner around the barn, "whether you're completely ready or not."

Olivia pointed to the empty corral. "Are they inside today?"

"These critters don't mind cold weather—up to a point. But this time of year we bring them in when the sun sets—at the latest. Matt saw to them while we were baking."

When they went inside the stable, Pebbles lifted her head and moved around like her feet were dancing. Heather went right to her and the horse nudged her shoulder. Olivia hung back and watched her friend stroke the horse's face and smooth her hand down Pebbles's neck. "You miss me, don't you, Pebbles?" Heather murmured.

"It's a special bond, isn't it?" Olivia said, thinking about how devoted Jillian was to Tulip, Olivia's one concession to having a family pet. "With you and Jeff as role models, and Matt, too, Jillian will learn to ride from the best." Carson might be teaching Jillian to shoot baskets, but Olivia was certain her daughter's heart had more room for horses.

"Since whatever block exists is entirely mine," Olivia said, "I have to be okay around horses myself. That's why I wanted to come out here and get a glimpse of what you see when you're around these beauties—and I can see they are beautiful creatures."

"Okay, then, Pebbles, the Appaloosa, prefers life outside, and we sometimes put a coat on her. Snow doesn't bother her, or Bo, Matt's horse. Bo is watching us now." She moved to the other horse's stall and patted the top of his head. "That's his favorite spot for a little love. These two enjoy each other's company." She pointed to the others who were nearby.

Olivia had heard about one named Night Magic. Heather went to her stall to greet the nearly all black horse. Like Pebbles, Night Magic lowered her head and greeted Heather with a light nudge. "I'll be riding her most of the time now."

Seeing Scrambler sitting at the open door of the stable, his tail thumping and listening to Heather talk to Night Magic in a low voice, her thoughts came together. Yes, with each day her conviction strengthened. She wanted this life for Jillian. "So, what if I were to get a horse for Jillian now? Let Jillian learn to take care of her—or him—through the winter and start riding her horse in the spring. Sound reasonable to you?"

Heather's face lit up in happiness and then she laughed. "Reasonable? Better than that, it sounds wonderful." She leaned toward Olivia. "And very brave."

"Your brother gets some credit. I see him with the Clydesdales and he patiently answers all Jillian's questions. Kind of boosted my confidence. Or, maybe he's helped me trust that Jillian can enjoy horses and also be safe." She held up her arms defensively. "I know, there's always some risk."

"Jeff's got the magic touch." Heather gestured to Olivia. "Come closer and give Night Magic a pat or two. You're a stranger, but she won't hold that against you. She's a good-natured horse, so you can build a degree of trust in no time." Heather stopped for a minute and then tilted her head. "Trust is a big part of dealing with horses. It works both ways."

Olivia reached out and stroked the horse's shiny neck, surprised by the warmth. "You're so smooth and soft," she whispered. "I know I can get used to having one of you around." She turned to Heather. "I'm going to give this a little more thought, but I'm about ninety percent there. Then I'll talk to Jeff."

"Good plan, Olivia."

"Speaking of trust, it won't surprise you that at first, I didn't trust your brother, even when he was so generous with me." Olivia waited for Heather's reaction. Not getting one, she added, "I'm not admitting anything you didn't already know."

"I had to learn to trust him again myself." Heather shook her head. "I was blunt with him. I will probably never understand why he turned his back on me for so long. It made me wonder if this homecoming was for real, lodge or no lodge. But watching him with Carson softened me up."

"You've forgiven him now, haven't you?" Olivia followed Heather as she approached some of the other horses in the stables, the ones Matt and Heather had bought, sold or leased.

"Could be the perfect horse for Jillian is in this group," Heather said, ignoring her question. "I'm not as familiar with them, but Matt will know."

Olivia took a step sideways and greeted the horses, who snorted and neighed back and moved restlessly. "You're not impressed, I see," Olivia said to them, "but what can I say. Hopefully, you won't be strangers to me for long." She felt a little foolish trying to sound conversational, the way Jeff sounded when he greeted the Clydesdales.

"You said you had two things you wanted to talk to me about," Heather said, as she gave one of the horses a pat. "Is Jeff the other topic on your mind?"

"Naturally you'd see through me." Olivia mulled over what she wanted to say, but it was jumbled in her mind. "I've been thinking so hard about this for the last couple of days. Even when I was measuring flour and sugar and dumping it into the mixing bowl." Olivia sighed. "In spite of myself and my fears, I'm falling in love with your brother… Oops, I should put that in past tense. It's already happened."

Heather let out a loud hoot. "Finally, the truth is out. You didn't fool me. Neither did my completely transparent brother. You were pretty cozy on Thanksgiving. Every time I see you two, what's happening is written all over both of you. You give each other that certain look."

Warmth rushed through Olivia as her heart fluttered in her chest. "Is that so? You never said anything."

"He brings you up in almost every conversation," Heather said, "but I was waiting for one of you to come right out and say something."

"He sort of grew on me," Olivia said, with a laugh.

"I think that's how love happens a lot of the time." Heather had a dreamy look in her eyes when she said, "Sounds kind of magical, huh? Or maybe charmed?"

"I suppose that remains to be seen," Olivia said. "We haven't talked much about, you know, what's next."

"Well get on with it," Heather teased. "Wow, you'll have a new family. Like me."

"I always thought I'd have more children…" Olivia stopped musing on that. She hadn't meant to say those words out loud. Instead, she said, "But, really, no matter what happens with your brother, my life is already looking up."

"Oh, stop. It's okay to crave it all, Olivia, including a great love. You deserve it." Heather's smile was amused and a little sly. "Something tells me the idea of more children in our lives is a conversation for another day. We better start back, anyway. The kids will be coming out here to find us if we don't show up soon."

Olivia studied the horses one more time before following Heather outside. "For so long, I've accepted that I had my one and only shot with love and family. That was it for me." She sighed softly. "I got stuck on the notion I wouldn't survive being abandoned like that ever again. But after dealing with Jillian's cancer and seeing her get a second chance at a full life, I wonder why that can't be true for me." She stopped and touched Heather's arm. "Turns out I'm stronger than I thought."

"And *you* get to decide what you want in your life."

"Much to my surprise," Olivia said, warmed by optimism. "I can hardly wait to see what's coming down the road."

"Good for you." Heather bumped her shoulder against Olivia's. "You've made room in your life for a new love."

"Seems that way." Olivia paused. "So, what do we do with this houseful of cookies now that we've baked them?"

"Oh, I suspect Stacey and Jen are already dividing them up. Try each kind and stock your freezer. They won't last long if you share with Carson and Jeff." She smiled. "Tell the truth now. Have we converted you to a cookie baker?" Heather's eyes were full of fun. "Did you enjoy it so much you can't wait to do it again next year?"

"Oh, you know me too well," Olivia teased back. "Not a chance. It was great being with all of you, though." She hesitated for a few seconds. "I'll never be much of a baker, or a cook, but I'm intrigued with Jen's wool. This winter, I may join one of her spinning groups."

Heather laughed. "You can learn to work with wool from Jen's charming sheep to go with your new charmed life."

Giving Heather a nudge with her shoulder, Olivia chuckled. "I knew you'd understand."

CHAPTER FOURTEEN

"THIS IS MUCH more exciting than I ever imagined." Olivia slipped her hand in Jeff's and gave it a quick squeeze as they walked toward Trey's corral. "It's because of you—and your sister—that I can take a leap of faith like this."

"I'm glad. I'm getting a kick out of it, too, actually." Jeff had been born for missions like this and was confident he'd help find a terrific horse for Jillian.

Trey, a man about Jeff's age, was waiting for them, along with three horses in his corral. When Olivia had posed her idea the other night, Jeff talked it over with Matt. Once again, Trey's name came up.

With a friendly smile, Trey nodded at Jeff, but spoke directly to Olivia. "I hear you're gonna bring a smile to your little girl's face this Christmas, huh?"

Jeff was amused by Trey's slightly exaggerated twang. He'd bet the guy brought out that particular accent when he wanted to impress a good-looking woman. With her green hat bringing out the color of her hair, Olivia was especially pretty that day. Maybe because her eyes sparkled.

"Jeff tells me you're the person I should see. I've been reluctant to catch horse fever for lots of reasons," Olivia said, "but I have faith in the advice I'm getting these days. Jeff assures me we can find a good-natured horse for my daughter."

Trey gave Jeff a quick glance before addressing Olivia. "From what Jeff said, you have some special circumstances involved."

"I thought it best to tell Trey about what Jillian has been through. And be open about your worries for her," Jeff blurted.

"It's okay. I don't mind talking about it." She looked at Trey and shrugged. "I'm just trying to minimize the risks. I thought it might be best—even safer—if Jillian had time to get to know her horse before she starts riding. Or, maybe it's selfish on my part. I'll feel better if I also get used to having the horse around."

As Jeff watched Olivia, he thought about how much she'd changed over only a couple of months' time. She exuded happiness that expanded by degrees every time he saw her. He had the same feeling about goings-on inside his heart. He'd been waking up with a smile every day for a while now.

"From what Jeff said, your girl is eleven years old and eager. That's probably the ideal time to get a horse." Trey nodded toward the corral. "I've got three good candidates here. All are experienced with young riders. Any one of them is likely to be a good fit."

Jeff went ahead to do his own inspection. He trusted Trey, but he trusted himself just as much. In the distance, closer to the shelter, Jeff spotted at least two dozen horses, among them a handful of Clydesdales and a couple of powerful Belgian draft horses. Jeff didn't interrupt Trey, but listened in as the dealer named and described the three.

It didn't take long for Jeff to have a hunch about one, a Morgan named Toffee. He almost laughed out loud. Heather would have called her a fancy-pants horse, a term reserved for horses with especially swishy tales and thick manes. That's what Toffee was like. Her coat fit her name, but her mane and tail were a rich dark brown, with two lighter markings on her face. She was eyeing Trey and took a couple of steps in his direction before stopping and again inching toward the fence. Jeff was drawn to curious horses and this one was certainly that.

The other Morgan, a little smaller than her two companions, had a grace about her, and the white-and-brown Appaloosa was a beauty, like Pebbles. When he was ready to buy more horses, he'd know where to shop first. Olivia was listening carefully to Trey's descriptions and the stats about their ages and previous owners. As far as Jeff could observe, Trey wasn't steering her in any particular direction, but he figured Trey probably leaned toward one horse over the others. Jeff expected the dealer had strong hunches like he did, about which horse would be the best fit for a particular customer.

Finally, Olivia turned to him. "Trey tells me they're all healthy, young and good-natured. I don't know how to make up my mind. What do you think?"

Jeff cocked his head and gave his lips a little smack. "I don't know if I should interfere…"

"Oh, don't be coy," Olivia mocked with a scolding tone. "You have an opinion, I'm sure of it. You always have opinions."

Trey chuckled, and so did Jeff. "Okay, if you insist. I've taken a shine to Toffee," Jeff said, "because she's hanging around as if she knows something's going on and it could involve her."

"Likely so," Trey said. "If it's any help, Olivia, I agree with Jeff. Something tells me Toffee would do well with a new rider. And she loves attention." He gestured to the other two. "Of course, so do these two."

Olivia nodded. "I had a feeling about her, too. It's not only that she's a beauty. I could see Jillian with her."

Trey's backward steps created a couple of feet of distance. "Why don't you think it over? I'll be around and ready to deliver any one of these beauties to your place."

Jeff explained that the horse would spend these few days before Christmas on the ranch with Matt and Heather, who'd agreed to keep the new horse with them until Christmas morning. "There's no way to hide a new horse at the lodge. If she's at the ranch, we can stick a bow on her on Christmas Day and lure Jillian to the stable."

"Sounds like fun," Trey said. "But, it's a big decision. Think it over. Take a walk." He pointed to a line of trees. "I plow the road where those trees are so my kids can ride during the winter. I'll be here when you get back."

"Good idea," Jeff said, turning to Olivia. "Okay?"

Olivia answered by glancing over Jeff's shoulder at Toffee before turning away.

They walked in silence at first, the only sound coming from their boots on the snow. Sunlight broke through the cloud cover, and the snow in the fields and on the buildings glistened. When they were a distance away from the corral and the house, Olivia stopped and raised her arms to the sides and spun around. "It's a winter wonderland. So beautiful."

"It's such fun to watch you enjoying yourself." Jeff cupped Olivia's face in his palms. "Your new life hasn't lost its sheen. I love that about you." He kissed her lightly. "I love you."

"My life couldn't have more sheen, as you say." Olivia flashed an intimate smile.

He shook his head and lowered his hands, amused by her expression. As Matt once said about his feelings for Heather, Jeff had it bad for Olivia.

"For a while I was afraid my job was going to

be the wild card that soured everything," Olivia said, "maybe threatening what I hoped to create here. But that changed with Clay's abrupt departure. I should call it his retirement."

"I feel a lot better now that he's no longer in a position to bully you." Once Olivia called the administrator, who confronted Clay, it was over. The doctor retired immediately and sought help.

"A sad way to end a long career—and I believe the doctors and nurses when they tell me what a good colleague he once was. That's why so many are hoping for the best for him. Thankfully, now, he'll be getting all the help he needs." She didn't want to speculate more about Clay's problems, so she returned to the subject of Toffee.

"As horses go, Toffee is quite the charmer." As Olivia stared out into the field, Jeff's thoughts jumped ahead to Christmas Day at the ranch and Jillian's joy when she realized her dream was coming true. Most of all, he looked forward to repeating history and turning Jillian into a skilled rider, the same way he'd taught Heather. It would be part of the fun of their shared life.

He leaned forward and kissed Olivia again. "Let's go buy that horse."

"HERE WE ARE AGAIN," Matt said pointing to Toffee, "busy with horse business."

"Nothing new about that," Olivia said, "except that this is the first time I'm a part of it." She might not be schooled in the way of these four-legged pals, but she recognized beauty when she saw it. Toffee was a horse right out of a storybook, with a personality to match.

"No regrets?" Jeff asked.

"Not even a hint of one." Everything felt right, from this gift to Jillian to the upcoming holiday and to her life with Jeff. With his help, she'd get used to Toffee, who had been put into the corral after Trey delivered her an hour or so ago. "Toffee seems calm and happy, too."

"That she does," Heather said "If you can tear yourself away from the fancy-pants horse, come up to the house with me."

Olivia wasn't eager to leave Jeff and Matt—or Toffee. But then she rarely said no to Heather.

As they walked toward the house, Heather explained she had a box of ornaments she wanted Olivia to look through. "Jeff took a few of them the other day, but I wanted you to have a chance to see if there were any you'd like for your tree."

"Oh, good. Our tree is a little sparse," Olivia said. "We had such fun on the day the four of us went to the tree farm and picked out the trees."

"That's what Jeff said, too." Heather grinned. "Are you and my brother more or less a done deal now?"

Olivia snorted. "What a phrase. But if you're asking if we're talking about making a life together with the kids, I'm pretty sure we're headed that way. I love him, he loves me." They hadn't exactly worked out every detail yet, but Olivia thought she and Jeff were committed to the same path.

"I can't say Matt and I didn't see it coming," Heather said smugly. "We're such romantics and you'd already told me you'd fallen for him. You're not showy about it, but anyone can see the spark between you two."

"Maybe we'll be one big family soon. For real. I don't think we'll wait too long. The kids know each other and get along." Olivia laughed from the happiness that she carried around with her like an unexpected shiny gift. "I've never had any of these emotions." When she and Jeff got down to serious talk about their future, it would be so different from her first time, when it had all the joy of fulfilling an obligation. Marriage had seemed like something she was supposed to do. But given another chance, she'd say those vows with her whole heart.

"You sound like a wedding will soon be in the works. Wow, you don't waste time."

"No, no, nothing like that… I mean, not yet, but I'm sure it won't be too long before we start planning what's ahead for us."

When they reached the house, Heather brought out a box of ornaments and Olivia chose a half dozen tiny clear glass birds, a perfect addition for their small tree. She gave Heather a quick hug and the two started walking back to the corral. Talking with Heather about her hopes for a life with Jeff led her to consider how much had changed. And all for the better.

The men were standing at the fence as Olivia and Heather approached. Olivia was about to say something, but then she heard Jeff's voice.

"I'm in no rush. Olivia might not feel the same way about this, but I think it's obvious we need to take it kinda slow," Jeff explained. "Carson's had enough to contend with, so I can't suddenly spring anything else on him. We have to see how this goes."

Olivia froze in place. She glanced at Heather, whose expression remained unchanged. Had she not heard Jeff?

Jeff turned and straightened; he'd noticed her and Heather. "Ready to go?" Jeff's voice was as casual as always.

Unable to speak to him, she nodded and glanced at Matt. "What about Toffee? Will she be okay now in the stable?" The strain in her voice was obvious, at least to Matt. He stared at her a second too long before answering.

"She'll be settled in very soon." He smiled. "We don't want the nosy twins seeing their new friend before Christmas."

"Toffee will be fine." Jeff smiled. As he went to leave, he held out his hand to Olivia.

All smiles, Olivia thought, as she stepped to the side, hoping it wasn't too obvious that she avoided Jeff's touch. The man had no idea what his words had conveyed.

As he drove through town, Jeff kept up his

talk about Christmas and the video production software he'd bought as a gift for Carson. The new monitor had already arrived and been hidden in the lodge. Olivia's contributions were updated speakers and a microphone.

"Do you need to pick up anything while we're out?" Jeff asked, his voice tentative now. "We can stop at the market in town."

She stared out the passenger window, seeing little but her reflection. "No. I don't need a thing."

"Okay. Just offering."

As soon as he stopped the truck, Olivia opened the door and got out and walked toward her cabin.

He followed her. "Olivia? What's up with you? Did Heather say something to upset you?"

Incredible. "Heather? Are you kidding? Why don't you play back what *you* said to Matt?"

Jeff's eyes narrowed, his lips pursed. "What are you talking about?"

"I know a brush-off when I hear one." She paced back and forth in frustration. "We went from kisses on the couch and declarations of love to you telling Matt we're taking it slow."

"Olivia, what's your point? I'm confused."

"No, you're not." Olivia put more distance between them. "Do you really think I'd do anything to hurt Carson? You told Matt you weren't sure how I feel about this. Well, why didn't you ask me? Because this feels much more like you're pulling away. And I can't… I won't…" She stopped talking because her thoughts were too jumbled to find the right words. Flashes of painful moments from her past were mixed with warnings that she was misreading the present situation. She headed for the cabin.

"I am *not* pulling away. And I'm not backing down." Jeff's voice carried across the parking lot. He jogged up the path to her cabin. "What's happened, Olivia? Why are you sabotaging us?" Jeff came close to the porch. "That's what you're doing."

"I can't talk to you now." She hurried inside the cabin and burst into tears. Confused? That's what her father had told her mother when he disappeared for good.

Only when Jillian came inside did Olivia pull herself together and pretend everything was the same. She thought about Toffee and imagined Jillian's face when her daughter saw her very own horse for the first time. At least she knew Jeff would take care of Toffee. "Hey, sweetie," Olivia said, "let's fix dinner. I'm on call tonight. Have to log in at six."

And then she'd get through the holidays.

"YOU BEAT ME AGAIN." Jeff threw back his head and groaned, "Your hand must be completely healed now. I don't stand a chance."

"You're not my only Ping-Pong challenger, ya know," Carson said. "You'd be surprised how good Mindy is. And Owen and Nina. You're better at pool. Olivia, is, too, but not as good as you." Carson laughed in a teasing sort of way. "You don't stand a chance at darts, though."

"Don't remind me." Jeff looked around and was pleased with what he saw. "We've gotten a lot of use out of this room, haven't we?" Jeff said. "We've got a fire going. We can have popcorn…" His focus changed when he caught the sweep of headlights coming around the curved road.

"Maybe that's the last of your guests," Carson said.

Jeff had four cabins filled, with the fifth confirmed, but they hadn't arrived or texted.

He'd been about ready to give up on them. He grabbed his jacket and went out to the porch. An older man and a woman were getting out of their car.

"Hope we're not too late," the man said. "We got lost on the way here."

Jeff assured them the room was waiting for them. When the man mentioned his wife had some trouble walking, he'd assigned them to the cabin on the flattest ground, where they could park close to the front door. Not a trace of snow was left behind on the stairs or porch. The couple was only staying this one night and leaving early the next morning.

"Come inside," Jeff said, "and I'll sign you in."

When the couple entered the lodge, they immediately reacted to the room.

"This room is so festive," the woman said. "Your tree is beautiful. It's like an old-fashioned postcard."

Carson introduced himself and the woman went farther into the room. "We've been spending a lot of time in here since we put the tree up," Carson said. "We play Ping-Pong, so the lodge gets a lot of use."

"Nothing beats a roaring fire, son," the man said.

The man followed Jeff to the counter and the check-in took only a few minutes. He circled the cabin on the map and gave his guest directions and the key. "Motion sensor lights will come on when you drive up the path. You can't miss it."

They joined Carson, who was nodding along as the woman chatted about going to see their son and his family and planned to arrive the next day, Christmas Eve.

"If we don't see you again, you have a good Christmas now," the woman said. Talking to Jeff, she said, "You have a fine son here. You enjoy every minute with him. They grow up so fast. Before you know it, you're driving hundreds of miles to spend a few days with him—and his family."

Jeff smiled and nodded, but Carson's face had turned an embarrassed pink. Without knowing it, though, his guest handed him an opening to talk to Carson about what was on his mind. The couple left and Jeff and Carson stood on the porch until they turned down the drive.

"I'll get the popcorn," Carson said, closing the lodge door behind them.

"The popcorn can wait." Jeff paused, but not for long. "Come sit down. I want to talk to you."

Carson looked a little pained. If Jeff hadn't known better, he'd have thought the boy's ankle was acting up. But that wasn't the cause of the expression. Carson always winced a little if he thought he'd be put on the spot. Given what happened with Olivia yesterday, Jeff would choose his words carefully.

Jeff sat on one end of the couch and pointed to the other end. "Seems like a long time has passed, but it was only a couple of weeks ago when you and I had that talk about your mom and how much she loved you."

"I remember." Carson's face was still red. "Does what just happened with that lady bother you?"

"Not at all," Jeff responded quickly. "That's the thing I'm getting to. You see—"

"But I'm not your son," Carson blurted, "and people like her will always assume I am."

Not expecting the conversation to take this turn so soon, Jeff regrouped and stated the obvious. "No, not biologically. But if you only envision family that way, my sister would never be the twins' mom. You can see for yourself how she feels about them—and they love her back. That's all that counts." Jeff got up and took the poker and pushed the logs around to get the fire roaring again. "In that earlier conversation I pointed out that you and I hadn't been at this relationship stuff for very long. You had the biggest loss any young person can have, and you didn't know me all that well to begin with." Jeff peered into Carson's face, trying to read his expression. "Right?"

"I suppose." Carson scooted to the edge of the couch and let his hands dangle between his knees. "Back when I was in the hospital, you never told me why you wanted to be my guardian," Carson pressed. "I was confused. I figured it had to be because you felt guilty about my mom dying. I didn't remember much at first, but I never blamed you. I know it wasn't your fault that she was killed."

"No, no, Carson, it wasn't ever about feeling guilty." He sat back down on the couch and turned to face Carson. "I want to be as honest with you as I can. I'll probably always wonder if I could have done something to change what happened that day. What if we'd

left one minute later? Or, we'd taken a different route to the ferry dock." Jeff sighed. "Use-
less conjecture. But guilt never played a part
in what made me want to be your guardian."

"You asked me if it was okay if you talked
to the social worker in the hospital. Why?"

"You're my good friend's son." Jeff extended his open hands toward Carson. "I did
know you…in a way. I didn't want anyone deciding what was right for you without being
involved."

"So? That didn't mean you had to take me
in."

"Whoa… I don't view it like that." This
conversation had taken detours he hadn't figured on. "Let's start over. Since you asked
the question, I'll come at this from another
angle. I suppose I could have walked away.
You would have gone to foster care. And I'd
never have been able to live with myself."
Those words hung in the air. Carson might not
understand them now, but one day he would.
"The alternative was clear. I wanted to do
right by your mom—and do the best thing
for you."

Jeff paused and nervously ran his fingers
through his hair. Carson nodded, but he of-

fered no other response. That was okay with Jeff. He had more to say.

"The first priority was to get you home and back on your feet. Then I needed to change jobs—not a big sacrifice." Jeff scoffed. "To tell you the truth, it lit a fire under me to get some direction in my life." Jeff gestured around the room. "Not too shabby, huh?"

Carson snickered. "Pretty cool."

"So, you were right, love didn't have much to do with any of these decisions. Not when we started." Jeff pointed to himself. "For me, though, things changed. Just now, when our guest told me I have a fine son, it was the easiest thing in the world for me to agree."

Carson gave him a skeptical look. Jeff could have sworn he saw a subtle eye roll. "Seriously? You rolled your eyes at me?"

Another little eye roll. "C'mon, that woman was just being polite."

Jeff waved his finger back and forth. "Not true, Carson. *You* were being polite." Jeff paused to let that sink in. "So, here's what I'm trying to say. I want you to be my son… for real." Jeff exhaled. "If you agree to let me be your dad."

Carson's eyes widened and his chin dropped in shock. "You mean, like adopt me?"

Jeff smiled at what he interpreted as Carson's pleasant surprise. "Yeah, Carson, adopt you." He took in a breath and his nostrils filled with the scent of the fire. He tapped his chest. "I want to be your dad. In your heart I want you to know that you can count on me, like a dad."

Carson's face still put his shock on display, but Jeff noted a hint of happiness in his blue eyes.

"We didn't talk about love before, but time has changed that. I love you, Carson. I've never been a dad, but I'm sure this is what it feels like to love a child."

Silence.

"You can think about it, Carson. Legally, I can't do this on my own. You're not a baby, so you need to agree to it. It's a big step for you, too."

Carson shifted in his corner of the couch. He shook his head. "Not that big."

Jeff took that in, but stayed silent. He sensed Carson had more to say.

"I didn't know you were thinking about

this," Carson said. "I never had a dad, but you already act like one."

Mission accomplished.

"So, when would this happen?" Carson asked. "We'd go to court, right?"

Jeff laughed. "First stop, a lawyer's office. We'll take it from there, but I assume we'll probably go to court. How about we invite Heather and Matt and the twins to come with us?" He paused. "If you're sure you're in."

"Oh, yeah, I'm in," Carson said. He thumped his fingers on his knee. "So, does this mean I'm supposed to call you Dad?"

Jeff had anticipated that coming up and had a simple answer ready. "That's one hundred percent up to you," Jeff said. "Let's not worry about *supposed to*." He put air quotes around the phrase. "I'm committed to you for always. It doesn't matter what you call me."

"I'm kinda used to thinking of you as Jeff," Carson said thoughtfully. "Maybe I can try something else." He had a faraway look in his eyes. "I knew a couple of adopted kids in my school in Seattle. But they were babies when their parents got them."

"This is an entirely different situation, which

is why I don't want you to worry about what you call me."

"Uh, did you tell Heather or Olivia or anybody else about adopting me?"

"Not yet." Jeff wanted to tell Olivia and would soon, as soon as they were talking again. "I needed to hash it out with you first. No one is going to be surprised, I can tell you that. Especially Heather. You're already a full-fledged member of her family whether you like it or not."

"Oh, I like it." Carson jumped to his feet and hurried to the kitchen. "I'm hungry. I'll put the popcorn in the microwave."

With Carson out of the room, Jeff stared into the fire. A legal document binding him to Carson probably wouldn't change much between them, at least short-term. But as the years passed, Carson would have a father who cared about him when he was an adult with a life of his own. In the past few days memories of his father rolled in fast and often. Dad would have liked Carson, but Jeff envisioned him as a grandpa trying to turn the kid into an authentic Wyoming cowboy. Jeff barely thought about that anymore. The teenager was as devoted to his basketball game as

Jeff had been to his horses. The commitment was what counted.

Jeff rubbed his eyes and massaged his temples, his thoughts turning to Olivia. He botched something. As he replayed his conversation with Matt, he heard nothing different from what he and Olivia had said themselves. At least along the lines of the future they had agreed on. Or so he'd thought.

Maybe she needed time. He didn't believe this was a permanent breach. It couldn't be. Impossible.

His thoughts drifted to the present he had for her. He'd planned it in secret and hid the wrapped box in a drawer in his desk. Only Carson knew about that gift.

CHAPTER FIFTEEN

"WELCOME TO THE Christmas Eve inaugural launch of the winter sleigh rides, sponsored by Stanhope's Woodland Cabins." Jeff spoke with a note of triumph in his voice and patted the neck of one of the Clydesdales. Since Olivia still had trouble telling the two apart, she didn't know if it was Sassafras or Bonnet. The sleigh was festive with bows and wreaths mounted on both sides of the wagon. Olivia had helped him decorate it before they'd gone to Trey's ranch and bought Toffee. They'd had such fun that day.

Three days ago was an eternity. First, they'd met up with Trey at the ranch to secure Toffee in her temporary home. Matt helped settle the horse in a stall and assured Olivia that Toffee could be kept a secret from the twins until Christmas Day. The more Olivia studied Toffee and practiced talking to her, the more endearing the horse became. It would still take time before Olivia overcame her apprehension around Toffee, or any of the horses. Not being terrified wasn't the same as the natural ease that others had around them. Jeff had assured her that if she was open, the magic would happen in her heart, as it had with Jillian. He claimed to have a strong sense about Olivia that way.

Now, they'd barely spoken all night. Determined not to do anything to mar the holiday for Jillian, or Carson, Olivia had been acting as if nothing had gone wrong. Talking to Jeff, trying to explain herself, would have to wait. Besides, she wasn't sure what she wanted to say.

After their Christmas Eve buffet dinner at the lodge, Jeff had harnessed the horses and set up for a ride on Rock Curve Road. Heather and Matt ran ahead with the twins, who squealed with excitement at the sight of the sleigh.

"It's like Santa's very own sleigh," Nick said, "only this one doesn't fly."

"And it doesn't have presents, Nick, only people. Can we climb in?" Lucy asked.

"I'm opening the back right now," Jeff said, nodding to Carson, who retrieved the wooden step and put it in place and then climbed in so he could help the twins settle in their seats.

"Time to get to work, Bonnet and Sassafras," Jillian said.

All the while, Olivia tried to pretend everything was normal. Maybe Jeff was faking his holiday cheer, too. Now she had deep regrets about things she'd said. It was as if all her fears had been waiting in her chest to bubble up and burst out. Given how she walked away, no wonder Jeff had said he was confused. It still infuriated her that he'd think she'd interfere with his bond with Carson.

She'd been so sure she was right, her early suspicions about him revealed as justified. She'd almost come to a place where she could accept that the romantic fantasies about him were over, but she wouldn't give up on rebuilding their footing as friends, forming the same kind of bond he'd had with Carson's mom. They'd be connected by Heather, a horse and Jillian.

Wasn't she made for exactly that kind of relationship?

Come spring, she'd start house hunting.

Only Heather seemed to notice that she was keeping her distance from Jeff, but her friend had always been attuned to other people and their shifting feelings. Olivia followed Matt's mom, Stacey, and her friend Grey into the sleigh, and Carson climbed in last and secured the latch.

"All set to go," Carson called out.

Jeff signaled the horses and off they went, bells on the harness trilling in the cold night air, their path ahead lit by the battery-powered running lights installed on the sleigh.

Behind her, Olivia saw the tracks they made on the fresh layer of snow that fell that morning. Jeff kept the horses at a steady but slow walking pace for a smooth ride across the pasture. When they reached the turn onto Rock Curve Road, they could see only the faintest lights in the distance. Matt started to sing "Jingle Bells" and Jillian and the twins joined in without hesitating. Adding her own voice to the chorus, Olivia took in the snowy landscape illuminated by the three-quarter moon. She attempted to cling to the magic of the moment, especially the voices ringing out. With the three younger kids between them, Matt and Heather had extended their arms across the back of the wagon to hold hands.

Olivia had never once had a holiday that matched the vision she'd longed for. She'd yearned to believe Heather and embrace the notion of having it all. Yet, rippling under the surface hadn't she known better than to trust that feeling? Never again. From now on she'd protect herself from ever believing lasting love was possible for her.

The horses picked up the pace, but not by much. When they'd finished "Jingle Bells" they moved on to "Deck the Halls," with the kids dragging out the final "fa-la-la-la-las."

"I think you can pull off this venture, Jeff," Heather called out. "This is great."

Olivia agreed. She'd been privy to the ads and brochures that Jeff, with the aid of Carson's sharp eye, was creating to promote winter weekend specials that could include a sleigh ride.

Matt kept the younger kids singing carols, but Olivia kept an eye on Carson across from her. They were a pair, because he also had little to say, but his gaze was fixed on the snow-covered trees lining the road.

Olivia leaned forward and touched his knee. "It's pretty, isn't it? It's so different from what I saw around me in Minnesota from our house in the city."

Carson nodded. "I was thinking that. No streetlights out here." He chuckled. "Not that many streets."

"You doing okay?" Olivia asked, hoping Carson would share his thoughts.

"Um, I'm fine. Most of the time."

"It's okay to have moments," Olivia said.

"Jeff and my coach at school said some meltdowns are to be expected," Carson said.

She hesitated for a second, but then asked after his grandmother.

"I talked to her this afternoon." He nodded with conviction, adding, "She likes my videos. *A lot.*"

"I'm not surprised. We all love your videos."

"I'm going to send her what I filmed at dinner once I've got video of the celebration at the ranch tomorrow."

"She'll cherish whatever you send." Olivia spoke just as they reached a Y in the road, each fork leading to a single house.

"This is where we turn around," Jeff called out. "Hot chocolate coming up!"

"Popcorn, too," Carson said, grinning down the row at Jillian. "Your favorite."

"And cookies, Carson," Jillian said. "The ones my mom made with your aunt Heather."

Aunt Heather… Olivia got a kick out of that. She looked around at the faces, and watched Jeff as he maneuvered the sleigh in a wide U-turn and headed back. Only a few jolts and bumps.

Olivia considered the assembled group, comforted by her sense of belonging. It wasn't only about the exuberance of Heather and her new family and their warm embrace of her. It went deeper than that. This was home. Pressure built behind her eyes when she watched Jeff guiding the horses. Jeff was home. So was Carson—now. She'd wrapped them into her new life. And now…

The other day when she erupted with Jeff, she'd been so quick to react, *overreact*. She'd raised the familiar fence around herself and Jillian. Created long ago to keep most everything and everybody out, it was wobbly now and wouldn't stay firmly in place. She had dueling voices in her head, each taking its turn. One of them kept reminding her that Jeff had been the generous one, the one to reach out, despite her snide remarks. If she misunderstood him, it was on her to probe more deeply.

It was being accused of sabotaging them that hurt the worst, but meant the most. What happened next between them was up to her.

Olivia closed her eyes and replayed the weeks since she'd met Jeff. Darts and dinners with the kids, buying Toffee, sharing Thanksgiving and sweet kisses by the fire. Her heart wouldn't let her go backward.

JEFF LINGERED IN the lodge, cleaning up after what should have been one of the happiest evenings of his life. He couldn't believe he'd made such a mess of it with Olivia. Neither could Carson, who'd been completely perplexed. Jeff hadn't figured out how to fix it before the get-together. He'd assumed he and Olivia would end up together, with the kids. A family. He'd even imagined the two of them having child of their own.

He was scrubbing the already clean counter one last time when his phone pinged. The message was simple: Can I see you?

Foolish question. He texted a reply: Your cabin? He was ready to grab his jacket when she messaged back that she'd be right over. He glanced toward the door. The tree was still lit up, and the fire was going strong. Might as well add a log to keep it blazing.

Olivia came inside and slipped out of her coat and dropped it on an empty chair as she approached. "I want a do-over."

Jeff wanted specifics. "Of?"

"The awful conversation."

"I wouldn't have called it a conversation." Jeff scoffed. "Maybe we need a *start-over*."

"You think so?" Olivia kept her distance. "By whatever name, it was my fault."

He waved those words away with his hand. "No, no. Don't take the blame. To begin with, I'm really bad at being close. I've shut most people out for way too long."

She cocked her head. "Like I do? Ms. Leave Me Alone?"

"At least Jillian can't score your performance. Carson came right out and asked me if I'd messed up."

Olivia's expression softened. "I've become fond of your teenager."

Jeff nodded to acknowledge that.

"When I replayed our argument, I saw my own overreaction." She shook her head. "It's so hard for me to admit I was sabotaging us in an irrational way. My familiar barriers popped up so fast. But I thought about it, and I know what you meant about wanting to avoid big changes for Carson—things happening too fast, too soon."

"I'm afraid to jump in now and explain myself and listen to you do the same until I know one thing for sure." Jeff ran out of breath at the end of the sentence. Aware of what was riding on this, his heart beat wildly in his chest.

Olivia stopped and stared at him, her soft eyes full of hope. "Tell me…what is it?"

He smiled. "This is going to sound really corny, but I thought I'd made it very clear that I want to be part of your charmed life. *Forever.*"

With open arms, Olivia rushed to him. He caught her and buried his face in her hair and inhaled her sweet scent. She rested her head against his shoulder, breathing hard. "That's what I came here to tell you, hoping you'd listen and give me another chance."

"I'd listen forever to hear the words you said. I love you so much, Olivia." He wanted to spill out the words to assure her she would live permanently in his heart. He caressed her cheeks and found her soft lips.

Many long kisses later, she took a deep breath before laughing with abandon and joy. "Oh, I love you, too. Whew! I said the words I never imagined I'd say to a man again."

"Say them again anytime because I love hearing them."

"But it's so much more than that. I love *us* as a family." She stepped back and held up her hand. "In time... I understand that we need time for the four of us to settle in and strengthen all these ingredients to make sure we're solid."

"That's all I was saying to Matt," Jeff said. "Maybe the words weren't as elegant as yours, but that's what I meant. If I hadn't been certain about wanting this life with you, I wouldn't have brought Carson into it."

"I get that now." Olivia pulled back and slid out of his arms. "So, we need to make a toast. Is there eggnog or cider around here?"

Jeff thought about the box in his desk drawer. This would be the perfect time to give her his gift, to seal their deal. "I think I can come up with something special. Wait for me on the couch."

Hurrying to his office, Jeff started second-guessing himself, but squashed that in a hurry. There would be no better time to make this holiday truly merry.

He slipped the box into his pocket and on the way back to Olivia he stopped at the bar and got the bottle of red wine he'd saved for a special occasion. Like this one. He picked up two wineglasses and joined her. She'd settled on the couch with her legs tucked under her, staring at the fire with a smile on her face. Now that was a sight he could get used to.

"Okay, time for my surprise," Jeff said when he'd opened the bottle and filled their glasses. "Well, two surprises."

"Oh? Tell me more."

Jeff took a deep, happy breath. "I'm adopting Carson. I asked him, and he agreed. He's going to be my son."

Olivia's eyes filled with tears she quickly brushed them away. "You and Carson belong together. You really do." She tapped her glass against his. "A toast to you and Carson."

"I've come to love the kid so much, why not make it official?" Jeff leaned back. "We're going to announce it at the ranch tomorrow."

Jeff then pulled the box out of his pocket. It was wrapped in deep blue paper with silver stars and topped off with a white bow. "Now for my second surprise."

"I've got a gift for you, too—it's in my cabin," Olivia said, sliding to the edge of the sofa. "I was going to give it to you tomorrow morning. I'll get it now."

He held her back. "Don't move. Tomorrow is soon enough. Trust me on this. This isn't really about Christmas at all." His gift was about promises, not linked to any particular holiday.

"Really? You're sure?" She held up the box and shook it. It made a shuffling noise. With a happy grin, she ripped off the paper and opened the box. She took in a breath and put her hand over her heart. "It's…it's…" With her eyes shining, she held up the silver charm bracelet. "Exquisite, Jeff, that's the only word that comes close."

"I tried to find charms for all the meaning-ful pieces of your life, even a sheep. I heard you were interested in Jen's spinning classes." It had taken help from Carson to locate some of them, including a cabin, a little girl, a hard-to-find dart, a pie to represent Thanksgiving, a Christmas tree, a cat, and he'd added a horse and a dog, along with a book because she read a lot. "The heart, which, as you can guess, represents my love for you, was easiest to find. But an X-ray machine was nowhere to be found."

"Oh, the stethoscope is perfect," Olivia said, putting the bracelet in her palm and separating each of the charms. "You sure are clever. You know how to create magic."

"A charming woman deserves a charm bracelet. How about we keep adding to it, year by year?" He leaned in and kissed her and when she ran her fingertips down his cheek, he captured her hand and planted kisses on her fingers.

With the fire still blazing they sat that way, exchanging kisses and talking about Christmas Day at the ranch, but mostly about their shared days ahead.

"Any chance you're sleepy?" Olivia asked.

He hadn't expected the question, but the answer was easy. "Nope. I don't expect to sleep much tonight."

"That's what I was hoping to hear."

"Is that so?"

Olivia wasted no time getting up off the couch. "Since neither of us can sleep, how about some friendly Christmas Eve darts?"

She was full of surprises. He could get used to that. He got to his feet. "I'm only a little intimidated. I know you bring your A game."

"Always." She flashed a bright smile. Jeff thought about the next winter months with snowy days and with any luck, cabins filled with paying guests. He'd teach Jillian how to take good care of Toffee, and her riding lessons would start in the spring. "We could also take a sleigh ride. You can sit in the driver's seat with me."

"I'm sure we'll find time to glide across this winter wonderland."

Jeff opened the dart cabinet and got ready to start the game. "We've got all the time in the world, Olivia. For us. And for our family."

JILLIAN HELD OLIVIA'S phone and was scrolling through the photos she'd taken of Toffee. Before they'd started their gift exchange in the living room, she and Jeff, Heather and the twins and Carson had walked out to the barn to introduce Jillian to Toffee, who wore a ribbon and bow. Jumping with excitement, Jillian also quietly listened to Jeff tell her about the horse and what owning the horse meant. They'd all taken pictures, including Jillian, and she was finally coaxed back to the house, where they'd all opened gifts. Olivia touched the jade-and-silver necklace, her gift from Jillian. As Olivia suspected, Jillian had bought it at the Christmas Market and Heather had kept it at the ranch. Of course, she'd worn her other special gift, the charm bracelet.

From Jeff's expression when he'd opened her gift, Olivia was positive the hand-woven saddle blanket was perfect. Jeff said he was especially touched by the framed photo of him with Carson that she'd taken on Thanksgiving at the ranch. Without either of them noticing her, she'd caught them on her phone camera with their heads together talking. She hadn't known they'd soon be father and son, but the picture caught the affection in Jeff's face as he cocked his head to listen to Carson.

As for the teenager, he'd given Jeff an oak carved horse and rider from the county gallery. "I thought we needed stuff on the mantel," Carson said with a shrug, not fully aware of the treasure he'd found. The sculptor was a well-known local artist.

All the adults in Heather and Matt's living room watched Jeff swallow hard as he held up the wood sculpture so everyone could get a closer look.

Olivia was in on the gift because she'd hidden it in her cabin. Even Olivia hadn't anticipated how touched Jeff would be by Carson's present.

When the gift giving was over, Jeff glanced at Olivia and mouthed the word *now*. With his eyebrows raised, it was a question, not a statement. She smiled and nodded. There would be no better time.

"I have an announcement," Jeff said, getting to his feet, "and I wanted to wait until we were all together." He gestured for Carson to join him and then put his arm around the teenager's shoulder. "A few days ago, I asked Carson if he'd allow me to adopt him, so I can be his dad officially. I told him I'd be proud to tell the world that he's my son." He glanced at Carson. "We're going to start the process in January."

Matt was the first to react with a loud cheer. "That's fantastic news."

"I'll say," Heather said.

Olivia stood aside as Heather put her arms around Jeff and Carson in a three-way hug. Carson's face was flushed. Embarrassed by the attention, maybe, but his smile let everyone in on his happiness.

"I want to say something," Jillian said, raising her hand as if in a classroom.

"Go for it," Olivia said, curious about her daughter's take on Carson's adoption.

"Will you adopt me, too, Jeff?" Jillian said. "Then Carson would be my real brother." The room went silent for a second before Jillian added, "I mean after you and my mom get married."

Olivia glanced at Jeff and her hands flew to her cheeks. "Jillian…that's… We haven't talked about that."

"Carson said it could happen." Jillian shrugged. "Why not? You two like each other a lot. And Jeff helped you pick out Toffee and he's going to teach me to ride."

Olivia watched Carson's pink cheeks turn red. She scanned the room and saw nothing but amused faces.

Carson cleared his throat. "I never said they were going to get married *soon*."

"Wait a second, I have something to say," Jeff said, turning to Olivia. "We might have known the kids were onto us."

She smiled. "I suppose."

"We've agreed to take our time. We'll all get used to being together more. And when we make that next step and become a family, Jillian, it would be my honor to be your dad. I've already had a little practice with Carson." He patted Carson's back. "Turns out, I like it."

"See, Carson? I told you so," Jillian said smugly. "We're already a family, sort of."

"A big family," Lucy said.

"What an amazing year." Heather turned to Jeff. "Before these kids set your wedding date for you, let's go visit Toffee again and say hello to the other horses. It's too cold to ride today, but we can visit our special pals."

"And when we come back," Matt said, "I want to see Carson's show—we were promised a real home movie."

"You'll get it. It's ready for prime time," Carson said. "And you're all in it."

It took a few minutes to get everybody into their coats, hats, boots and gloves, but they soon filed out to the barn on the frosty, sunny afternoon. Carson and Jeff walked along with Matt and Heather, but Jillian ran ahead with the twins. Olivia hung back, still trying to grasp all that had happened. Jeff waited until she caught up with him and they stayed a few steps behind the others.

"This is the best day of my life," Jeff said, taking her hand. "Or, two days, in fact."

Last night they'd cuddled on the couch and talked about nothing and everything. Olivia stopped walking and put her arms around him and planted a quick kiss on his mouth. "I've never been so happy and optimistic about my life—our future, and Jillian's and Carson's, too."

"No matter what happens, I'm here with you for the long haul—all of us together." Jeff held both of her hands. "We're a family, Olivia."

"And to paraphrase my daughter, we like each other a lot."

As they walked to the stable, Olivia thought about the bracelet on her wrist. She'd soon add more magical charms to her circle.

* * * * *

More great romances are available from acclaimed author Virginia McCullough and Harlequin Heartwarming, visit www.Harlequin.com today!

Get 4 FREE REWARDS!

We'll send you 2 FREE Books plus 2 FREE Mystery Gifts.

FREE
Value Over
$20

Both the **Love Inspired®** and **Love Inspired® Suspense** series feature compelling novels filled with inspirational romance, faith, forgiveness and hope.

YES! Please send me 2 FREE novels from the Love Inspired or Love Inspired Suspense series and my 2 FREE gifts (gifts are worth about $10 retail). After receiving them, if I don't wish to receive any more books, I can return the shipping statement marked "cancel." If I don't cancel, I will receive 6 brand-new Love Inspired Larger-Print books or Love Inspired Suspense Larger-Print books every month and be billed just $6.49 each in the U.S. or $6.74 each in Canada. That is a savings of at least 16% off the cover price. It's quite a bargain! Shipping and handling is just 50¢ per book in the U.S. and $1.25 per book in Canada.* I understand that accepting the 2 free books and gifts places me under no obligation to buy anything. I can always return a shipment and cancel at any time by calling the number below. The free books and gifts are mine to keep no matter what I decide.

Choose one: ☐ **Love Inspired**
Larger-Print
(122/322 IDN GRHK)

☐ **Love Inspired Suspense**
Larger-Print
(107/307 IDN GRHK)

Name (please print)

Address   Apt. #

City   State/Province   Zip/Postal Code

Email: Please check this box ☐ if you would like to receive newsletters and promotional emails from Harlequin Enterprises ULC and its affiliates. You can unsubscribe anytime.

Mail to the Harlequin Reader Service:
IN U.S.A.: P.O. Box 1341, Buffalo, NY 14240-8531
IN CANADA: P.O. Box 603, Fort Erie, Ontario L2A 5X3

Want to try 2 free books from another series? Call 1-800-873-8635 or visit www.ReaderService.com.

---

*Terms and prices subject to change without notice. Prices do not include sales taxes, which will be charged (if applicable) based on your state or country of residence. Canadian residents will be charged applicable taxes. Offer not valid in Quebec. This offer is limited to one order per household. Books received may not be as shown. Not valid for current subscribers to the Love Inspired or Love Inspired Suspense series. All orders subject to approval. Credit or debit balances in a customer's account(s) may be offset by any other outstanding balance owed by or to the customer. Please allow 4 to 6 weeks for delivery. Offer available while quantities last.

Your Privacy—Your information is being collected by Harlequin Enterprises ULC, operating as Harlequin Reader Service. For a complete summary of the information we collect, how we use this information and to whom it is disclosed, please visit our privacy notice located at corporate.harlequin.com/privacy-notice. From time to time we may also exchange your personal information with reputable third parties. If you wish to opt out of this sharing of your personal information, please visit readerservice.com/consumerschoice or call 1-800-873-8635. **Notice to California Residents**—Under California law, you have specific rights to control and access your data. For more information on these rights and how to exercise them, visit corporate.harlequin.com/california-privacy.

LIRLIS22R3

Get 4 FREE REWARDS!

We'll send you 2 FREE Books plus 2 FREE Mystery Gifts.

FREE
Value Over
$20

Both the **Harlequin® Special Edition** and **Harlequin® Heartwarming™** series feature compelling novels filled with stories of love and strength where the bonds of friendship, family and community unite.

YES! Please send me 2 FREE novels from the Harlequin Special Edition or Harlequin Heartwarming series and my 2 FREE gifts (gifts are worth about $10 retail). After receiving them, if I don't wish to receive any more books, I can return the shipping statement marked "cancel." If I don't cancel, I will receive 6 brand-new Harlequin Special Edition books every month and be billed just $5.49 each in the U.S. or $6.24 each in Canada, a savings of at least 12% off the cover price, or 4 brand-new Harlequin Heartwarming Larger-Print books every month and be billed just $6.24 each in the U.S. or $6.74 each in Canada, a savings of at least 19% off the cover price. It's quite a bargain! Shipping and handling is just 50¢ per book in the U.S. and $1.25 per book in Canada.* I understand that accepting the 2 free books and gifts places me under no obligation to buy anything. I can always return a shipment and cancel at any time by calling the number below. The free books and gifts are mine to keep no matter what I decide.

Choose one: ☐ **Harlequin Special Edition**   ☐ **Harlequin Heartwarming**
          (235/335 HDN GRJV)   **Larger-Print**
                                 (161/361 HDN GRJV)

Name (please print)

Address   Apt. #

City   State/Province   Zip/Postal Code

Email: Please check this box ☐ if you would like to receive newsletters and promotional emails from Harlequin Enterprises ULC and its affiliates. You can unsubscribe anytime.

> Mail to the **Harlequin Reader Service:**
> **IN U.S.A.:** P.O. Box 1341, Buffalo, NY 14240-8531
> **IN CANADA:** P.O. Box 603, Fort Erie, Ontario L2A 5X3

Want to try 2 free books from another series? Call 1-800-873-8635 or visit www.ReaderService.com.

---

*Terms and prices subject to change without notice. Prices do not include sales taxes, which will be charged (if applicable) based on your state or country of residence. Canadian residents will be charged applicable taxes. Offer not valid in Quebec. This offer is limited to one order per household. Books received may not be as shown. Not valid for current subscribers to the Harlequin Special Edition or Harlequin Heartwarming series. All orders subject to approval. Credit or debit balances in a customer's account(s) may be offset by any other outstanding balance owed by or to the customer. Please allow 4 to 6 weeks for delivery. Offer available while quantities last.

Your Privacy—Your information is being collected by Harlequin Enterprises ULC, operating as Harlequin Reader Service. For a complete summary of the information we collect, how we use this information and to whom it is disclosed, please visit our privacy notice located at corporate.harlequin.com/privacy-notice. From time to time we may also exchange your personal information with reputable third parties. If you wish to opt out of this sharing of your personal information, please visit readerservice.com/consumerschoice or call 1-800-873-8635. **Notice to California Residents**—Under California law, you have specific rights to control and access your data. For more information on these rights and how to exercise them, visit corporate.harlequin.com/california-privacy.

HSEHW22R3

THE 2022 LOVE INSPIRED CHRISTMAS COLLECTION

Buy 3 and get 1 FREE!

May all that is beautiful, meaningful and brings you joy be yours this holiday season...including this fun-filled collection featuring 24 Christmas stories. From tender holiday romances to Christmas Eve suspense, this collection has it all.

Get 4 FREE REWARDS!

We'll send you 2 FREE Books plus 2 FREE Mystery Gifts.

FREE Value Over **$20**

Both the **Romance** and **Suspense** collections feature compelling novels written by many of today's bestselling authors.

YES! Please send me 2 FREE novels from the Essential Romance or Essential Suspense Collection and my 2 FREE gifts (gifts are worth about $10 retail). After receiving them, if I don't wish to receive any more books, I can return the shipping statement marked "cancel." If I don't cancel, I will receive 4 brand-new novels every month and be billed just $7.49 each in the U.S. or $7.74 each in Canada. That's a savings of at least 17% off the cover price. It's quite a bargain! Shipping and handling is just 50¢ per book in the U.S. and $1.25 per book in Canada.* I understand that accepting the 2 free books and gifts places me under no obligation to buy anything. I can always return a shipment and cancel at any time by calling the number below. The free books and gifts are mine to keep no matter what I decide.

Choose one: ☐ **Essential Romance** (194/394 MDN GRHV) ☐ **Essential Suspense** (191/391 MDN GRHV)

Name (please print)

Address   Apt. #

City   State/Province   Zip/Postal Code

Email: Please check this box ☐ if you would like to receive newsletters and promotional emails from Harlequin Enterprises ULC and its affiliates. You can unsubscribe anytime.

Mail to the Harlequin Reader Service:
IN U.S.A.: P.O. Box 1341, Buffalo, NY 14240-8531
IN CANADA: P.O. Box 603, Fort Erie, Ontario L2A 5X3

Want to try 2 free books from another series? Call 1-800-873-8635 or visit www.ReaderService.com.

*Terms and prices subject to change without notice. Prices do not include sales taxes, which will be charged (if applicable) based on your state or country of residence. Canadian residents will be charged applicable taxes. Offer not valid in Quebec. This offer is limited to one order per household. Books received may not be as shown. Not valid for current subscribers to the Essential Romance or Essential Suspense Collection. All orders subject to approval. Credit or debit balances in a customer's account(s) may be offset by any other outstanding balance owed by or to the customer. Please allow 4 to 6 weeks for delivery. Offer available while quantities last.

Your Privacy—Your information is being collected by Harlequin Enterprises ULC, operating as Harlequin Reader Service. For a complete summary of the information we collect, how we use this information and to whom it is disclosed, please visit our privacy notice located at corporate.harlequin.com/privacy-notice. From time to time we may also exchange your personal information with reputable third parties. If you wish to opt out of this sharing of your personal information, please visit readerservice.com/consumerschoice or call 1-800-873-8635. **Notice to California Residents**—Under California law, you have specific rights to control and access your data. For more information on these rights and how to exercise them, visit corporate.harlequin.com/california-privacy.

STRS22R3

COMING NEXT MONTH FROM

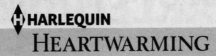

#451 THE COWBOY'S RANCH RESCUE
Bachelor Cowboys • by Lisa Childs

Firefighter paramedic Baker Haven will do right by his orphaned nephews—even keep his distance. He couldn't save his brother, and he can't give his heart to the ranch's beautiful cook, Taye Cooper, either...despite the hope she brings to their home.

#452 HIS PARTNERSHIP PROPOSAL
Polk Island • by Jacquelin Thomas

Aubrie DuGrandpre and Terian LaCroix were rivals in cooking school—and now they're vying for the same restaurant property! When Terian approaches her about a partnership, she agrees. Can a past grudge lead to a lifetime commitment?

#453 A RANCHER WORTH REMEMBERING
Love, Oregon • by Anna Grace

Matchmaker Clara Wallace avoids skeptics—and Jet Broughman, her new client's best friend, is the ultimate nonbeliever. He's also her teenage crush! Now Clara must help Jet's friend find love *without* falling for the gorgeous, stubborn rancher she's never forgotten.

#454 THE OFFICER'S DILEMMA
by Janice Carter

Zanna Winters and Navy Lt. Dominic Kennedy wanted to escape the small town of Lighthouse Cove. But Zanna's surprise announcement might tie them there...and to each other. Can two people who dream of adventure find one with family?

HARLEQUIN
PLUS

Announcing a **BRAND-NEW** multimedia subscription service for romance fans like you!

Read, Watch and Play.

Experience the easiest way to get the romance content you crave.

Start your **FREE 7 DAY TRIAL** at
<u>www.harlequinplus.com/freetrial</u>.